RYAN KURR

THE
BLACK
HEN

A NOVEL

"A wonderfully imagined and gripping conclusion to the *Esoteric Alchemy* trilogy. *The Black Hen* is an intense ride rich with all the magic, character growth, and twists that make Kurr's books impossible to put down."

—Sarah Day, author of *Ora and the Old God*

"*The Black Hen* is beautifully written, creative and imaginative. Its energy and pace will have you captivated right from the start. Kurr's insight into human nature is taken to new depths through his character portrayal and the life choices these characters make. The attention to detail is absorbing. He is a master of the written word, his knowledge of witchcraft and the human soul. An inspired end to a magical trilogy and powerfully thought provoking. All three books are a must read on everyone's must read list."

—Laura O'Rourke, *Witches Magazine*

"With *The Black Hen*—Ryan Kurr's *Esoteric Alchemy* series is complete. He beautifully brings our beloved coven members full circle in his unique and magical way of telling their adventurous journey to create balance in the world and to find themselves."

— Sandra Szatkowski, Owner of *Merenwen's Runes*

THE
BLACK
HEN

The Black Hen/ Ryan Kurr. -- 1st ed.
ISBN 978-1-7347245-6-1 (Hardback)
ISBN 978-1-7347245-7-8 (Paperback)
ISBN 978-1-7347245-8-5 (ebook)

Jacket and cover design by Allison Layman

Visit the author's website at **www.ryankurr.com**

The universe is full of magical things patiently waiting for our wits to grow sharper.

Eden Phillpotts, A Shadow Passes

For those who feel darkness and light,
And see the growth after every plight
Beyond the odds and armed with ambition
The strength is found in our ever-present intuition
Together in spirit, we're here at the end
A new beginning, collectively we transcend
From The Fool to The Universe, and up the mountainsides in between
All of it, a journey that needed to be seen
Sage, oak, metal and feather, a witch's brew
Words are spells, and these are for you

CONTENTS

*Elucidations for text marked with this symbol are located at the back of the book in the Esoteric Compendium.

THE
BLACK
HEN

Utica, New York; Nineteenth Century

Francis Barrett's unusual mind was a vast and bottomless ocean where normality went to drown. A quirky Englishman whose interest in science and chemistry was overshadowed by his fascination with the arcane, he enjoyed things that were divisible by four, inexplicably loathed and equally feared exotic chickens, and would sleep only if he knew his head was facing due west. He rarely slept, and was up by sunrise for his daily meditation that always lasted until his stomach growled twice, no more, no less. He would break his fast with porridge and a wedge of bread, and clean his face four times with water, each pass with a clean table linen. Francis also had an eye for art, and saw it in everything. What didn't have art had science, and what didn't have science had magic—they all had beauty.

Francis lived a life that was centered on mastery, discovery and appreciation, not so much on transcendence, a concept he felt was best to experience briefly and return from, not to strive for. The magic of transcendence was experienced after he returned to his physical body, with all the secrets of the ether. It made him ultra-productive in ways that allowed him to sleep for only four hours a night when he slept at all. For years he couldn't quite explain why he felt the need to remain so dedicated to his meditation, a habit that left him a brilliant new shade of enlightened after every session. It felt as necessary as breathing, a function that controlled the omnipresent fear that he might not actually ever find what he was looking for. It was tricky, because he didn't even know what he was hoping to find, he just knew that he had to do it.

One extraordinarily quiet morning in early January, the answers found him. He realized the answers had been there all along, as if crystalized in amber—waiting to be unearthed.

Finally, after years of endless productivity and the fear of crushing defeat in the back of his mind, his persistence showed him what happens when you do something long enough through all manner of hardship without going insane. Francis wasn't a skeptic, but he was relieved when he pierced the Somnium plane and found his theories answered with a spiritual verisimilitude. In that heightened state of awareness, which only grew more sensitive over time, he was allowed to think deeply and without restraint—his finest talent. The truths came heavily coated in exhilaration and laced with superciliousness, which felt appropriate for an autodidact as dedicated and unapologetic as he. It was his neuroticism that allowed him to have that sort of creative, spiritual breakthrough in the first place, so how could success not come with a little pride?

Francis had always believed that *his* normal was something of great value. The truth was—he was a witch. Day after day, night after night, he embraced his spiritual and intellectual humility and learned all that he could about magic, the world that existed within the natural world.

Francis learned that he was of the second nature of witches to evolve, the Transcendents—the most intuitive, empathic and clairvoyant, the witches adept at healing trauma in addition to twisting the will and manipulating the minds of others. Francis, like many Transcendents who came before and after him, had his own heap of trauma to process, but he concluded that learning as much as possible with the intentions of sharing that knowledge was a much higher priority than healing his own wounds. Instead, he focused his attention on creating an archive—books that he wished had been around for him, everything about magic and esotericism specifically for mystics, witches and occultists—that was irrefutably his own. The only true way for him to achieve such a thing was to publish them himself. He survived on the freedom he felt by bypassing the gatekeepers who wanted to edit, judge and ultimately decide what was best to publish, all with a subjective perspective that was rooted in profit instead of quality of content.

First, he published a book all about the Union of the Divine Dualities and the black hen. Immediately after that he published *The Magus* in 1801, a book that moved beyond the nuances of ritual magic. Not just in theory, or by writing something with a wider audience in mind, but by writing it with such passion that it entranced its readers. Paschal Beverly Randolph was one such reader who fell under the book's spell. A well-traveled sailor who made an art of never knowing when to shut his mouth in a bar, he couldn't hold his liquor in the sense that after a drink, he would vomit up words. It earned him several black eyes and a few missing teeth, because his words always seemed to be secrets that patrons wanted to take to their grave. He never once considered that some people didn't want their dirty laundry aired, or whether they were ready to hear their own subconscious, especially after he'd had a little whiskey.

On his second visit to the Bell & Barnacle pub on Ballast Quay, Paschal sat at the bar and ordered a whiskey, and his life changed forever. He'd sat right next to Francis Barrett, the author of the book that had enchanted him to his bones and beyond. Francis bought him another whiskey and introduced himself, smiling with satisfaction when Paschal pulled out a tattered old copy of *The Magus*. Francis would wax poetic about that detail for the rest of the night while they bonded over their mutual interest in astrolatry and their love for and fascination with magic. Paschal asked a train of questions, until Francis caught the scent of his breath. It wasn't whiskey he smelled, but cucumber and freshly fallen rain—he smelled a witch. After all those nights of reading the ether, for once he left the bar without losing any teeth and without a scratch on him.

Francis began teaching Paschal everything he knew about magic out of his small apartment at the edge of London, and tried to convince him he'd be more intuitive if he slept with his head facing west. *It worked for me*, he insisted.

Paschal was the first famulus, but he was not the last. Francis introduced a woman named Mary Jane to Paschal one afternoon. He had decided to take a quotidian walk at four o'clock that day, and that was when he found her. She smelled of sulfur, and had been using her powers to grow and cultivate marijuana to heal ailments. She didn't know how she was doing it, until Francis explained everything. Francis knew everything was falling into place.

A few months later, the three witches moved to America. Francis had had a dream in which he had been given many messages. They all were to be rewarded with inspiration and magical expansion, which would lead to bigger, richer, and more magical lives if they relocated. In the dream, Francis saw a wedding, a farmhouse, and a new wave of creative thought. He knew it would all manifest once they actually touched foreign soil; moving was a desideratum. When Francis spoke of their plans, Paschal felt an electricity in him, and he trusted him, even if the plans made no sense. Francis was not only a neophiliac, but a charismatic and convincing one.

Francis bought a cheap farm on a plot of land with a shabby farmhouse in Utica, New York, just like he had seen in his dream, and that's when he officially initiated them into a coven. He was creating structure and order for himself and those closest to him, and not even a coop full of exotic chickens was going to stop him from pushing forward. He began to sleep less and less, and each meditation proved to be more fruitful than the last, flooding him with new ideas that emerged like mushrooms after a heavy rain. He was more than the unsophisticated eccentric on the periphery of town; he was a creator, a powerful manifester with a throat just buzzing to confabulate and maunder.

He sequestered himself in a room at the west end of the farmhouse and thought about their future as a coven. They had been successful every step of the way, but it wasn't enough. There had to be others, he knew there were. He just needed to find them—lead them. Francis had become an opportunist, and when the moment appeared without obstruction, he seized it. In all his findings in the Somnium plane, he never saw a vision of an official, structured system of magic anywhere. His heart beat wildly with excitement. It had never been done before, and that was how he knew he could do it. If it could be done with two, it could be done with many. He decided he was now Proctor, and head of what he called the Advisory, a central authority over all things magical. Since witches had no choice but to live among the rest of society, there needed to be a tight system of checks and balances, especially in regard to property and finances. Paschal had a head for numbers, so Francis named him the Keeper of Books and Assets. Francis was elated at the systems he put in place, which he intended to be permanent. Soon he would be able to usher magic into a new age. All he needed was a way to dive deeper into meditation and mine for bigger gold.

Mary Jane had a marvelous aptitude for farming, but her most prized crop was the magically enhanced marijuana formulated specifically for ritual and meditation. She named it Mary Jane, after herself, and Francis used it religiously to search for what he called the song of the universe, a stream of consciousness from Source.

It was 1850 when Francis's dream came to fruition and Paschal and Mary Jane were married. *I must be close, I have to be,* Francis thought. He assumed he was right on the precipice of all he sought, and that all he needed was a little help to make the leap. Francis stuffed his pipe with Mary Jane until it overflowed onto the floor, covering it in a layer of sticky, purple-green nuggets. He welcomed the spirit of plant and flame, beseeched them for guidance and inhaled all the smoke his lungs could hold. He looked out the west-facing window and into the resplendent, midsummer-gold setting sun. The shafts of light illuminated the grassy knolls and cast arcane blankets of shadow into the shallow valleys of the undulating hilltops. *I can hear it already,* Francis thought as he lay back onto the floor and crossed his hands over his belly.

Francis stared at the ceiling until he was lost in the hazy euphoria of the spirit of Mary Jane and had to close his eyes. A buzzing filled his ears first, then his chest. He exercised his third eye with newfound multitudes until he slipped beyond the borders of where he'd been before and passed into a realm entirely new. It required patience and skill, but also kindness, leaving space for failure while always striving to be better.

Four minutes later, the storm of buzzing slowly dissolved and the thoughts of another filled the space. *Who is this? What is this?* The name Volustina streamed through his mind before it flashed away. Information had never arrived in such a way, not like this. It was a surprising new shade of mental strength, even for someone with an already astounding gift. In one flooding rush, he absorbed an abundance of knowledge. He tried to process as much as he could: his reincarnation as a woman named Bisa, the spirit and power of all natural elements, rituals, spells, how to connect with Spirit, and much more, enough to fill books.

When he broke from his meditation, he rose from the floor with a gasp. It felt as if he had lived lifetimes over the course of a few minutes. It would've been exhausting for most, but Francis was invigorated. He spent the next three weeks writing down everything he could remember, information that had carved itself into his memory. He had finally achieved the next level of success and now needed to document all that he had learned for future witches. He didn't want fame, even though he had the disposition for it. He wanted to make magic more accessible to the many who would come after him, important ones—in a sense, that included him, reincarnated.

In the thick of his scribing, he spent nine solid days without food or sleep, often finishing a full chapter a day, all while using Mary Jane to maintain his flow state. It was a lonely, isolated existence, but he had to do it. Finishing was its own best reward. When he was done, his fingers had blistered and calloused, but he'd completed two full book-length documents: *Metaphysical Manifestations and Sharpened Senses*, and *The Secrets of Magic and Other Curious Practices*, neither of which he wanted his name to be associated with because he hadn't truly written them; he'd channeled them. He was merely the vessel.

It was then that everything changed. Paschal started working as a medium to the curious and the grieving, until Francis planted the idea that he should start a publishing company with the money coming in. It may have been a selfish request, with two unpublished books ready to be bound. Nevertheless, as Keeper of Books and Assets, Paschal made it happen. He not only published but authored many books on magic and spirituality. They published Francis's two books off the record, with no author or publisher listed, for a limited run of a few hundred copies.

The coven separated when Paschal and Mary Jane divorced (amicably) in 1864 and the enchanted strain of marijuana was gone. It wasn't long before Francis sniffed out a new member, Kate, another Primordial, who found her soul mate in Paschal. By now, Francis had thought that he had served his purpose and fulfilled his destiny, only there was more. He lay down one Monday evening for his evening meditation, and what he received was a new form of inspiration in the form of architectural drawings. He wasn't the best with math, and always thought numbers were best divisible by four, so he sat with the information for a while. He would have drafted them all by himself, but this was far too important to not get right.

Walter Basil Harvey was just the man—and witch—for the job, a practicing architect who rendered Francis's drawings into engineerable sketches. The time and the place weren't right, Francis just felt it.

A short time later, Francis, Paschal and the coven relocated to Nova, Colorado—it was where he felt his soul was drawn to. The Advisory and the Proctor system continued on, until one day, long after everyone had passed, a protégé of Walter's found the sketches and built the house on a plot of land owned by the Keeper of Books and Assets. It was a beautiful marvel, 444 Smoky Quartz Drive.

Many years later, Rosemary Cherry joined the Advisory and renovated the house before passing the role of Keeper to a man named Nix.

THE
BLACK
HEN

CHAPTER 1

Nova, Colorado, March 2020

Ollie could feel Bisa's energy on the page of Avery's grimoire, and for a moment he felt a tightness in his chest. He cleared his throat and blinked away the deep-rooted pain that struck him without warning. Ollie understood but didn't always appreciate how grief was never consistent and how it always found a way to show itself at any given moment. It was easier to address when it was happening to someone else, when it was somebody else's pain. The more he choked back his feelings about losing Bisa, the more it dug up a trauma he thought was buried so deep that it would never be found again. Yet, there it was, rising up from the depths, free from all the shackles Ollie had placed on it. It was always there, like an evil ghost, one you thought you had escaped, only to be surprised that it turned up years later, reflected over your shoulder one chilly morning. It was the reason the Devil, Nine of Swords, the Moon and the Tower always showed up in his tarot spreads when referring to his past or his subconscious mind.

Ollie felt another stab of pain and began to perspire. He took a deep breath and tried to swallow the pain back down, acknowledging it just enough to try to get rid of it, like a mosquito in need of a good slap. But no throat in the world could've downed the beast in his body. Before he could even think about burying it again, the grief had welled up and percolated out of his eyes. Ollie shifted his body and wiped his eyes. He didn't dare look up at Avery. He knew his eyes were far too red. A few more blinks and a throat clear later and he'd won—for now.

"Are you okay?" Avery asked.

He knew she would be able to tell if he lied, he knew the cost of admitting the truth, and he didn't feel comfortable doing either. So he told a version of the truth. "Yeah, but no. I'm still kind of reeling about everything that happened. Bisa. And Nina. Everything." *There,* he thought. *That wasn't a lie, it just wasn't the whole truth.*

Avery nodded, feeling a little emotional herself. "I know," she said. "Hopefully this all will be, I don't want to say worth it, that sounds awful, but…I don't know. I just hope all of this wasn't for nothing."

Ollie returned his attention to the grimoire. His eyes passed over the lines and patterns that filled the entire page—they were words.

"'Find me at the end,'" Ollie said.

"What?" Avery turned to Ollie. "What are you talking about?"

Ollie ran his fingers over the page. "'Find me at the end.' That's what it says."

"Those are words?"

Ollie nodded.

Avery was entirely confused as she tried to make sense of how Ollie had determined that a page full of scribbled lines made any sense. "That's…just…art, those aren't words."

"Bisa's words. Look." Ollie handed her grimoire back to Avery. "Look at it like this, and close an eye. Do you see it?"

Avery let out a gasp. "Oh my stars, get outta here. You're right." She paused for a moment. "The end. The end of what?"

Ollie shook his head, as confused as Avery was.

Seeing Bisa's message in the form of a mysterious riddle was frustrating. Avery never had time for riddles. Avery always trusted her gut, and her spirit when her gut was too difficult to read. But her friendship with Bisa was strong, and understanding how she thought was becoming clearer. She grabbed hold of the pages and flipped to the very back of the book. When she turned the final page, a shiver ran through her entire body. Tucked into the binding between the end page and the case was a small piece of paper, folded and sealed with wax. The edges of it had been gilded in gold leaf. There was art in everything Bisa did—even this, whatever it was. Avery plucked it from its hiding spot and broke the purple wax seal with a swift swipe of her forefinger. A wisp of fragrance filled the air as Ollie unfolded the paper: an epicene, olfactive magnetism that was auspicious and spectral—unmistakably Transcendent. *How long has this been here?* Avery wondered.

It was a handwritten letter—instructions, a spell. The words *renascence of spirit* was written across the top of the paper in bold blue and purple ink. Ollie's eyes hurried over Bisa's words, and he could hear Bisa's spirit calling out from between the lines. His temperature rose as he read. The paper was as hot and alive as he was. When he finished, he narrowed his eyes at the title of the spell. *Is this really what I think it is?* He was certain there was no way to bring someone back to life. That was something no witch could do. Nina had always been very clear about that. One could communicate with the dead, but never return them to a physical body. Would that be enough to stop Bisa from trying?

"What is this?" Avery asked.

Ollie took a deep breath, exhaled, and read the instructions aloud. "'This ritual is designed to bond my spirit from the afterlife with a physical body. To tether my spirit is likely an impossible task, and this is more of an experiment than an actual tested spell. I may return in dreams, through speech, tools of divination or even an auric presence, for life is just the transference of energy from one place to another. However, there is no guarantee the spell will work as intended. Four items are needed, all personal to me, each representing one of the four elements. One: the feather of an owl; this represents my connection to air. Two: purple ocher or violet pigment made from earth deposits; this represents my connection to earth. Three: a gem elixir made with rose quartz, malachite, amethyst, citrine, blue kyanite, sunstone and moonstone and set out under the full moon to infuse until just before dawn; this represents my connection to water. Four: a piece of volcanic basalt rock from the Bachit Basalt Rock Formation in Nigeria; this represents my connection to fire, as well as my homeland. Once all items are in your possession, build a fire of palo santo and birch wood, and chant the following: "Bisa Bello—your spirit exists in the scent of amber, your voice is heard in the flutter of an owl's wings, your blood flows in the droplets of potions, your heart pulses like lava. Your body, of this earth, lives in the purple pigment of the earth. Hear my call—with pure love and light, *invoko te—invoko te—invoko te.*" Cast all items into the fire along with my self-portrait and burn to ash. Bury the ashes in the ground.'"

Avery looked up at Ollie and waited for him to speak. When he didn't, she said, "Then what? That's it? Is she going to just sprout from the ground?"

Ollie looked up into space. "Self-portrait?"

The words echoed against Avery's enthused silence and racing heart. They bolted to Bisa's room and pushed the door open. Ollie stopped in his tracks once he entered, and stared into space, looking for any sort of energetic guidance. Avery rushed in and rustled through the pile of canvases in the corner. She checked behind each one, her teeth biting an anxious tongue.

Paintings of landscapes, abstract dreams and dark psychedelic milieus, but no portraits.

Ollie closed his eyes for a second and approached the easel in the opposite corner with a steady stride, as if he were being pulled by a wire. One step, and another, and his eyes opened and landed on the painting with deep crimson tones. "Here," he said as he reached a hand out toward the painting. It wasn't a portrait, but some sort of still life with interleaved sheets of reality, fantasy and bestial unexplored emotion.

Avery whipped her head around and faced Ollie. "You found it?" she asked impatiently.

Puzzled, Ollie removed the painting from the easel and looked behind it. Leaning up against the wall, half hidden in shadow, was the face of Bisa staring back at him. The visage of someone suspended in time, embodied in tones of crimson and cherry, showcased by an aura of gold. Her eyes conjured the fever of meditations spent in the Somnium plane, and a destiny crowded with juxtaposition. There was beauty, and truth, and power in those eyes. Ollie approached the painting, lifted it from the corner and brought it to the light of the window. He explored the canvas with his fingers and experienced the textured paint as if it were a sort of energetic Braille disguised as a painting. He grabbed hold of it and turned it around to see the back. Nothing.

"Could this work?" Avery asked.

Ollie shook his head. Doubt was everywhere, like stars in the night sky, bringing reason and logic to everything he'd learned. "I don't think so," he said. He tried to sense any other spirits in the room that might have an answer, but there were none. "I mean, maybe? I don't know. Nina would know."

Would she? Avery thought. *I'm not so sure.* Instead she said, "Nina always said that she knew a lot, but not everything. But if I took anything away from knowing her, it was that boundaries can always be pushed."

"But we're talking about laws here, proper laws of nature," Ollie said. "And as far as we know, facts. No one has ever been able to successfully do something like that. Surely we would've come across that by now, or heard about it. Someone would have said something like that. If it were true, no one would be dead." Ollie looked out the window, now doubting his own stance. He turned to Avery. "Right?"

"We're not gonna know unless we try," Avery said. "What do we have to lose at this point? I'm not really one for rules or laws unless they're my own. I don't think I would've had half the life I've had if I had followed every rule."

"Getting these ingredients is going to take a little time," Ollie said.

Avery nodded and checked the full moon app on her phone. "We have until April ninth to get everything if we want to do this right away. Eighteen days. That's the next full moon."

A thousand and some miles away in Cayucos, California, Mitch was headed back to his parents' house after an early morning trip to Morro Rock Beach, where he intended to have a healing meditation followed by some yoga, a long-neglected hobby that he had lost interest in. As the darkness in the clouds above faded to light, Mitch listened to the waves crashing onto the shore. Even the beach in all its majesty couldn't truly rouse him from his suffering. He'd barely even made it to the beach to begin with. It was exhausting enough to get out of bed, and thinking about brushing his teeth felt like—a lot, too much. He couldn't meditate, and he couldn't bring himself to do any sort of yoga except shavasana for a half hour after thirty minutes of nothing.

His hair was getting long. An unkempt, greasy lock fell across his forehead and flapped in the breeze. *I told you this was pointless. You can't even bring yourself to wash your hair right now…Sally,* he thought. It was Leo who had given him that offensive nickname, but it proved to be useful at a time like this when he was so down. It was easier to stay there. He wondered if this was how Leo always felt on the inside. Had he ever been happy? Had Mitch just been pretending his whole life? How could he even tell anymore?

He looked down at his thumb, bloody from picking that he hadn't even known he was doing. *What the fuck is the point anymore? Did you really think life was ever going to get any better?* For a brief moment he thought about how annoying Leo was with all of his negativity, and then he instantly felt repulsed: he was the same way. He couldn't stop ruminating. Even magic couldn't make him stop, because he couldn't bring himself to try. *What's the point? It probably wouldn't even work. Magic just seems like another way for me to fail and not be good enough. I'm probably going to be five hundred years old and still be sitting on this fucking beach, with my one skill being picking the best yarn for a hat.*

Mitch's heart skipped a beat, and he clutched his chest. His body heaved as he battled for breath. A sudden tightness in his lungs seized him completely. He gagged and coughed as if ghostly hands were at his throat trying to collapse his airway. It was gone, as quickly as it had come. *A bug, probably,* Mitch thought as he slowly fell back into his train of thought.

Mitch had even given up on his Etsy store and shut it down. He was already fed up with them taking a portion of his sales. After thirty-two hats, three robes, seventeen scarves and enough mittens to prevent the entire state of New York from ever having frostbite, he'd finally determined that nothing really mattered. He'd been home for only a short while, and in that short while he'd decided to stop answering his stepmom's questions when she asked if he was still selling crocheted clothes. What she was really asking was *What are you doing with your life? You're too old for this.* At least that's what he told himself. It indeed was what his stepmom wanted to know when she hugged him and asked if he was eating. Showing up practically uninvited only to be bombarded with questions he didn't really have answers to, the energy to respond to, or anything for them to be proud of all made for a truly self-disinviting experience.

Only he had nowhere else better to be. The benefit of being with his dad and stepmom was that he could distance himself from all the trauma he'd been through, because they didn't know that Mitch. Mitch didn't want to know that Mitch—at least not for a while. He hadn't heard from his biological mother in such a long time, it didn't make sense to try to see her. It occurred to him that he didn't have her number anymore, so he couldn't call her to say he was in town even if he wanted to. His dad and stepmom *were* his parents now.

When Mitch arrived back home, his stepmom was hysterical in the most catatonic way he'd ever seen. She was draped over the back of a living room chair, surrounded by a heaviness that Mitch felt but couldn't see. The fingers of her right hand savagely stroked the length of her forehead over and over as she stared at the memories in her head that fought the reality of the news she had just been given. Mitch stayed quiet for a moment as he stared at Diane. He knew that disposition well. Maybe something had happened to her adventurous daughter; Diane never liked how she galivanted around the world, climbing mountains on every continent. Her parents were both deceased already, so it couldn't be that. But it couldn't be...*that*.

Diane turned to Mitch and locked eyes with him long enough to deliver two words. "Bad morning."

Mitch took a step backward. "What happened?"

Diane's hand fluttered down from her forehead to her mouth before it rested nervously on the side of her neck. "Your dad went to the store"—she paused a moment—"and he had a stroke." Diane shook her head in disbelief. "He was going to make us all breakfast." She let out a pained gush of air as her chest tightened.

Mitch felt it before he knew it.

Diane locked eyes with him one more time. "He's dead."

Mitch ruminated over her words until they muddled together and didn't seem to make any sense. He almost ran out of the room, but he was already running—had been running. Mitch felt the bug in his throat again, but this time he knew it wasn't a bug at all. His father was gone. To his surprise, tears weren't the first thing to arrive next, but memories, nostalgia and even some regret. Instantly he tried to recite the prayer his dad had taught him when he was little. He made sure he said it every single night no matter how tired he was or what work he still had to finish—only now Mitch could remember only the first few words. He repeated them over and over in his head, hoping it would trigger the rest of the prayer, but the rest of the words never came.

Memories of his childhood came flooding in next. Mitch thought of the neighborhood he explored as a child, where all the streets had names specific to Mormonism: Mosiah and Ammon Court, King Benjamin, Zarahemla, and Helaman streets. Everyone called the main road that connected them all the Book of Mormon. Its real name escaped him. He used to walk down that street every day after school in tears because the other kids would tease him all day. Mitch suddenly heard all of their taunts as if they were right there in the room. *Are you a boy or a girl?* Mitch would never answer, but they would always laugh. Why are kids so mean? *I should have told my dad*, Mitch thought, but he never did. Instead, he started tattling on everyone to get revenge. It only made things worse, and everyone called him Mitch the Twitchy Snitch because of the numerous tics he couldn't hide. It might actually have been laughable if it hadn't been so painfully accurate.

Back then, his father said they could pray his tics away at church in the prayer circle and it would get better. They had prayed—a lot. It never helped, but that was where Mitch met Bethany, who taught him to cross-stitch. He enjoyed how it made his tics disappear because he was so focused. But staring at the fine crosshatch patterns being pierced by a needle made his eyes uncomfortable and gave him a new winking tic. When summer rolled around, he would dance to "Gypsy Woman" by Crystal Waters in his bedroom and then try to sell his stitched creations around the neighborhood. It turned out there wasn't really a market for small linen squares of cross-stitched robins, snowmen and snowflakes, but it did encourage change. The kids started to call him Cross-Stitch Mitch instead. He never told his dad any of this, but also, his dad never asked. *And now he'll never know any of this. Or maybe he knows it all now because he's gone?*

Mitch loved that his dad had been so receptive when he'd come out. He was such a proud Christian father, going to church and trying to be good to his family, until religion seemed to disagree with many things his son naturally was. It felt like he turned on a dime without vacillation, but Mitch never really knew. What he did know was that he loved his father just a little more from that point on, but he didn't truly realize it until he was told he was dead.

It was like there was a cloud of suffering above Mitch that rained on him no matter where he went. His only relief was that his brother, Chad, didn't speak to him during the funeral, the burial or the wake. He had been dreading exchanging dialogue with him in any way, and when they made eye contact for the first time at the funeral, Chad immediately looked away, as though he'd seen an old boss in the produce section who hadn't been given a fair two weeks' notice. Finally, a moment without heavy rain—albeit no sun.

A week passed, and Mitch had nowhere to go, but he couldn't stay at home any longer either. He did what every other bored, lonely or depressed gay did—downloaded a sex app pretending to be a dating app, rife with headless torsos, profiles filled with *masc4masc, no fem, can host, dtsd,* and *looking for top.* He snapped a pic that gave face but said absolutely nothing.

Within minutes, the digital dogs smelled fresh meat. Messages arrived from all distances and, oddly, in groups of three every few minutes: *Woof. Hung top on PREP do you have nice feet? Into?* Mitch escaped from the nightmare of reality into a whole new kind of netherworld. He understood very little, it seemed. He'd been out of this kind of world for longer than he could remember, and it had evolved to a sort of perverted, to-the-point shorthand. *Woof? Into? What does that even mean? I...don't even know how to answer that.* He continued to weed through profiles and judge them based on their profile photo and info alone. More messages came, this time with images: *(dick pic) hot af—flood me plz, I want you to glaze me like a donut (cumshot).*

Mitch was exhausted from everything. He wondered how he could want company but also *not* want company. He had spent the good portion of three days collecting dick pics, corresponding with randoms, and making plans to meet and hook up with them right before ghosting them. It was easier to ghost when they didn't know your real name and had been fed nothing but a banquet of lies ranging from being a Coppola to being a sign language instructor. He left the apps open all the time, allowing them to drain his battery and steal the attention of nearby gays when the infamous chirp of a new message went off inside his pocket while out and about.

There was nothing particularly special about NathTech, he just happened to be the first one who talked about yarn. Mitch was so low and worn down from ghosting that he eventually had no option but to give in. His name was Nathan and he was an IT specialist. Some malady in his youth had left him partially blind in one eye, which meant that his other eye worked overtime, but not nearly as much as his mouth. The guy just wouldn't stop talking. It didn't matter if Mitch answered one of his questions or replied to one of his disorganized thoughts, Nathan found a way to dominate the conversation regardless. In a way it was darkly comedic, being assaulted by his incessant monologues, like having to sit front row through a full comedy show where no one laughed.

Somehow Nathan's conversation seemed more entertaining via messaging. His tedious storytelling delivered via rapid-fire text on Scruff was absolutely mind numbing when face-to-face. Any chance of him actually finding someone who could tolerate him long enough without leaving was slim to none. It was undoubtedly the reason why he talked so much; Mitch was the first person who stayed around long enough to listen, at least since his last boyfriend, Jake—who jerked off to gay porn so much that it turned him straight and he couldn't get aroused by men anymore. Probably wasn't true; it was probably just really hard to get head when Nathan wouldn't stop talking. Which was true because Mitch tried—twice. Not to say they didn't fool around—they did—but Mitch never made the first move, and he always had to be just a little drunk.

Mitch wasn't even attracted to Nathan, and honestly, he didn't like him any more than he liked himself, which wasn't very much. He kept him around partially because he felt he deserved it; misery loved company. When it came to coping mechanisms, tedious, one-sided chat was a hell of a lot better than picking skin until it bled. Now he only had to worry about his ears bleeding. Mitch kept Nathan around because it made him feel better about himself—because at least he wasn't Nathan.

How can this guy actually have any friends? And as soon as he thought it, he felt it. Maybe it was his witchy intuition finally beginning to bud. His eyes went wide as he waited for what he knew was coming: the invite.

"What are you doing tomorrow night?" Nathan asked as he sprawled his leg over Mitch and nestled into his side on the bed.

Think fast, say you're busy! "I don't know." *Shit!*

Nathan hardly waited for him to answer. "Come with me to my friend's party."

Has he even met me? What makes him think I want to meet his friends? "I can't," Mitch said.

"What do you mean you can't? Of course you can. Ugh, you never want to do anything. I make time for you, I invite you to do things all the time, I buy you dinner, I tell you everything."

I really wish you wouldn't. "Why is everything always about you?" Mitch finally made some serious eye contact and analyzed him. "You're such a selfish, arrogant...Virgo," he said, but he wasn't even sure if Nathan was a Virgo. He couldn't remember because there were just too many details. A night with Nathan was like being forced to listen to all of Wikipedia read aloud using text-to-speech.

Then something amazing happened. There were a few seconds of silence where Nathan couldn't tell if Mitch was serious and annoyed or joking and just mean.

Nathan rubbed his leg up and down Mitch's thigh and truffle-pigged into his armpit. "We could have hot sex in this bed," he said, smirking.

Ha! "Oh really?"

"Yeah. It's about time. We've been messing around for like, what, two weeks now?"

Unfortunately. "I don't have sex."

For the second time in history there was another break in Nathan's talking. His head cocked up from the bed. "You don't? Are you an alien? You don't have sex?"

"No, not unless I'm seriously dating someone."

"Would you date me?" Nathan asked, unreasonably hopeful.

Hell no. "No."

"I would date you," Nathan said.

"I don't date either," Mitch said.

"Oh…so you …don't have sex then?"

Just get up, Mitch, just leave. Do it before you accidentally, or deliberately, set fire to him. "No, I don't like it. Being a top doesn't get me off, and bottoming hurts."

"So you don't suck cock now either?"

Ugh, I was hoping he would ignore that I kept resisting that. "Nope."

"So that has changed in the last week or so?"

"What?" *Okay, now he's finally done it, he's finally confused the hell out of me.* "What are you talking about?"

Nathan pulled his leg back and sat up. "Are you kidding me?"

"No?"

"Um…you went down on me?" he said.

Mitch stared into Nathan's good eye until it was uncomfortable. "I did?" he said, confused, partially amused and a little disgusted with himself.

"Yes, when you were drunk off that bottle you brought over."

I remember the bottle. I wish I could smell a lie like Avery. "Well, I don't remember that."

Nathan pursed his lips and narrowed his eyes. "Mmmmm…" he grumbled.

"What does that mean?"

"It means there's a limit to my tolerance level."

"I see." *I don't care.*

"And you call *me* self-serving."

Mitch agreed to go to the party, mostly out of guilt, and ended the night. For as much time as he had spent with Nathan, he felt relieved when he was gone.

CHAPTER 2

What the hell are we going to do here? Leo thought as Merlot drove through a crumbling part of town, past treatment clinics and tent cities, massive warehouses and graffitied buildings for rent. He reached up and scratched an itch on his nose, and sniffed a few times.

"Hey, when I plug my nose, like, after, it smells really bad. Like I can smell the inside of my nose. It smells really bad. Is that normal?" Leo squished his nostrils together and took a deep sniff.

Merlot shook her head and kept her eyes on the road. "Is this really what you think about?" she asked, although she didn't actually want an answer.

"Well, yeah, that's why I asked."

Merlot let out a sigh as she turned onto a side street.

This can't be it, Leo pondered as Merlot pulled up to a long, one-story building where street trash fluttered in the breeze around the entrance.

Leo shook his head, utterly confused. Merlot parked and walked to the entrance, her stride confident and composed, like she owned the place. Leo shut the car door and slowly followed her. The whole vibe felt uncomfortably familiar; it felt like she was pretending to help, only to lure him into a treatment clinic where she'd have him sign in and he wouldn't be able to leave. Only he would have the means to make sure that never happened, and also that Merlot wouldn't ever take another breath.

"Hey, yo, I thought we were going to try to manipulate my blood or whatever," Leo said.

"That's exactly what we're doing here," Merlot reassured him.

"Here?" Leo asked as he took another look around the neighborhood. The only signs of life were a few homeless people across the street, a few sirens in the distance, and a rustling coming from the alley that he assumed was a rat, maybe several rats.

Merlot entered a code into the keypad at the front door, the only thing within a five-block radius that had no graffiti, and the door opened with a click and a swoosh. Leo heard the sound of silence, the kind of medical science silence that was laced ever so gently with the humming of machines and equipment and the whirring of centrifuges. When the door shut behind him, Merlot led him through the hall of fluorescent lights and down a stairwell to another part of the facility. Leo gazed around apprehensively as Merlot led him to the room at the end of the hall. A plaque next to the door read *LAB 4*.

Merlot retrieved a keycard from her pocket, swiped it through the sensor and pushed open the door. "After you," she said.

"What are we doing here? Leo asked, his voice tense. "I feel like you're just fucking with me. Are you gonna help me or not?"

"Ay dios mio, we are going to work on your blood *here*, where we have the proper equipment to do it."

"What is this place?" Leo asked.

"A sex club—my goodness, what does it look like? It's a lab, my lab—I own it," she said as she waved for him to enter the room. "You poor babies, you have no idea the things you can have if you just *use* your powers instead of wasting them trying to light candles from across the room."

"What do we need a lab for? I thought we were gonna do some sort of weird magic shit. What are you gonna do?" Leo asked as he passed through the doorway.

"A blend of science and magic."

"And what's that?" Leo scratched his head and took notice of the world of expensive equipment around the room: blinking lights, beakers and flasks, high-powered microscopes and machines that measured and analyzed blood chemistry and various other instruments that most people never see once in their entire lives. It looked like a small city, or the face of some electronic music producer's studio cabinet.

"Miracles," she said as she shut the door behind him. The sounds of the equipment sounded louder and more menacing with the door shut. "Take off your jacket."

"Why don't you show me how to—"

"I already told you I'd help you *after*, so stop asking or you'll get nothing. Either you agree to that or you leave."

After Leo choked down his anger, he peeled off his jacket and took a seat on a stool. Merlot remained unflappable, but with a little smirk. She picked up the phone on the wall and called a technician into the room. Leo knew she was in complete control and he had no choice but to play along.

The technician entered the room, a young, fresh graduate with brains that could've swallowed both Leo and Merlot whole.

"Do they...know?" Leo asked.

Merlot smiled. "They know what they need to. I've made that so." She pulled out a little joint from her coat pocket and lit it.

"Should you really be smoking in here?" Leo asked.

Merlot sucked the smoke into her lungs, held it, and then blew it toward his face. "This is my fucking house. I do what I want here."

Leo watched the technician prepare things that looked like he was going to be broken down like a chicken and prepped for roasting. "Is this gonna hurt?"

Merlot waggled her head back and forth. "First, we have to extract your blood, then we have to try a few different things after that, then some incantations, spell and ritual work trials to see if any of that will work. It's all very experimental. So, we've got a lot of things to get started."

"What kind of things? Will it hurt?"

"Yeah, probably," Merlot said casually.

Hours full of pricks and prods passed slowly, almost like they were enchanted to be as such. Each passing minute seemed longer than the last, and when there were no needle pricks, there were aggressive injections. Merlot tried a few magical experiments off in the far corner of the room when Leo had provided enough blood samples to get started. *I should be closer than this by now*, she thought as each failed attempt at creating the miracle blood drove her closer to believing it just wasn't possible. She had several brains working for her at the lab, and with a team that smart, she was certain she could do the impossible. Merlot could remember only one other time in her life that she didn't get what she wanted: when she wasn't chosen for the position in the Advisory. She wasn't going to let that happen again. Everything she had done since then was proof of her unstoppable ambition. She *would* make this happen, regardless of all the other things she had on her plate.

Merlot retrieved the final blood sample for the time being and added it to a small beaker. She added various other elixirs, potions and distilled liquids before she held her palm over the opening and recited various incantations. She could see her desires on the insides of her eyelids, and her heart skipped a beat right before she opened them, only to be disappointed that the blood remained unchanged. Sometimes the beaker shattered, or turned acidic. However, she reminded herself that to be successful, you have to fail—repeatedly.

Merlot had to try to forget about how many steps the head technician told her were left. She had to—otherwise the goal felt too unattainable. The blood had to be extracted, altered, reinjected for at least a full day, then extracted again, and altered once more with an incantation. Only then would it finally turn gold. All the books and all the mind digging she did on all the technicians had proved this was the only way it would work. She would have to knife through the tests of defeat no matter how exhausted, upset or uncooperative Leo became. He had no choice but to be stuck until his arm went numb.

Merlot looked at the clock and knew if she was going to make it where she needed to be, she needed to stop for now. Which is exactly what she reluctantly decided to do. She turned to Leo, who was sipping juice from a small paper cup, and put on her coat.

"Are we done?" Leo asked. His face was pale, his lips had gone a little blue and his shirt was damp with stress sweat.

"We've just started. I'm going to have them continue a few more things and then we can try again tomorrow. So tonight, rest up. Eat well. And we'll return tomorrow."

"You're leaving me here? Where are you going?"

"Yes." Her aggravation over a day of failure was relieved only by a little callousness here and there.

CHAPTER 3

There was no turning back now, at least not without making a huge scene. Mitch and Nathan stood in the hallway of his friend's obnoxiously opulent apartment building, listening to the boisterous epidemic of catchy electro-dance pop that spread straight through the door. Nathan knocked on the door using the dainty silver knocker.

"This is a gay building," Mitch said as he looked around the hyper-stylized hall: a sleek black concrete floor covered in shiny lacquer, walls painted a bordello red, and vibrant, tailored lighting that lit the halls like the runway at Paris Fashion Week.

"Oh my God, you have no idea. So many gays live in this building. Half the people who live here are probably already inside. Or they're pregaming at the grand bar on the top floor."

That wasn't what Mitch meant, but he took satisfaction in calling it for what it was. Nathan knocked again, and suddenly the door swung open and a man three sheets to the wind answered.

There was a moment of hesitation.

"Oh! You came!" Jeff said in a tone that was crowded with disappointment. "I thought maybe you wouldn't come because I changed the date and I didn't—forgot to—tell you," he slurred. Nathan seemed oblivious to the fact that he wasn't actually invited this time and maybe wasn't even welcome. If first impressions mattered, then Mitch made a horrible one just by being the friend of the buzzkill.

Nathan stepped into the apartment and pulled Mitch inside, where a bomb of boysmells stormed his senses. "No, yeah,

Perry told me it was tonight instead of next week like usual," Nathan explained as he shut the door.

Jeff scoffed and lifted his drink into the air, and a small wave splashed out onto the floor. "I'll have to tell—talk to—Perry, so that *next* time…" Jeff shrank his eyes, pointed a finger at Nathan and waved it back and forth.

"Is he here?" Nathan asked.

"Perry's not here tonight." Jeff clicked his tongue and raised his eyebrows. "But *you* are!"

Nathan grabbed Mitch's butt as he said, "This is Mitch!"

"Hi Mitch," Jeff said with a great deal more respect and civility than he had given Nathan. "Come in, have drinks, state your boundaries, be safe, and no photos." Jeff ran his fingers through his hair and analyzed Mitch before he asked, "Are you a watcher?" He didn't even wait for a response before continuing, "We need more watchers. Vincent always wants more watchers. You'll meet him, he's like a Muppet, he doesn't have any lips. But if you wanna watch, just wear the blueballs sticker. There's a big bowl of them by the bar." His eyes were glazed.

Jeff cut them loose and invited them to explore the massive apartment. Mitch panicked a little upon realizing what kind of party it was. Before he could say anything, Nathan was gone, chatting up people who didn't care about anything he had to say. Mitch found the bar and the bowl of blueballs stickers. He couldn't bring himself to actually put on a sticker, because that would mean he was participating, and he just couldn't have that, even if he wasn't actually participating. He poured a drink as stiff as the gaggle of gays in the corner under the cover of the smoke machine playing some kind of drinking game. The crushing sounds of Gaga finally had a break with a hint of

Deadmau5 and some fleeting tracks by queens of hip-hop. The energy was insufferable, like a three-hour drag brunch with second-rate mimosas, rafter gymnastics and mobs waving dollar bills, when all one wanted was a well-seasoned soft scramble and to hear themselves think.

Mitch finished a gin and tonic in about as much time as it took him to mix it. He didn't even like gin; he thought it tasted like vomit. Which he was moments away from doing between the company, the music and the gin. He helped himself to the fancy charcuterie board before setting the cheese back down because it felt too warm and he didn't like the way it felt against his skin.

It was then that Nathan shouted his name. There was no escaping a shout from Nathan; it could be heard from space. Mitch poured another drink and listened to Nathan scream his name again. Mitch rolled his eyes, turned around and made his way toward Nathan, who was standing next to two other guys, who were also shaking their heads and rolling their eyes. *I would almost feel sorry for him if I didn't actually detest him so much. He has no idea that he's so irritating. I hope I'm not like that. I probably am.* He wondered for a moment what would happen if he grabbed one of the other guys and started kissing him. Maybe Nathan would hate him forever. But then again, maybe not—it was a sex party. The younger one was clearly a seasoned regular, Mitch could smell it. The older and more attractive one seemed to have a type by the look in his eye, and it wasn't Mitch. Both of them were already as irritating as Nathan in their own way, and he hadn't even spoken to them yet. *Why can't I ever go to a party full of gays that I actually like? Do they even exist? Where the hell are they? Why is this gay culture?*

Nathan rubbed the older guy's back and smiled. "This is Travis. He posed for *Playgirl* once and was in a Sean Cody video back when that was a thing, but his porn name is *Ståle*," Nathan said mockingly.

Travis shot Nathan a look full of scorn. His final seal of disapproval on Nathan as a person. "Why do you do that? I really hate it when you tell that to strangers." He walked away. "It wasn't even Sean Cody," he said to no one.

"So this is a sex party?" Mitch asked the younger, seasoned regular.

"I like to think of it as Christmas meets Halloween," he said proudly.

Well, it is scary, so...you've got something on Halloween. "What do you mean?" Mitch asked, dying to find out what the regular was going to say, and also wondering why Nathan wasn't the one talking for once.

"Well, everyone loves Halloween and it's like a big house full of presents," said the regular.

"Sorry, I still don't get it," Mitch said.

"It's like a holiday, only we celebrate it every month instead of every year." He gave Nathan some side eye. "It's usually *next* week, but..."

"Huh. Weird," Mitch said without hesitation, his voice full of disdain.

A bitch face rolled over the seasoned regular. "What's wrong with our holiday?" he said, heavy on the bitters.

Mitch took a sip of his poorly made cocktail with high-end liquor and shook his head."This isn't a holiday."

"Why not? Don't you have days where you get together with people to celebrate and play games?" the regular asked.

Mitch snorted, "Yeah. But not *sex* games."

A million eye rolls. "Don't be so *unwoke*. Evolve," he said with the type of judgment that Mitch had grown to expect from the community that seemed to love to revel in attitudes and exteriors and never have anything of substance. At least according to Mitch's experience.

Disgust filled Mitch, only this time it wasn't Nathan, or the warm cheese, or the pine-like booze, or the ground-shaking pop music that only seemed to get louder, stronger and deeper. "Evolving isn't...having sex," he said plainly.

"Actually it is," the regular delivered in an arrogant tone.

"You know what I meant," Mitch said, thinking he might just be in a fight. Somewhere in the room a disco party light started spinning flurries of fluorescent magenta, sapphire, and sour apple green across the seasoned regular's chest. For a moment, Mitch wished they were bullets, forcing him and his judgmental, horned-up arrogance to go away. *No wonder so many conservatives think we're crazy perverts. Sometimes I feel like the only gay who isn't like this.*

Mitch had nothing in common with anyone there, and he started to feel the Mitch the Snitch energy explode inside him. As he downed the last of his icy drink, he thought he saw Nina in the back of the room. But what the hell would she be doing at a gay sex party, and not even a good one. He started to turn away from them, but before he could, Nathan grabbed his arm. "Where are you going?" Then he began talking about something that Mitch didn't care about. Had he paid a little more attention to something that wasn't *him*, he might have noticed that Mitch looked practically catatonic and was drowning out everything he said.

"I have to use the bathroom," Mitch lied. He could just leave, but Mitch was madly in love with being miserable, and if one is in love—they don't leave. He had power, but he didn't think he was any good at using it, so it only made him feel like more of a failure. At least he was a fucking champion at being depressed.

In the bathroom he found a few moments of peace. He flushed the toilet he didn't use, ran the faucet and touched the towel as if someone was that obsessed with detail and might be checking. He left the bathroom and found his way back to the kitchen, where he grabbed a beer, walked into one of the hallways and sank onto the floor. He propped himself up against the wall and raised his knees up. He listened to the thumping music and got lost in his own thoughts. At least he wasn't picking at his skin. When the smoke machine paused, Mitch looked down the hall and into the gaggle in the other room. He didn't understand them any more than they understood him. Everyone just felt like attention-seeking, sex-craved relentless partyers whose personality was Gaga, Britney or Beyoncé. Mitch was never really a gay culture gay; he was just Mitch. The person he had become had a poisonous contempt for the entire community, especially those at the party, and he was so fond of his own perspective and condescending authenticity that he wasn't aware that he was doing the exact same thing that he accused everyone else of doing to him. Well, he knew a little bit; it just didn't matter. This was a kink and coke community with brunch in the morning, and *no one* knew how to crochet. Except for Nathan. But that didn't count.

"Not your scene, huh?" said a voice from above.

Mitch looked up to see a sweet-faced man with eyes the color of weathered bark, a good seven to eight years older, elegant, and out of place. A welcome sore thumb in the middle of a nightmare that was quickly beginning to mature into pandemonium.

Mitch chuckled and let out a *psssh* noise. "No," he replied as he tore his eyes away from the man long enough to look around at the rapidly shifting energy. He looked back up at the man, who was gazing back at him with a good-natured stare that one only gets when someone says *I like you* for the first time.

The man nodded, smiled and lifted his eyebrows. "Mine either," he said as he leaned up against the wall and slid down to sit next to Mitch. The edge of his knee brushed ever so innocently against Mitch's, and when Mitch turned his head to look at him at eye level, he saw his aura in rose gold. There was an earthiness to him, but also an artsiness that Mitch could almost taste, but definitely see and feel. *Taurus...maybe.* Mitch instantly tried to put together an astrological profile.

"What do you do?" Mitch asked. He always hated that question, as if someone was defined by the work they did and judged for it in some way. But it was the only thing he could think of in that moment under the rose gold light.

"I'm a screenwriter. Mostly. I also make music. I have kind of a hobby band with some friends. Lots of distorted guitar, heavy on the drums, and loops of moody, metallic feedback. Things like that. I have my hands in a lot of things. So whatever they call someone like that, that's what I do."

Steven Soderbergh Sun. Jim Jarmusch or Christopher Nolan Moon. Timotheé Chalamet Rising.

"I'm Jace," the man said as he held out his hand.

"Mitch," Mitch said as he shook Jace's hand and inadvertently let his well-guarded wall begin to crumble.

Everything else dissolved, and the energy between them suddenly ignited. There was a unique kindness to Jace's temperament, and when he smiled, it never felt like it was being polite.

Jace looked around cautiously for a moment and then leaned in a little closer. Mitch would've flinched had it been anyone else. He stopped a few inches from Mitch's ear and whispered, "I'm also…" and then inside Mitch's head, "a witch."

Mitch's eyes went wide as saucers, but the gentleness in Jace's eyes kept him from panicking.

They shared a moment, something that other people wouldn't value, of unspoken recognition, a knowing, the kind that could happen only when both people are thinking and feeling the exact same thing. The second most outstanding thing was how casual and easy their energy was. Jace didn't break eye contact. Mitch almost looked away and considered saying something, but Jace reacted in precisely the same fashion. They looked into each other's eyes as if their souls were enjoying a warm conversation with the cosmos within each other.

Right then, he knew it: for the first time, he was in love. Mitch couldn't explain it. Nothing he could say would articulate any of the feelings he was having. It felt good—right. It was beautiful. He was beautiful. It felt like an epic joke as Mitch thought about all the times he'd thought he was in love and that the person was surely the one, someone who had done far more than start a conversation on the floor. And here was Jace, doing next to nothing and making Mitch rethink what love means in the matter of an instant.

"Is…" Mitch looked around the apartment.

"Anyone else here a witch? No."

"How did you know? About me, I mean. How could you tell?"

Jace considered how to answer. "I could smell it."

"Are you in a coven here?" Mitch asked.

"No, these are all vampires," Jace said jokingly.

Mitch laughed and noticed how it felt like something that hadn't happened in millennia. "No, I mean—"

"I know what you mean," Jace said with a smile, and shook his head. "I'm not. I know a lot of the witches in a couple of the Southern California covens, but…after a few years"—he paused—"it just wasn't for me anymore, you know?"

Mitch understood. "Did something happen?"

There was a pause, then a deep inhale and exhale. "I was really excited—crazy excited—when I first learned about witchcraft. I mean, who wouldn't be, right? Especially someone like me. I go to work, eat sushi, and spend all day making up shit to film, just like tons of other people here. One day, everything changed. I joined a coven; this was all years ago. It was kind of a rough time for our Proctor. There was this other witch who became obsessed with magic. All kinds of it. Someone in the coven at the time. They were triggered by magic a little differently from the rest of us. I don't think they were inherently a bad person; I don't know if anyone really is. But just the wrong chemistry, I guess. Something in them was kind of unleashed when they learned magic was real. It's kind of like trying to stop, I dunno, an extinction-level asteroid from hitting Earth when it's already barreling toward us. Or like herpes, you know, you just can't kill it. It changed how they were and how they thought. How they reacted.

"Anyway!" Jace took a breath. "To make a long story short, something the studios are always on my case about, one night things got really bad. And this person was really strong, had gotten really powerful and knew he was powerful. He got into an argument with a friend of mine, another member of the coven, and it got violent. I intervened, and that's when he said he'd stop if I was able to read his mind and tell him what his high school mascot was, like it was some kind of security question to log in to your bank app. If I couldn't do it, he was gonna kill them."

Mitch sat in thought for a moment and nodded. He didn't have to ask what happened; he knew.

"So, a few weeks after that I was standing outside in my backyard charging some ritual tools on a folding chair in the moonlight. It's winter, and it's cold enough to see my breath for once. And I'm staring at my tools, almost through them, where I can see my thoughts, and I start thinking, *When did I become this person who bathes altar tools in moonlight?* I don't know, everything changed from that point on. Left the coven. Still a witch.

"Everybody has something dark. But there's definitely a power to gain from darkness. If you accept it, you can leverage it, create something with it. For me, it just made sense, you know, as a screenwriter and filmmaker. My job as a filmmaker, or *our* jobs as creatives"—Jace reached toward Mitch to include him—"is to discover and illuminate whatever it is that's in the dark, breathe a new kind of fire into it. Rebrand it, give it a new life, make it share its story, give it a whole new identity or force it out of the dark.

"Most people in the industry hate actors, but I fucking love 'em. I think it takes a lot of empathy to be an actor. You have to assume whatever role it is, without judgment or bias, at least if you want that performance to have any sort of genuine truth to it. I think interrogating the dark like that, and really going through it, feeling it, makes you more empathic. It can even be therapeutic, because you also have to make sure you aren't destroyed and slaughtered by it either. Acting, or any art, is its own kind of magic. Art can show us who we are in a way that we can identify with or understand, or accept in some way. I mean, how do you feel after you see a really good film, or read a great book or wear a well-crocheted hat?"

Mitch's ears perked up.

"It's amazing to build something and then share it. We're all just trying to be seen and heard and understood," Jace said, realizing that Mitch had taken his monologue pretty well.

Mitch nodded and his mouth tightened with empathy, his eyes glistening with fascination. Then he scoffed and almost giggled in shock. "I can't believe you just, like, told me all that. I met you, what, a few minutes ago?" He was floored by Jace's direct and honest what-you-see-is-what-you-get attitude.

"Take it or leave it. You're the first witch I've come across in a while. I also felt like it wasn't going to scare you off. Or that maybe you needed to hear it. I mean, if this party didn't scare you off, then that story didn't stand a chance."

They laughed.

"Do you celebrate this *holiday* too?" Mitch asked.

Jace shook his head. "No. I don't really celebrate any holidays."

"Not even like, Christmas? Or Hanukkah? Or…whatever this is."

"No, not really. None of them really mean much to me. People don't even know what they're celebrating anyway, so it seems kinda silly. Except birthdays, and maybe things like weddings, things like that. The actual thing being celebrated is pretty clear."

"Who do you know here anyway? Do you always come to these things?" Mitch asked, genuinely confused.

"An actor friend invited me. I didn't know it was going to be a *sex party* sex party. Not really my vibe. I was going to just have a beer and slip on out undetected, but that's when I caught your smell."

Mitch had lived his entire life with people staring at him or not seeing him at all, but he'd been waiting for someone to look at him the way Jace looked at him. In the multicolored oceans of Jace's eyes, Mitch felt in an instant that someone saw his core beneath the knitwear, the skin, and all the other sheets that covered the real Mitch. The thought of being seen felt really good, but it was also terrifying. *What kind of fucked-up person would see me and not run?*

Mitch never liked how easily he fell in love with people. It often didn't take much. He was slightly ashamed of his track record of choosing people who would never or could never love him back, people he loved only because he'd built them up as the perfect lover simply because they smiled at him from afar. The rest he filled in with fiction, crafting something out of nothing like it was one of his crocheted garments. Maybe it was time to start living his life in a different way. Maybe this was his chance. Something about Jace made Mitch want to be a better person, not just for him, but for Mitch too. It wasn't going to be easy. Mitch could count the number of people he liked and trusted on one hand.

"I know you're a Primordial guy, but what kind of witch are you?" Jace asked.

"A really bad one," Mitch jibed.

Jace rephrased, "What do *you* gravitate toward?"

The question dampened his spirits a little, but he forced himself to answer it honestly out of respect for trying to live his life in a different way, and once he answered, he was relieved. "I honestly don't really know yet. Nothing seems to really vibe with me. It's almost like the magic doesn't really understand me. Or maybe I don't understand *it*. Or maybe I'm just not very good. You'd think magic would make it easier to get your needs met," Mitch added, laughing.

"One thing that my Proctor drilled into us was that magic is really active. It isn't just a way to fix something, or get what you want, or have your needs met—we still have to put in the work. Magic only goes so far; we have to meet it halfway."

"Okay, yeah, but we can still light the fireplace without having to get up off the couch," Mitch reminded him.

"I mean beyond that. Deeper than that."

"Why do you ask, anyway?" Mitch asked.

"Just curious. No judgment. Everyone has their own magical path, and I'm in no place to judge it. Your path is your path. I just want to know more about how you work and what your experiences are. I'm not gonna say what you're doing is wrong or that I'm doing magic right."

For a heartbeat, Mitch felt his defenses begin to melt away as he nervously twisted his malachite ring off and on his finger. He was about to ask a magic-related question, but a loud moan from the other room stopped him. They laughed and continued to talk. The attraction grew as precious as the stones in Mitch's rings. He had never expected to meet someone new who made him as comfortable as someone he'd known forever. A fire began to burn inside him, and for once, he didn't want to rush anything. He wanted to get to know Jace bit by bit, over a long period of time. A huge part of his brain told him to jump head-first into whatever *it* was between them, because he felt that they *could* skip so many steps. But for the first time, he didn't want to.

If Mitch was to be completely honest with himself, which was something that even a spell had trouble coercing him to do, he'd never been able to see a future with someone, anyone— not even himself. He didn't tell Jace any of what his heart was singing, because he didn't want to scare him or cause any sort of trepidation, but he could see a future with Jace. And he wanted to see what happened next with their dynamic, with all the hopes and aspirations that it would develop into a long-term dynamic, with growth and changes and maturity, which he'd always looked for in other situations but never really found. Part of that was his style of treasure hunting—but *this* revealed that everything prior was just a pale imitation of whatever was happening. It was more than he imagined was actually possible. For the first time, he considered that even if their relationship did end in a worst-case scenario, it would still have been worth it. It was wild to feel he inherently knew someone he didn't know at all.

An hour later, Jace gave Mitch a ride home. Mitch didn't even think about Nathan or any deaths he may have caused from his loquaciousness. He looked out into the wet streets. It had rained, and he hadn't even noticed. He noticed that it'd stopped. When they arrived, Mitch's eyes were soft with ado-ration. *I've dreamed of this before,* he thought. The night ended with an exchange of phone numbers and without a kiss.

The chill in the evening air caused his fingers to shrink, leav-ing one of his rings free to slide off without his noticing. It fell in secret to the back of the passenger seat, where it became wedged between the cushions and shrouded in the dark of night.

By the time Mitch got into bed, he was feeling the weight of doubt upon his chest once again, and the familiar hopelessness that was cozier than any of his blankets.

(allow something good to happen...don't shit all over it)

He wasn't sure if that was Nina, some*thing* else, or just his heart trying to be heard in the choir of his depression. But at least he heard it this time.

He lay back on his bed, plugged his ears with his earbuds and fired up "Blue" by Joni Mitchell and stared at the ceiling. When it finished, he listened to Bon Iver's *For Emma, Forever Ago* in its entirety. Immediately afterward he dug through his belongings and looked for something that he'd thought he wouldn't need ever again—or at least for a long while. He thumbed through the pages of one of his notebooks filled with spells and rituals he'd collected while under Nina's tutelage. His thumb fingered a section, and he opened right up to the page he was looking for. The ritual that he'd always wanted to try but never actually had. Hand painted in gold ink across the top of the tea-stained page was *the gold spell—to become the highest version of yourself.* He skimmed through the instructions and read the first line of the incantation aloud: "Let me speak the truth, see the truth and hear the truth of others."

CHAPTER 4

Two days after Ollie and Avery discovered Bisa's renascence spell, they had nearly all the necessary provisions to attempt it. Avery, being the second most artistic and the biggest crystal enthusiast of the coven (what was left of it), gathered all the crystals mentioned for the gem elixir from the gem store in Golden, and procured the special purple pigment thanks to Amazon Prime. Ollie had ventured out the night they discovered the spell and searched for an owl. He could've been a wonderful Primordial witch had nature not decided he was meant to be a Transcendent. His interactions with the forest animals under the cover of night would've impressed Avery, had she not already been occupied with preparing the gem elixir. Maybe it was the relationship Ollie had with the plant world that allowed him to be so well received in the pines. He imagined it was a home made of wood, needles, bark and cones, decorated with fascicles and a billion leaves. He just needed to be polite, and the trees would help him find what he was looking for, and he was always polite when entering anyone's home for the first time.

Ollie found himself wishing that he had brought a trowel along in case he discovered something that he might like to take with permission—a rock, a plant or some other gem of the forest. *Where can I find an owl?* Ollie asked of the forest. The wind rustled the pines a few moments later.

"Is it this way?" he asked as he intuitively began walking to the east after the breeze had subsided. After making a small path of his own through the trees, he looked up and saw an owl watching him from a branch above. It began to flap its wings repeatedly as if about to fly away. *May I please have a feather?* Ollie asked of the owl. Surely it would've been easier had it been molting season, but it was winter, and he had to ask. Ollie watched the owl from the ground and waited for a gift. It arrived a few moments later, falling down from the owl like soft snow.

"Well done, Ollie," Nina said to him.

Ollie turned around to find Nina standing behind him—in spirit, but as clear as day, solid as a rock. He felt a giddiness when he locked eyes with her. All the feelings and thoughts of how much he appreciated her, missed her and respected her rushed through his heart.

The forest fell dark and silent again, and they talked all the way back to the house. "You know what this is for, don't you?" Ollie asked. "The feather, I mean."

"I do," Nina said with a nod and kind eyes as bright as they had been in life.

Ollie smirked and shook his head. "But you're not gonna tell me if it's gonna work or not, are you?"

"I don't know," Nina said as she looked at the house.

"You don't know if it will work or if you're gonna tell me?" Ollie asked. There were almost tears in Nina's eyes, and Ollie had no idea if they were happy or sad.

Nina had never been so mercurial in life, but as a spirit she seemed to have more information than she was able to articulate at any given manifestation.

Finally, she spoke. "Ask me again after the next full moon."

Ollie scoffed, then laughed and waited for Nina to say more, but then she was gone. He took another look at the feather in his hand, walked up to the house and entered.

Avery was in the kitchen, cleaning all of the gemstones physically and energetically: a bath of salt water and then a quick mental incantation. When it came to small tasks, she was always so delicate and focused that it made Ollie sometimes forget how powerful she actually was. Enemies wouldn't even know what hit them if Avery was motivated enough—angry enough.

"That was fast!" Avery said as she nodded toward the feather in Ollie's hand, a chunk of moonstone clutched tightly between her palms.

"How's the elixir coming?"

She dropped the moonstone, the last of the crystals to be cleansed, into a small bowl with the rest. "It's ready. All we have to do now is wait for the full moon; then we can mix it."

"Is this silly?" Ollie asked her, but he was really asking himself.

Avery tuned out the question as she wiped up some salt water she had spilled. She was hoping that Ollie wouldn't ask her that again. She wasn't entirely confident, but she was great at pretending at times.

"What if it doesn't work?" Ollie asked. "Or worse, what if something else happens that we don't want?"

"Ollie, this is what we're doing," she said sharply. "I'm telling you, I think this is…going to work." But she wasn't saying the rest of her thoughts, which were an army of concerns and doubts. Of course she was skeptical, as any witch would be. For a quick moment she thought about calling it all off, but then she remembered how much she admired Bisa and determined that there was nothing to be gained by not trying. She hadn't snapped at someone in a while. Leo hadn't been around, and he did nothing but set her teeth on edge, but if she was really honest, she liked the conflict, even though it wasn't healthy or pretty. Arguing with Leo made things make more sense for her, made her magic a little stronger. She swished the crystals around in the bowl, and the shiny ones flickered under the light of the room. Avery realized she had snapped at Ollie and looked up at him to apologize. "It just...It has to work. It has to."

CHAPTER 5

Waiting is bullshit, Leo thought. When he thought about how obedient and patient he'd been, it made him want to throw up. For a couple of days, he actually thought what Merlot was doing was beneficial. At times he thought he might actually experience some personal growth by having some discipline and exercising patience. Only Leo, at his very core, didn't care. It hardly seemed worth it to have to sit around being poked and prodded and drained of blood so Merlot could carry out her end of the bargain.

Two hours into their lab work, Leo interrupted Merlot's incantation. "Hey, now seems like a good time for you to teach me how to bring someone back from the dead." He rubbed his arm where the needles had drawn his blood. It reminded him of his heavy druggie days, only a lot less dark and nowhere near as euphoric.

Merlot let out a sigh and opened her eyes. The blood sample still hadn't reacted how she wanted and needed it to. *Maybe it would if he would shut the fuck up.* "I don't know how many times we have to talk about this," she said. She spun around and was about to say something nasty when the technician handed her another blood sample with a smile.

"Do you even know how to do it?" Leo asked. His tone chafed Merlot's patience. Then something he hadn't considered before popped into his head. Suddenly, he felt really exploited and stupid. "Why didn't you ever do it with your coven when they died?"

Because there isn't a witch alive or dead who can bring someone back from the dead, Merlot thought. *No magic, object, or spell can either. It's impossible.* Sometimes, in between experiments, she considered that maybe there was a way and no one had discovered it yet.

Perhaps the rafkolite, if that was even real. She wasn't much for prophecy, or erudite witches, and a dead witch was one less witch to get in her way; she wanted power—the highest form of it. For she was ambitious if nothing else, and no one, not even a dangerously powerful witch like Leo, was going to stop her. *He might figure out that I'm just shining him on. He's growing more and more impatient, more anxious. He could kill me and not think twice if I keep this going much longer. But I'll have what I need soon. And once I have what I need, Leo, you'll be dead and I won't care.*

"Those who can't do—teach," Merlot answered. "I could never do it, because it requires the summoning of a spirit of death that is pure danger. It's unpredictable and kills indiscriminately at will for being summoned. It is known that the spirit could easily kill me before I even make a request."

"A spirit would instantly kill you?" Leo wasn't convinced. He might not have been incredibly book smart, but he was street smart, and it sounded like bullshit. "Why? Just for summoning? How?"

Merlot always loved how fast she could think on her feet. It was part of what made her so threatening. "It's rumored that it sucks out all of a witch's astral fluid. I assume you know what that is by now," she added condescendingly before finishing the story she had concocted in her head moments ago. "It sucks all of their power, destroys their mind, and leaves them with a terrible disease. It looks similar to tuberculosis." *Too much?*

"You've seen this?" Leo asked as he sipped some orange juice and took a bite of a sugar cookie.

"I haven't. But historically, every witch who has tried it has failed and died. I'm not talking about only a few over the course of history. I mean thousands and thousands of witches."

"Thousands and thousands?" Leo repeated with disbelief.

"Yes. It's a fact. Ask any witch who knows anything about our history and they'll tell you." *I know you have no one else to ask.* "I trust in facts. In history. Not speculation." Part of what she was saying was true: there were entities that could harm witches and their powers under the right circumstances, entities that had been poisoned by dark magic or the will of other dark witches, that…if called upon, could destroy someone. Merlot had a way of cherry-picking to suit her needs that served her very well.

Leo tipped the cup above his head and downed the last few drops of juice. "So what happens exactly? What do they have to do?" he asked, hoping to catch her in a lie.

Don't test me, I can play this game until you're dead. "The witch has to summon the spirit into our world. But, if they aren't strong enough, not witch enough, they'll fall victim to the influence of the spirit." Merlot waved her hands around the sides of her head as she continued to explain. "Their consciousness then instantly slips into the spirit's world and they're trapped for eternity. Their physical body can't sustain itself, so the person falls into a coma and never returns."

"You think I'm strong enough to do it?" Leo asked.

If it were possible, you'd have a chance. "I do," Merlot said, almost whispering.

That was all Leo needed to hear. He'd never done magic like that before, but he believed he could. "What do you mean strong enough? Strong how? Is there some kind of magic or spell I need to learn to protect against it sucking me off or whatever?"

Merlot slowly nodded, drowning in the drama of her own performance that was so expertly acted that it could've made her outrageously famous. She was half thrilled that even she was starting to believe her lies. "There is rumored to be one sure way to prevent the spirit from acting against you, falling under its influence." She paused.

"Rafkolite?" Leo guessed.

Merlot gave a truly disarming smile, the kind that made him forget how far he was from actually finding it. "Rafkolite, yes. The witch can use its power as a shield. A guarantee that you'll be safe." Merlot let out a sigh, checked the time and looked back at Leo. She popped his balloon of hope with her sharp tongue. "But of course no one has ever found it, so no one has ever been able to try to use it and find out for certain if that's actually true."

"Do you think it is?"

"Yes, but again, where is it? How do we find it?" Before Leo could respond, she lifted a finger in the air and waved it back and forth. "But you may not need to resort to that." *Keep him interested. Keep him on track.* "There is a way to test whether you're strong enough to resist the spirit's pull. It's an old kind of magic that witches have but have a hard time using because it's…complicated. Oddly enough it's not that different from how Salem would determine a witch. You know, tie them up and drop them into a deep lake. If they sank, they were only human—innocent—but if they floated, well, they were a witch and they were killed. The test pulls on an ancient magical skill of survival. It is achieved through mind, spirit, will and magic.

If you survive, you can be confident you'll be able to resist the influence of the spirit." Merlot sat in a chair and leaned back, awaiting Leo's response. Even the technician, who was under the influence of Merlot to conduct business, was interested.

"Do you think I can pass the test?"

"Yes, I do," she said with such conviction that it cut exceedingly deep through all of his doubt.

There was a time when Leo ignored his fear of heights and climbed to the tops of tall, abandoned buildings just to see the world from an unsafe perspective. A seemingly inconsequential phobia, an occupational hazard that came with being a self-styled urban explorer, more rooted in thrill seeking than seeing the world from another angle.

Now Leo was standing on the edge of yet another tall, abandoned building somewhere on the outskirts of Denver, only he wasn't there to admire the view before climbing down.

"Jump?" asked Leo, as he squinted his eyes and furrowed his brows. "The test is me falling twenty-something floors and hoping that I live?"

Merlot nodded and rubbed her hands together devilishly. "Yes! Oh…" She reached into her pocket and retrieved a necklace with a small silver charm on the end. "This will ensure that you don't somehow project yourself back to safety." She slipped the necklace over Leo's head and onto his neck.

"Are you crazy? I'll die!"

Merlot rolled her eyes. "Don't be such a defeatist. Use your mind, use your will. I know you can do this; you have great, great power."

"I can't," Leo said as he peeked over the edge of the building. It looked a hundred times farther than it actually was.

Whirling snow devils, like columns of sparkling sand, danced across the ground below as the wind whipped and whistled, giving a mesmeric and dreamlike condition to the spot where he would surely explode on impact like a bomb of flesh, bone and blood. A wave of nausea surged up from his stomach and into his throat before it eventually spread to his wobbly knees. He imagined what patterns his body would make splattered across the snow- covered ground. A messy Russian roulette–red inkblot against a canvas of white. What kind of noise would it make on all that soft snow? Would it hurt? *Will I feel it?* There was no ignoring his fear of heights now. The safety of knowing he could always climb down to safety was gone. He had to jump headfirst, literally, into his fear. What was he even doing this for? he wondered. Was it worth it? Would he ever have jambalaya or pancakes again?

Leo swallowed a lump in his throat. It turned out he wasn't as ready as he'd thought he was, not even a little bit. "Oh Jesus, fuck," he said as he closed his eyes. He couldn't jump. He was as frozen as the earth below. "I can't do it."

"Here, let me teach you," Merlot said as she shoved her hands into Leo's back and pushed him off the roof. He shot out into the air like a discarded work rag. The world was all cold air and blinding snow as he fell toward the ground. He tried to scream, but only a few high-pitched shrills came bursting out of his lungs. Only moments ago he was thinking about food, because what the hell was the point of living if you couldn't eat good food that you loved, and if he wasn't able to pass this test, he would surely never have such earthly pleasures ever again.

There was so much fear, fear that replayed everything he had ever done, good and bad, and made falling go much more slowly. Which was worse than the actual impending impact.

The anticipation was always worse than the actual event. It was the kind of fear that made him forget what he was supposed to be doing in the first place, using the power of his mind and will. He was certain that in a different timeline or lifetime, or whatever else there was, things wouldn't be this fucked up. Maybe he wasn't adopted, and maybe there weren't things like witches at all.

Leo closed his eyes right before he made impact, only he didn't. He fell into a patch of air that was warm against his skin, even in the middle of gusting sheets of snow. Below him was the ground where, until seconds ago, he'd thought he was going to be spread like jam. He tumbled and flipped like a leaf caught in a violent breeze, suspended in the air, held hostage by a warm breeze he didn't understand. When he finally was able to make sense of which direction was down, he saw a small trinket on the snow—a talisman. Bronze, with a small emerald in the center. Now that his stomach had caught up with the rest of his body, he felt sick again, bobbing in the air like a buoy in the sea.

"Merlot?" Leo shouted over and over, until she finally exited the building from the entrance on the ground floor. "Merlot! Get me down," Leo shrieked. "I wanna get down! Get me down!"

Merlot let out a sigh as a wicked smirk appeared on her face. "What happened?" Leo asked, still tumbling above her.

"You failed," she said plainly as she walked over to the talisman she'd secretly placed on the ground on their way into the building. She bent down to retrieve it, and instantly Leo came crashing down. "You're not ready. Now you know you're not ready. I wasn't going to have you jump without some insurance first. I need your blood." She shook her head. "Meditate more. You're lazy."

"I'm not lazy, I just—"

"Yes. You. Are," Merlot said. "We can try again...once I have what I need." She took a breath and clapped her hands as she turned toward the car. "Come on, let's go. Back to work!"

Leo fell forward onto all fours and threw up.

CHAPTER 6

After Mitch woke in the early morning, and after he'd watched the sun fill the sky, he hoped that he would start to feel the effects of his spell. Only nothing had changed. He stood on the dock at Morro Bay Marina and wondered what he'd done wrong. Why didn't his spell work when he really wanted it to— needed it to? He looked around the marina. It was surprisingly empty. The gray overlay of clouds that covered the sky had already proved too strong for the sun and had swallowed it before Mitch could even appreciate it.

There was a numbness in his heart, and no matter what spell he cast, or how many inspiring people he met, or how many parties he went to or how much skin he picked, nothing could lift his spirits. He stood at the edge of the dock for several minutes, staring into the rippling water, hating himself for not even being able to witch himself out of his own way.

Mitch was exhausted. Nothing was ever good enough, and there had been so many failures, he'd experienced so much trauma, that it was impossible to think of anything ever being any different. *If people only knew what this was like. No one actually knows what this feels like. All people ever say is snap out of it, stop being so negative, but they just...don't get it. They'll never get it any more than I'll understand why they don't get it. I'm not choosing this. Why would I choose this?* He'd tried to choose to feel differently so many times that he'd started to think things working out was just some crackpot theory designed by whoever made *good vibes only* a thing. He suddenly could understand Leo in ways that he hadn't before.

Maybe that was the attraction all along, the darkness, the darkness that had been part of their genetic makeup.

Then, Mitch felt a presence. He didn't know how long it had been there, but he felt it now—behind him. His shoes scuffed a tiny bit of sand on the dock as he turned around. His eyes darted down just in time to see a large frog—his totem—make an impossibly high jump toward his face. The only thing he could see were the two bulbous eyes as he slipped on the sandy dock and fell backward. His chin smacked against the wooden dock, and he crashed into the water as the frog let out a *ribbit*. Everything happened so fast that fear and surprise were the only things he felt when he hit the surface of the water. He didn't even feel the pain of hitting the dock. The world was a wash of black water and glistening silver air bubbles, the dock dissolved and the bubbles engulfed him until there was nothing but the frightening vortex of effervescence that surrounded him.

In what seemed like a fraction of the smallest increment of time scientifically possible, everything around him melted and ran like hot wax down to a hollow of luminous light. His eyes snapped open, teared with panic, his cheek embedded in cold, damp sand. Mitch sucked for air as he propped himself up onto his knees. Everything was sepia, and there was no end to it, like a dense fog that bled into infinity in every direction. The air smelled like early morning rain. Mitch felt dizzy, but only for a moment; he blinked and rubbed the sand from his eyes. That's when he saw it—his totem, some indistinguishable distance ahead of him in the amber fog. He was no longer alone in the mysterious, misty abyss. There was nothing and no one else, so he walked to meet it—for the second time.

He was sopping wet and dripping, but there was no more water, he was somewhere else now. Like a sleepwalker, he proceeded forward through the fog. His footsteps slapped along the damp sand as he closed the gap between himself and his totem. When he was close enough to see clearly, he stopped, stared at the frog and waited for his breathing to return to normal.

"G'day, Mitch," the frog said with a heavy Australian accent.

Mitch wasn't sure what to expect, but it was safe to say that he hadn't expected his totem to talk, and why with an Australian accent? "You talk?" Mitch whispered through wet lips.

"That's right! Well, here I can, anyway," said the frog. Its eyes blinked and its throat billowed in and out.

Mitch's mouth opened wide and closed as panic ripped through him. "Here? Where's here? Oh my God—am I dead?" He looked around for signs of an afterlife, realizing quickly that he wouldn't recognize it even if he saw it.

"Not at all. You're still very much alive," said the frog.

"What happened?" Mitch asked. Had this been somewhere else, he would've taken off running, but there was nowhere to go, not this time. He looked at the totem and shook his finger at it. "You. You jumped at me. You pushed me off the dock."

"Yes, I did!" The frog's tone was oddly gleeful.

"Why would you do that?"

"Because you need to hear a few things," the frog said.

Mitch's breathing had finally returned to normal, but he was still a little pale from shock. His body still shook with anxiety. "Why do you sound like that? Why do you have an accent?"

The frog cocked its head in a way that seemed impossible for a frog to do. "I don't have an accent; *you* have an accent."

Mitch remembered his descent through the watery vortex. "How did I get here?"

"I brought you here, silly, to have a yarn. I want to talk to you about land mines."

Mitch looked confused. "What?"

"Growth and healing, the very process of it...*is* to step on land mines. To explode. To learn. To fail," the frog said.

Mitch scoffed through a set of still-wet lips. "Oh, so is this like a self-help thing? An intervention?" *How the hell did this happen? I thought I was going to learn magic and establish balance, and all I've done is be repeatedly traumatized, and now I'm here in some underwater hotbox having woo-woo therapy with a talking frog.*

The frog blinked and sat in silence for a moment. "I heard all of that, you know."

"Good!" Mitch snapped. "So maybe you can help me out then. What am I supposed to do, huh? How do I fix *everything*?"

"There are hundreds of ways, you're just not looking for them. Well, you're choosing not to."

"I don't know about hundreds, but let's, let's start counting!" Mitch held out his hand and started with his index finger. "Um, Wellbutrin, Zoloft...twenty-five milligrams—horrible sexual side effects...Mirtazapine—crazy, *crazy* diarrhea...Trintellix at three hundred dollars a month—it was either that or purchase a mansion in the Hollywood Hills, but I opted for mental health." Mitch continued to rattle off the various medications and methods of self-help that never seemed to actually help anything. "Should I go on? Or can we skip all of that and you can get me outta here?"

"Get out yourself!"

"Is this like an escape room or something? Do I have to find a clue somewhere?" Mitch asked sarcastically.

"Your thumb is bleeding," the frog observed. "Have you been picking again?"

"Yeah, well, be glad I'm not slitting my wrists," Mitch said with a scoff. "But, let's be honest, we both know I'd never do it because I'm too afraid to. Instead I just Google 'I'm tired of existing but I'm too scared to die.'" He rolled his eyes.

"You don't want to die, Mitch, you're just not searching in the right places," the frog said in a friendly, matter-of-fact way.

"Where should I be looking then?"

"Right there, you bloody galah."

"Where?" Mitch looked around the vast and endless fog to find nothing. "And what are these words? I have no idea what you're talking about."

"If you'd stop your whinging, you'd see it! All the time, it's nothing but whinge, whinge, whinge," the frog said.

Mitch's eyes glittered with anger. "What? Do you mean *me*? Are you trying to say I should be looking *within me*?" he asked mockingly.

"Good on ya! That's right! Start taking care of yourself!"

Mitch stepped back and shook his head. "I take care of myself."

"Do you, though?" the frog said, rich with skepticism.

Mitch didn't want to lie, but he also didn't want to tell the truth. He didn't know what to say, so he looked down and began to ruminate.

"What is it?" the frog asked.

Mitch struggled with what to say, because he wasn't sure if he could truly identify whatever it was that was making him so...whatever he was. "It's just all too much."

"What is?"

"Everything!" Mitch shouted. "The world is such shit. People are so shitty and fucked up." He started to shake as he allowed all that was inside to come out. "Everything just seems to be getting worse and worse, nothing seems to get any better, it's just, like, what's the point? The world is just…beyond hope. The longer we're here, the more obvious it becomes that we really have no idea what we're doing besides making horrible decisions. And we're awful, and ugly. To everyone. If not living, but just surviving, is really this fucked up, then I don't think I wanna be mixed up with a bunch of people I can't trust to make anything better. And I know, *I know* there's a shit ton more going on in my brain and everything else isn't, like, the sole reason for my shit, but that doesn't make it any easier." Mitch let out a heavy sigh. "And isn't this what we're supposed to be doing anyway? Helping to bring the world back into balance? It doesn't feel like anything is balanced. I don't think we'd even realize it if it were. It sure as hell doesn't feel or look like it ever will be. So what's the point?"

"The point of life is to live. Aren't you doing that?" the frog asked.

"Nothing I do is worth anything. I don't like anything about myself. Sure, I crochet a bunch of shit and some people like it, but so what? I'm a witch—so what? What difference does any of this make? It's all been so hard. Even when it's been easy, it's still been really fucking hard and nothing ever changes. It just gets more difficult and more complicated, and I just get older and older and watch everyone else handle it all better than me. Or make more money than me. Or cast spells better than me."

"This is all getting a bit tedious. You're being self-indulgent and defeated. You're not celebrating any success, whether it's small or not."

"I'll celebrate when there is something worth celebrating!"

"You're not confronting anything, you're complaining."

"Oh, fuck off! That's what everyone always says!"

"You don't have to be perfect, Mitch. Nothing is perfect. But don't ruminate on what you're not. Chasing after the so-called genius of others or the life of others is a chase you'll never win, mate. You don't need to idolize anyone else, or anyone else's talents. You're already doing what you love and living how you want, so why are you torturing yourself?"

"I'm not! This world just isn't set up to help people. Living my life the way I want isn't encouraged or rewarded…but being a Kardashian with excessive privilege, resources and opportunities up the fucking ass—is. What, am I just supposed to be a banker so I can buy a new washer and dryer like everyone else? Everyone thinks I'm a loser and I need a real job and I need to grow up. Everyone talks about art…but no one actually encourages artists."

"Why do you turn what others think into a weight that is impossible to lift?"

"It's always been this way," Mitch said, his eyes welling up with tears. "Kids used to make fun of me for being weird, or gay, or…anything that wasn't them, and all I kept thinking was that none of that makes any sense. I didn't get how I was supposed to be a *normal* kid like them but also be *me*. How could I be a kid, and they be a kid too…if I was so different and they were so awful?"

"Mitch, darling, the only person you have to worry about making you feel ashamed of yourself is you. Life isn't fair. It's not even easy. Grow, Mitch. Growth doesn't feel good. Stepping on emotional land mines doesn't feel good. But it's necessary if you want to grow. And that happens at different times in different ways for everyone. You can't compare."

"Sure, says you, who doesn't have to live in this world as someone like me."

Mitch hesitated again and thought about his pattern of always running, always seeing the cloud instead of the sun behind it. He wondered if this was all some really cruel trick, and his own totem would end up laughing at him, making him feel even more defeated than he already did. He couldn't handle that. Or could he? "And what if I'm not any good at that? What if growth is just…not in my skill base?" His voice started to crack.

"Are you going to try?" the frog asked.

"I have been trying. I've tried so many times," Mitch said as his face puckered into a mess of tears. "And if I see one more fucking influencer making millions by giving people stupid advice that no one cares about or twerking on a scarecrow for likes, or selling their farts in a jar and having people actually buy them…I'm gonna throw up."

"Are you going to try?" the frog repeated kindly.

"I don't know. If I'm not automatically amazing at something, or I don't immediately reach the goal, I just—"

"Quit," the frog finished for him.

"So what do I do?"

"Try harder, try again, put in the work," the frog said softly.

"What if it's just more of the same? What if it's just more of the same until I die of exhaustion? Maybe that's not who I am meant to be. Maybe this is just who I am…how I am."

"What kind of witch are you? What kind of person are you?" the frog asked, but it didn't wait for an answer. "A fucking good one. Do you believe that?"

"I don't know," he said. Something about the way his totem had asked the last question made Mitch dig a little deeper. "Do you?"

"I know you are. It's time you knew that too," the frog said, and it jumped forward at Mitch. Suddenly, everything was white, and the air was warm and cold all at the same time and full of shimmering bubbles. They bled away into the dark water, and Mitch found himself still underwater, looking up toward the rippling surface where he had fallen through only moments ago. With hardly any air left in his lungs and armed only with a will to live, he flailed his arms and swam upward.

His hands burst through the water's surface, and behind them was his head, gasping for air. He grabbed hold of the dock and pulled himself from the water, finding strength he hadn't known he had. He flipped over onto his back and stared at the sky. *That was one hell of an emotional land mine,* he thought as he spit out the water pooling in his mouth.

When Mitch returned to the house, he immediately drew himself a bath with enough salt to mimic the Mediterranean. He peeled off his soggy clothing and stepped one foot into the bath, then the other. Mitch sank under the water until only his face remained on the surface. His face was calm and stoic, but his thoughts were running wild. Having to kill Jasper, who had had Leo's soul, being locked up in a Plexiglas box, the endless traumas of childhood and adolescence and adulthood—all of it bubbled to the forefront of his mind, where he doused in it salt water.

The pain was heavy and dark, and his body was too weak to carry it anymore. *Could I just decide to be blissed out?* he wondered. *It can't be that simple. It can't be as simple as making a choice. But maybe it is? There's a chance that it actually is that easy.* Making the choice was the easy part; doing the work was more hellish than heavenly. Mitch sat in the water, letting his eyes fall into a soft gaze as he passed over all the events in his life up to the present. Some experiences were abandoned and hidden far in the back but still sharp enough to cut, and others were fresh and life sapping, like invasive weeds across a lawn. He wondered if he had only been coping, and if maybe coping wasn't the path he needed to take. Some of his traumas puzzled him: he didn't understand why they made such an impact. *Maybe that doesn't matter, maybe I just need to create some kind of plan...some kind of resolution going forward instead of just more of the same. I can't change any of the past. I have to make peace with that in some way. My God, is that why I was so obsessed with Leo? Was I just attracted to what was a mirror of my own shit? My own suffering?*

Mitch cupped his hands, collected some bathwater and poured it over his face. *I guess it's all about choice. Right? It has to be. As much as I hate saying that, maybe that's part of the problem. Maybe making a choice goes deeper than what I think. There's nothing...wrong with me. Maybe it's more about...what happened to me and how I choose to heal? Well...that won't be easy, and it sounds scary as fuck, but so does...staying the same, so does...not being happy. I'm more than just what happened to me.*

When he opened his eyes, nothing had changed, but everything looked different, like the difference between seeing a tree from the ground and seeing it from the sky. When he was ready, he pulled the bathtub plug and listened to the drain gurgle away all the weights he no longer needed, the weights that had cut into him day after day, that had given him calluses and fatigued him.

CHAPTER 7

It was finally the full moon, and Ollie and Avery were fully prepared with the elixir.

When the moon was high enough, they set the elixir, with all its ingredients, under the moon's light. Avery spent the next few hours somewhere between sleep and awake, until her alarm went off. It was almost dawn. She retrieved the elixir, removed all the stones and transferred the liquid to a brown glass bottle.

"Ollie, wake up, it's time," Avery said as she shook his arm gently.

The sky was no more awake than Ollie was, but the sun was coming. They cleared a spot in the snow and brought all of their provisions outside. Outside it was quiet, as if even the world around them was eagerly awaiting the spell, wondering if they would succeed. Avery, with fire-starting in her wheelhouse, stacked a few logs of birch wood and then stuffed shards of palo santo into the gaps like kindling. She breathed out a few puffs that instantly turned to vapor in the cold morning air. The moment had finally come. Her eyes found the center of the woodpile, and it roared to life with a rumble as everything caught fire. Ollie stepped back as the heat whooshed across his face. The icy snow crunched under his feet. Avery locked eyes with him, held out her hand and waited for him to grab hold.

Avery recited the incantation slowly, as if reciting and ap- preciating poetry. The wind rustled her hair, and Ollie gripped her hand a little tighter. He could feel a presence, but when he looked around, he saw nothing and no one. Maybe it would work after all, he thought.

Avery took a deep breath and finished the incantation. "Hear my call—with pure love and light…"

Then together, "*invoko te—invoko te—invoko te.*"

The fire snapped and popped, primed and hungry, eager to be fed.

Ollie took a deep breath and grabbed hold of the portrait that glistened in the flickering light of the fire like it was alive. Bisa just had to be there. Ollie felt it so strongly that he could almost smell her. For half a breath, he almost forgot she was gone.

First was the owl feather. Avery dropped it into the fire and watched it curl and flare up in the flames. Next was the paint, and the rock. Ollie hesitated a moment, thinking they had only one chance to do this, there was only one painting. But it felt right. He tossed the painting directly into the flames, where it slid just a little off to the side. He nudged the corner with a snow-covered foot, repositioning it into the heart of the fire.

Ollie lost the scent of Bisa as the painting cooked and melted on the fire. He looked over toward Avery. She was holding the last ingredient, the gem elixir. He nodded. Avery stepped forward and dumped the contents of the bottle over the fire. For a moment, she thought it might extinguish the flames. But the liquid met the fire like kerosene. It spread out across the melting painting in rivers as bright violet and magenta flames surged up ferociously in a current of hot, smoky air. They took a few steps back and marveled at the small fireworks display before them.

Avery looked over at Ollie, his face coated in all the colors of the fire. She chuckled. "You look like a character in *Euphoria*. Do you watch that?"

Ollie had no idea what she was talking about. "I don't really watch TV anymore."

What she was really asking was *Do you think this will work?* She looked up into the sky, watching the smoke trail off into the air above, then back down to the fire that was quickly dwindling. She smiled, feeling a little proud of both of them for giving such an impossible magic task a try.

When the fire was nothing but smoking ash, Ollie picked up one of the shovels.

Everything had been incinerated, even the piece of basalt rock. Magic did impossible things. As he began to dig a hole in the frozen ground beside them, he wondered what *impossible* meant. Was *impossible* just a word for something they hadn't figured out how to understand?

Together they dug and filled the space with the ashes. They pushed the frozen snow and dirt over the top and buried it. Ollie was familiar with this process; it was like starting a seedling. He grunted as he slapped the last bit of earth with his shovel. It was done. He was a little dizzy, sweaty and exhausted. His shirt a little damp and icy in the cold winter air. Right then, the sun peeked over the hill and bathed them in golden light. The way the sun was shining somehow seemed more hopeful than normal. All they had to do now was wait.

CHAPTER 8

Merlot had been very busy—and not just with Leo's blood; she had a full schedule. Any downtime was spent away from Leo, and although he always wondered why she was meditating for so long, he also knew what he was like: people could only take him in doses. But like Leo, Merlot had secrets and goals of her own. She wasn't retreating to her room just to get away from Leo and his obnoxious personality. She could tolerate that. She didn't love it, but she could tolerate it. Merlot was sequestering herself so that she could astrally project herself to different parts of the world. Why? Ambition was behind every choice.

She had always been the type of person who lived for ambition, partially because she believed she'd achieve everything and believed it so blindly that any doubt was easily overshadowed by her tenacity. She broke it down into very simple steps. How would Merlot rise to the very top of the top? She had to feed witches hope, and the best way to unite witches and get them to like her was no different from how it was with most humans: free food and drinks. No matter what her intentions were, she figured out that if she could throw a good party in the name of unity and peace, people would show up and magic would take care of the rest.

Step one: find a reason to celebrate. That part was easy. What she really needed to succeed at was getting them to reconsider the way magic is governed or not governed globally. It was the best way to strengthen the magical community and establish—keep—balance, which was the whole reason for their existence. How could hundreds and hundreds of witches tell her that wasn't genius?

That's how Bacchanalia parties became a thing again. Merlot hosted them across the globe in witch hot spots, trying to spread the word like a zealous club promoter who promised free drinks but neglected to mention the forty-dollar cover and the fact that the only free drinks were cans of Bud Light. Merlot was a lot of things, but a cheap-ass she was not. The parties were extravagant, resplendent, indulgent and decadent, and lured every witch, from the ones who wanted to party to the ones who cared about unity. A flurry of champagne fountains, dazzling lights, candles and candles and more candles, sumptuous food and a killer vibe. She had somehow managed to throw a classy party that was actually fun. The parties always began with a clear, concise and inspiring speech, followed by an impossibly wild and fun time, before it all faded into a serene afterglow with everyone in support of Merlot. How did she achieve that?

Step two: contagious magic. The Bacchanalia parties were truly just rallies designed to do one thing: gather as many witches as possible in one spot and dose them all with a contagion spell. It worked out well for her that she had a decent singing voice. In another life, she could've been a party promoter, an event planner, or even a pop star, given the right circumstances, but that shouldn't suggest she would let those skills go to waste. When the DJ began to build their set to a feverish, sexy, pounding rhythm, she took hold of the microphone and sang—well, chanted—a spell.

Music was often overlooked as a strong form of magic among witches. Merlot used it to her advantage. She fashioned her spell into a song, an intimate, personal and thoughtfully crafted spell. Each verse correlated to a period of time in her life, adding magical layers to the spell, making it more powerful. Merlot was always good at magical layering. She thought of it like cooking. She wouldn't just write a spell on paper; she would first soak the paper in a tea made of herbs associated with the spell's intended goal, then burn it and use the ashes to anoint her candles. It's the reason why when other people made potatoes, they were just potatoes, but Merlot's potatoes were freakishly divine. She put the gold in Yukon gold potatoes. She built layers of flavor, and her spellwork was no different.

Every time she finished singing at a party, the witches were never the same. The spell seeped in through their ears and slowly drained their powers away until they had nothing left, but not before spreading to the aura of the next witch they came in contact with. She had to account for all the stubborn, homebody witches who didn't like fun. Any sort of budding or newbie witch, she wasn't concerned with. They were no match for her.

She organized a Bacchanalia world tour and over the course of a couple of weeks had hit Chicago, L.A., New York, London, Madrid, Montreal, Santiago, Cape Town, Tangier, Berlin, Oslo, Istanbul, New Delhi, Melbourne, Moscow and Tokyo.

Merlot's magic was as dangerous as her ambition. Combining the two was how she had managed to kill Nina; infect witches across the globe; and own a comedy news channel and HelloMerlot, a conglomerate beast that included real estate, publishing, wine, media and entertainment, a marijuana company that developed, cultivated, manufactured, packaged, shipped, and distributed regulated recreational and medical-use cannabis, and of course the med lab where she was conducting experiments on Leo's blood.

It wasn't the contagious magic that she was most proud of, although it was truly a ridiculous feat to pull off. She was most proud of finally figuring out how to successfully manipulate Leo's blood. She had been reading an old alchemy book when she found a way to achieve what she had been aiming to do for days. The blood had to be magically altered, then returned to his body for a full night, then drawn again and magically altered again with an incantation. It should turn gold after that, per the writings of ancient texts by an alchemist she'd overlooked. That's all it took. Then she could consume it, and she would be more powerful than any other witch—well, any witch with powers, anyway.

Merlot knew that tonight was the night. An incense burner on her Moroccan coffee table filled the room with oud smoke and created halos around the lit pillar candles. She nestled into her plush love seat, tucking herself between two large, super-fluous pillows. Before her on the table were three vials of Leo's blood that the technician had given her earlier. They had been taken through the entire process, injected into his body, left to germinate and then redrawn for Merlot to use. They looked almost black in the soft candlelight. It was quiet, and she was ready. Merlot closed her eyes, held her hand over the vials and took a moment to ground herself.

The quiet turned to noise. Classic rock to be exact, which to her was one of the most dreadful forms of unbearable racket. She took a deep breath and tried to focus, but it was impossible with the shredding guitar and hectic drumming. She was so close now. She wished she had started just a little earlier like she had wanted to. Had she already finished, she could've walked right into his room and slit his throat right there. Merlot opened her eyes and lost herself in her own little hate fantasy. Until the guitar broke through. She cracked her neck, shook her frustration out through her wrists and tried again. Performing magic with distraction wasn't something she'd normally had trouble with. Perhaps it was what was at stake that made it so difficult to concentrate. Again and again she tried, but each time she couldn't focus. It was like trying to fall asleep with a screaming baby, or a downstairs neighbor having a frat party.

Leo was jamming out in front of a portable speaker, high as fuck for the first time in a long time. He couldn't even remember where the weed had come from, he just knew it was in the cargo pants that he hadn't washed in…well, he didn't know how long. It was dry, crumbly, like dead leaves, but it still had a little kick to it. Even ditch weed could be pretty good in a pinch, even if weed just wasn't enough anymore. *This must've been some kind of happy, energetic sativa,* because he was wired. Spotify shuffled from "Moby Dick" by Led Zeppelin to "Toad" by Cream, two songs that reminded him of the K holes he used to be in once upon a time, back when he dreamed he could do the things he actually *could* do now. Some three minutes into the song, Leo had an inspired idea. *I bet I can summon that spirit. I bet I don't even need the rafkolite. I can do it.* There he was, the good ol' Leo he had almost forgotten about. Foolishly brave, stupid and addicted to bad decisions.

He grabbed hold of the sweetgrass on the end table, shoved the end into a lit candle and filled the room with the smoke. For a moment he remembered that Nina had once mentioned never to use sweetgrass without using some other kind of cleansing smoke first, but no one had time for that, not when he was having so much fun being a new version of the old Leo.

Summoning the spirit without any sort of actual knowledge of how to do it—or even what spirit it was—was a formidable task, to say the very least. But he was feelin' it, and not just the drum solo. He had seemed to have pretty good luck when he didn't overthink things, so he just let himself dance. The kind of dancing that only someone really high would think was good, the kind that would clear out a dance floor. He didn't think about failing, he didn't think about all the horrible things he'd done and would probably still do, he just focused on finding that spirit, whatever it was.

The drumming continued, and Leo smiled as he wiggled his fingers. He caught a glimpse of himself in the mirror, and for a hot second, he thought he looked like Aaliyah in *Queen of the Damned*. Without thinking, he quoted a few lines with the same hissing inflection she had in her voice. *Stop! You're getting distracted*, he said to himself, and he continued to try summon or invoke or whatever it was he was trying to do, hoping he could do so without actually knowing how to do it.

As he spun and hopped around the room, his hair flailing down in front of his face, he managed to bridge the gap between planes, and that was when he saw it. A shadowy silhouette down the hall in the doorway to another room. Leo smiled, feeling successful, feeling like he was the shit. The figure revealed two bright yellow eyes, like tiny mirrors reflecting the candlelight at him. Leo bumped into a stack of old books and jars of herbs on the floor, but he didn't care. He reached out toward the figure and smiled, beckoning it to come to him. After all, that's what he had summoned in the first place.

It finally obliged and slipped closer, slithering along the wall like a snake. The sight of it would've been terrifying had it not been so exciting. The reassuring strength of his power, the security of his connection to the spirit, the danger of the invocation and its intoxicating trance, the intensity of the music…It was enough to give him an erection, he was so in love with his own experience. The risk factor was so high that adrenaline consumed any and all logic.

Leo didn't care about what he was actually doing—he wasn't thinking about that at all. If he had been, he might have thought twice about trying to summon a spirit that would dissolve a witch's blood and, along with it—their powers. It was the type of spirit that some witches would call a psychic vampire spirit. Normally, witches can't detect the spirit, and are made aware of it only once it already has a hold on them, draining them away to nothing. But Leo was different. His powers were a little more advanced than other witches', even at the most basic level.

He continued to dance with the spirit, a sort of dark courtship, teasing it with his dry fingers and calloused hands, feeling he was in complete control. As the shadowy spirit glided along the walls toward Leo, he watched—unblinking, smitten with his own recklessness. Leo giggled and begged for the spirit to come closer, and closer. It did. The spirit penetrated Leo's mind and began to feast. Leo's heart beat faster and faster, and only then did he realize that he was no longer in control—the spirit was.

Merlot entered the room and gasped as she saw the spirit before her. She had a split second—less than that, really—before the spirit would consume her too. She was cat-quick, and surprised the spirit. As the sinisterly mesmerizing yellow eyes turned toward her, she already had her arms outstretched toward it.

"*Relinquo!*" Merlot shouted.

The spirit spun around wildly with a *whoosh* as the spell sent it flying down the hall, leaving a tornado of white-hot dust and sparks in its wake before it imploded and disappeared. A sulfuric smell was all that remained. Leo reached up, grabbed hold of his chest and gasped for air. He didn't realize how close to failing he had come until he looked at Merlot and saw a venomous look of disdain. Leo doubled over his knees, looked back at Merlot once more and smiled a smile that said, *I almost died.*

"You stupid idiot," Merlot shouted as she charged toward him and slapped him repeatedly.

Leo wasn't bothered at all; the weed buffered his mood just enough to allow him to see the humor in his near-death experience. Merlot continued to hit him, and the more hits she landed, the harder Leo laughed, like an older sibling who took joy in teasing someone half their size.

"If I had known you were stupid enough to try something like this in my own house, I would've locked you up!"

"Chill!" Leo ducked away from her.

"You could've killed us *both*!"

"But I didn't! Now I know better!"

Merlot shook her head, tired of his juvenile insanity. "You don't get it, do you? It doesn't matter if you're still alive, because it's going to come for you. You don't even know what you summoned, do you? Without clear intent, you could very well manifest the very thing you are trying to avoid into existence. From the energy left in this room, I'd say that's exactly what you did. And now…it's seen you and your powers. It won't stop until it has you." Merlot walked over to the doorway the spirit had vanished through to make sure it was actually gone. "You sloppy half-wit." She slammed her fist into the frame of the door, where it landed with a heavy thud. "It's not done. It's going to keep coming back, and not just for you, but for every witch you've ever met. Why would you even attempt something like that after I told you how dangerous it was?"

Leo shook his head. "I thought you got rid of it."

"Well, yeah, for now. Only because I caught it off guard, by half a second."

"What do you mean?"

"The spirit is hard to banish. I can make it leave, but I can't remove it from our plane entirely."

Leo squinted in confusion into Merlot's scowl. "But, I thought hundreds or thousands of witches have done this before. Isn't that what you said?"

"That was a long time ago. I may know a lot, but I don't know everything. I don't know how to stop it from coming for you or me. You've released it from wherever it's been for however long it's been there. It's not going to just go back. Can't say I blame it. If you'd been trapped for an eternity, wouldn't you put up a fight if someone tried to trap you immediately after you were released?"

Leo thought about her statement for a minute. He'd been locked up before, and it hadn't taken an eternity for him to want to run out of the cell screaming for mercy and explaining they weren't even his drugs. "So what now?"

"Now I manipulate your blood. Perhaps with that, we won't need to worry about how to banish it for good. I'll just be able to do it." Merlot left the room to retrieve the vials of blood, a couple of books and her notepad.

Leo followed behind like an excited puppy. "Wait, did you figure it out? Finally?"

"Yes, all I have to do is do it." Merlot waved to Leo to follow. "Come on, let's go. You can't stay here on your own in case it comes back for you. It'll be safer to keep moving for the next few hours. Let's go to the lab…finish this."

When they arrived at the lab, Merlot got right to work. Leo hovered near the wall in the back as she prepared her magical work space. Merlot begged for silence so she could concentrate. She poured the vial of blood into a shallow dish and set it before her. She leaned down to smell it, and breathed out gently. The words of the incantation rested on the edge of her tongue, waiting to be said. Merlot placed both hands around the side of the bowl and focused her intention. She repeated the words over and over in her head but had yet to say them.

A strange sort of smell began to fill the room that Leo could smell all the way over by the door. It was so strong and distracting that he wondered how Merlot was able to continue. This wasn't like any other time. Something was different. It was like the blood knew it was about to go through some sort of transformation. Leo kept looking around the room and out the door, expecting there to be a spirit ready to eat him alive. Merlot saw only the gold that the blood would be momentarily—she saw success. Everything in her life, every obstacle, every small victory and sacrifice was finally about to become worth it, just as she always knew it would.

She closed her eyes and recited the incantation, each word delivered with purpose and fierce determination. The air went thick, like the humid summers that Leo was used to in Louisiana, and then came the smell, the smell of gold, the scent of transformation, the signal of change—like the melancholic deliciousness of freshly mown grass.

Leo sat in silence, watching from a distance like a wall-flower at a high school dance. He listened to Merlot finish the incantation as her gently breathed words echoed throughout the cold, sterile room.

When Merlot finished, she hesitated and kept her eyes closed, waiting for the right moment to see the result. The heaviness in the air no longer lingered, and the strange smells had all dissipated. The darkness of her shut eyelids began to glow. There was light. She opened her eyes. Slowly at first, her eyelids lifting like drawn curtains, her eyes began to focus on the blood before her, no longer red, but a glistening, shimmering gold. She'd done it. Its radiance gilded the whites of her eyes. The blood's radiance was intense, and her eyes started to water—not from the brightness but with happy tears. They were the eyes of a mother finally able to hold her newborn child after hours of labor. Merlot was a mixed bag of emotions, and there was no telling which one Leo would get if he decided to reach inside, which of course he would. He had to; he still needed something.

"Did it work?" Leo asked as he walked toward her, curious about the lustrous glow that outlined Merlot's body.

Merlot chortled and smiled wide, her eyes manic and wet. "Yes!" she said as she gently dunked her finger into the metallic surface of the blood. A ripple bounced out from around her fingertip.

Leo stopped and stood still for a moment. He listened to Merlot's giggling intensify and furrowed his brow. *What the fuck*, he thought as he mouthed the words silently. Then he nodded and said, "Okay. Now show me how to bring someone back. Right now. You've got what you need."

Merlot lifted the vessel and brought it to her lips. The smell of it wafted across her nose. She moaned. "Oh, it smells like champagne and sovereignty," she said as she tipped the vessel and poured the gold contents into her mouth. She tilted her head back and swallowed every last drop. Her body surged with warmth and a childlike excitement. It hit hard and fast, more than any drug Leo had ever tried or Merlot had ever concocted. Leo was almost a little jealous that she didn't share some with him.

"Hey, we had a deal, right? So, come on," Leo said more sternly. "Right now."

Merlot tipped her head back down and with one quick swing, swept the menagerie of lab equipment off the table. Shards of metal, glass and blood sprayed across the room with a gigantic crash as she turned around toward Leo. It was all she could do not to simply crush his head right there. But she was too high for that kind of violence just yet.

"There is no way to do that. No one can do it. Not even me, not even now."

Leo looked stunned. "But you said…"

"I said whatever I needed to say to get what I want. Get it through your thick fucking skull! It can't be done!" Merlot said, relishing the anger in Leo's face. "It's not personal, *dulzura*. But I have what I need, and I don't need you anymore." Leo wanted nothing more than to burn her alive or crumple her body with a quick flick of his hand. His anger was even more vengeful than ever, and he didn't care how strong Merlot had become, he could take her.

"Go on, try it, I can see it all over your face," Merlot said. "You're idiotic, arrogant and stupid. Reckless. I'm stronger than you even at your peak—now." She winked.

Leo pooled all of his hatred into his hand and lifted it to crush her body like he'd done to so many necks already. But she was too strong, too fast, too superior. With hardly the amount of effort used to blow dandelion seeds off a stem, Merlot deflected his magic with a quick flash of her hand. Leo flew backward at lightning speed and crashed through the door as a storm of debris sprang out from along his path until he slammed into the wall in the hallway.

Merlot's fingers were hot with energy, and she waved them in the air to cool them off. She would get used to the heat in time. She walked through the mess and scoffed at Leo on the floor, writhing around and sputtering guttural moans underneath fragments of door. Within moments, she was gone, although Leo hadn't come to enough to know she had left. He looked down at the gash on his arm and touched the edge of the bloody flesh. He licked his upper lip and tasted blood. Now he was out for revenge.

When he went to Merlot's house after taking the car she had left behind, he was surprised to find no sign of it. He knew he had the right place, because he saw the can of soda he had left out in the snow by the edge of the property. But the house was gone. She'd enchanted it somehow. With a deep groan of self-hatred, he took the only option he had left—he returned to the coven. He thought long and hard for a few minutes about everything he'd done, everything that had brought him to the cold patch of snow he was standing in. For the first time in a long time, if not ever, he closed his eyes and asked for Nina's guidance. If he could summon that crazy spirit, then surely he could connect with Nina, if she was willing. He didn't really know how these things worked. Typical Leo, he didn't really know or care much for how things worked, or the consequences of doing them, he just did things.

Leo reached his right hand up and placed it on his heart. "Please," he said softly. "Nina, I need help." He took a deep breath, holding the cold winter air deep inside his chest as he concentrated on his connection to Spirit. He exhaled and breathed again, longer and calmer this time, hoping against hope that he had just a fraction of the Transcendent skill that Bisa had. Leo blinked and fluttered his eyes open, and his heart skipped a beat as he saw Nina standing a few feet in front of him. She looked the same but different, more otherworldly, oddly nocturnal. *Perhaps that's just how spirits look*, he thought.

"Nina!" Leo said aloud as he lowered his hand from his chest. His fingers were stiff and cold from the winter's chill, and he made a fist and rubbed them together. Before he could utter another word, Nina dissolved into the freezing breeze. He had made the connection, but wasn't strong or skilled enough to maintain it. He tried again and again, but she never returned.

CHAPTER 9

Avery's talents were growing stronger. Even passive talents like bibliomancy had grown especially sharp. She whispered her intentions to herself as her fingers ran along the length of the bookshelves. The room was dark, and the only sound was the soft sweeping of her fingers across the tattered books. Avery scanned three shelves before she felt a buzzing in her index finger as her fingernail grazed the binding of a black book. *This is it.* She plucked the book from the shelf and cracked it open at random. *I wish Nina were here to see this*, she thought, but she knew that Nina was indeed there, it was just that Avery couldn't see her. Maybe one day her powers would evolve and expand beyond Primordial and into Transcendence. Avery was becoming a witch with little uncertainty, self-assured and at the ready, but she still doubted whether they would ever complete what they had set out to do. At least according to the prophecy.

"I know how to restore spiritual balance," Avery told Ollie fifteen minutes later. They were sitting by the fire, hovering over the book she'd found. "Well, I know where to start, anyway. It's all right here." She tapped the page three times.

Ollie leaned in toward the book to study it. "Okay, but what do we do when we get there? There's nothing else here."

"We have to pass through the veil of spirit. After that, I don't know," Avery said. She wanted to believe that it was as simple as doing just that, but she knew something as delicate as spiritual balance would be anything but simple.

Ollie stared into the fire, unsettled by the idea that there were no other instructions and there was no one else to ask. He considered that it wasn't even that important for a hot minute. After all, nothing truly seemed to be getting any better. It didn't take more than a cursory glance at the daily news to have that impression. The world seemed to be getting darker, more unaligned, more unbalanced than anything else. It even crossed his mind for a second as he was lost in his own thought that perhaps all of it was pointless. *Is any of this making a difference? Will it ever? Has it ever? We only seem to be getting worse.* Ollie headed to his room and played with his plants and tinctures until he had something that he hoped would bring answers during meditation. Information had been flooding in quickly recently, but he needed more.

"I know what we have to do," Ollie told Avery a little while later over a cup of turmeric, oak bark and burdock root tea, dazed and spacey from his concentrated meditation. "We have to free the Muses."

Avery frowned with skepticism. "Muses are real?"

Ollie shrugged. "They're apparently trapped, or entranced, in some way by an entity that is feeding off their abundance of gifts, using that energy as food. It's like a virus."

"How long have the Muses been captive? Wouldn't someone have known about this by now? If this prophecy was made"—she waved her hands wildly in the air—"whenever it was made, wouldn't that mean that *someone* knew they were going to be imprisoned? Right?"

Avery waited for an answer, but Ollie just sipped his tea and breathed a little more deeply. He rubbed his forehead with his fingers, finished his tea and looked Avery right in the eyes.

"Maybe? Maybe not? Maybe only part of it was known, and the other part needed to be discovered…because it hadn't happened yet. Like whatever energy made the prophecy, Source or whatever it was knew that something would happen, but didn't know what. Maybe Source doesn't know everything. Maybe I was just meant to do everything that I just did and *that's* how we discovered what to do!"

"So how do we free them? What does that even mean?" Avery asked.

"I guess we'll figure that out when we get there?" Ollie said. They had proved to be a rather good team, and the uncertainty about what to do was only a minor snag.

After Ollie was a little more grounded, he refreshed his face with some cold water. He slipped Rosemary's garnet ring—which he'd been given after her death—over his finger and created a door to wherever it was they needed to go.

Avery looked at the wall of rock inside the newly formed door and scoffed. "That's solid rock. There's no way through."

Ollie stepped forward, held his hand out only inches from the rock and slowly moved toward it. His hand punctured the rock like a gentle jackhammer as he pushed forward with ease. Chunks and large sheets of rock tumbled over him as he entered into the unknown. On the other side, he emerged out of the large boulder fit into the side of a mountainous cliff, full of trees and uneven terrain, shrouded in the black of night. There was an eerie silence, which seemed unnatural for a landscape so lush. Somewhere in the shadows, the spirit was hiding, sucking the energy of the Muses as it had been for what must have felt like an eternity to the Muses. Avery followed Ollie through the rock and into the darkness. They assumed they were alone, but they were mistaken.

Avery picked up a large stick from a fallen tree, snapped it in half and set the end of each ablaze with a blow of her breath. She handed one to Ollie, and they chased the dark away with their torches. The shadows bounced around and made the strange land look more alive. There was a crude trail to Ollie's left that looked like the only walkable path.

"Where do we go?" Avery asked. Her face filled with uncertainty for the first time in a while. She bit her lip and suddenly found herself uneasy. Avery thought back to their time in the forest when they had attempted to find their totem animals. The thick, swampy forest had been full of snakes, spiders and gators that had all made her skin crawl. That was before she had truly found her power. Yet, even now, that same feeling struck her heart. She caught a set of eyes from underneath the leaves of a nearby shrub. The beady, stalking eyes of a serpent. Avery's breath was trapped in her chest as she locked on to the snake. Its coiled body glowed amber under the light of the torch, its head like the tip of a spear, aimed directly at them. Her eyes were drawn to the tree next to them, where another snake was wrapped around a branch, stealthily observing from above. A dozen snakes seemed to appear all at once, free from their camouflage, like some kind of twisted version of Where's Waldo? made of Avery's nightmares. She grabbed hold of Ollie's arm cat-quick and drew his attention to the growing number of snakes.

"Where the hell are we?"

"This is where we're supposed to be!" Ollie said. "I don't know where that is though," he added. Ollie closed his eyes for a moment, chanted something under his breath and then looked around with his third eye. "I think it's this way. I can feel it."

"We have to get out of here. I don't think I can do this," Avery said in a panic, imagining ten different ways the snakes would attack.

Ollie whipped his head around to look at Avery. He repeatedly called out her name with vigor until she stopped rambling about the snakes. "Get it together! You're the Primordial here. You have the strongest connection to animals—use it."

"These aren't animals…these are—"

"Avery!" Ollie repeated. "Concentrate! Connect with the snakes."

Avery took a moment to control her breathing and found the fire inside her. She thought about the lion at the zoo and channeled that energy. They weren't there to harm them, and she thought hard about how much they insisted on not being attacked. It was a conversation that she hadn't thought would ever happen, but found herself having in the ether. A conversation predominantly about respect, one that made a request rather than demand. The first snake she saw uncoiled its body and slithered away into the brush. The snake wrapped around the limb was next. The snakes along the path, the ones hiding in the crevices of the rocks, then others that were close but that she hadn't seen. Large ones, smaller baby ones, and all the other many proportions that surrounded them. All of them twisted and slithered away from their hiding spots and vanished into the depths of the dark jungle.

Ollie listened to the sounds of the snakes slipping away and looked to Avery with pride. "See?"

When the path was clear, Avery coolly led the way, consistently removing the threat of a potentially fatal snakebite with each step forward, flinching only when sharp branches occasionally poked at them. As they battled through the strange brush and often jagged, irregular landscape, they took guesses as to where they might be. It was much warmer than Colorado and incredibly humid. It had to be somewhere tropical, Ollie thought, or maybe somewhere in South America. They were always on the cusp of the answer but never quite landing on it entirely.

Thirty minutes later, they finally made it to a small stretch of what they realized was an island. They could see and hear the ocean now, and there were lights at some unknowable distance across the water. They turned around to see they had descended a stretch of a small mountain, and there was a faint outline of a white tower in the distance. Neither of them could be certain what it was or where they were.

Ollie kicked a few rocks around on the ground in front of him. "I think it's here," he said.

Avery looked around and saw nothing but rock. "Where?"

Ollie proceeded down a trail of stones into a small cavity. "This. Here," he said as he reached out toward a large sheet of rock that was wedged up against the side of the shallow crater.

Avery descended to meet him and held her torch out to see. "Here, really?"

Ollie nodded with certainty. "Give me a hand with this," he said as he grabbed hold of the large rock.

The two heaved and pulled, and the rock began to loosen from its resting spot. A few minutes later, they managed to pull it out from the side of the crater to reveal the opening to a cave. By the time they caught their breath, their torches had already begun to burn out. Avery searched nearby for another piece of wood to use and set it on fire. Ollie entered first, but stopped when Avery called out to him from the entrance.

"I can't go in," she said, sounding surprised. She tried to take another step forward but couldn't. "It's like I'm being repelled. Is this the *veil* we need to pass through?"

Ollie came back out and Avery tried to enter again, this time with success.

"I think there can be only one at a time," Ollie said. "One of us is going to have to go."

Avery scoffed. "Who goes?"

"I think you should go. There's not a lot I can do as a Transcendent. At least not without invoking some other spirit and using their power."

Avery shook her head. "Which we didn't do."

"No."

"We just left immediately," Avery said as she let out a deep sigh. "Well, we don't have time for that now. You're right. I might be able to do more. All right, fuck it. Here I go." She took hold of the torch and brightened the flame with a wave of her hand. "Keep an eye out."

Ollie furrowed his brow. "For what?"

Avery waved the question away like an annoying insect.

"Please be careful," he said. "If you get into trouble, there isn't anything I can do. I won't be able to come in and help."

"I got this," Avery said sharply as she caressed Ollie's shoulder before turning to descend into the cave. The torch popped and sparked as the fire roared to a near white hot.

What a badass, Ollie thought. He didn't want to give her a big head.

The cave was deeper than it looked, and colder. Avery pressed into the cave and followed the narrow path until it opened and spread into a massive cavern with stalagmites and wet cones of rock that hung from the ceiling like icicles. There were two openings, two paths. The first path led her to a dead end. Avery let out a sigh, retraced her steps and started down the left path. She was surprised to realize that she was way more adventurous than she had ever given herself credit for. Back-packing around the country was one thing, but she would've never assumed she would be exploring caves by torch. As she proceeded down the dark path, she recalled the moment she'd stepped off the train in Charlotte from New York City, with her notebook full of banal thoughts and trivial reflections, the start of a whole new way of life. And now she was somewhere in the outrageously wide middle, a fire in her soul and in her hands, her skin glossy from the sweat of a dangerous jungle hike past golden lance-head vipers and jagged rocks, treading fearlessly into the unknown, a shockingly robust variety of Avery that she now knew she had always been but had never embraced.

The torch fire broke through the darkness in full when she rounded a corner and found herself in a small room. A sheen of gold covered her skin as the light of the fire bounced off what she saw before her. Treasure. It was nearly like every movie she'd ever seen that featured something of the sort, only more tactile. Avery never cared much for jewelry or money, and certainly not gold, but seeing it stashed in piles around her gave her a rush of unexpected joy. It felt like the moments just before she woke from a good dream, in that limbo period when she was half awake. Only this was real. She was awake. Avery blinked a few times just to make sure she wasn't making it all up. It was all still there, glistening in the torchlight like a blanket of birthday presents under the amber glow of a lit birthday cake. Avery realized she had explored the entire cave. There

were no Muses, and there was no spirit holding them hostage—
only gold.

Avery's eyes drifted across the treasure. *Did Ollie get it
wrong?* Under the babbling brook of her own thoughts, she
heard a peculiar melody coming from a gold bottle just beside
her, a sweet euphony of whispering voices. She listened closely
as she took a step toward the ancient-looking bottle. Behind the
voices were deep gongs, like heavy wind chimes. Avery's
breath was heavy with tension as she reached out to grab the
bottle.

Everything was different. She was no longer standing beside
the bottle but was inside it, and it was not a bottle, but a lofty,
spacious and exceptionally decadent room, lit by a chandelier
of a thousand candles that would never extinguish. She had
passed through the veil of spirit that the prophecy so vaguely
articulated. The air smelled sweet and rich like orange blossoms, amber and forest berries—rife with beauty, creation,
passion—and an overflowing abundance of love-induced in-
ventiveness and transformation. A harp stood in a corner of the
room next to a table of dewy fruit. In another corner was a large
cage, fashioned into a bedroom with plush furniture, blankets
and pillows—and three ethereal beings. An aura of nurturing
energy encapsulated them. They were beautiful in ways that no
human could ever achieve, with a beauty beyond symmetry and
decoration. The honey-colored candlelight gleamed off their already luminous skin. Their faces, although beautiful, were
sullied with sadness, visages of ones who had nearly forgotten
what freedom outside of slavelike servitude was like. *The
Muses?* Avery speculated.

The figure closest to the edge of the cage nodded in affirma-
tion.

Can they read my thoughts?

The two other Muses joined the first, and they pointed toward a corner of the room that Avery had yet to discover. There, atop a bed of shimmering satin, was the spirit. Nothing like she expected, it looked human, but in truth it was a paradigm of indulgence and vampirism. She watched its chest rise and fall. It was sleeping. Avery sneaked over toward the cage until she was face-to-face with the Muses. She could feel their energy radiating from them like sunbeams.

"You must help us," the Muse said softly. "We cannot leave without a key." The Muse lifted a finger and pointed toward the spirit. Running along the top of the ornately carved headboard of the bed were three hollows, each filled with impossibly beautiful marble figurines. In the middle hollow was a large skeleton key, made from the bones of a Muse who had attempted to escape.

"How am I going to get *that*?" Avery wondered in a soft whisper.

"You must retrieve it—carefully. If the spirit wakes, there is nothing we can do to protect you. Your magic won't work in this space, nor would it harm him if it could."

Avery turned to look at the key once more and studied the rise and fall of the spirit's chest. She looked all over the room for something to help her retrieve the key while keeping her distance, but there was nothing. She thought about the prophecy. *Me being here right this second should be proof enough that I can get the key and end this, right?*

She took a deep breath and released it softly as she took her first step toward the bed. Outside the cave Ollie had noticed a sudden reappearance of snakes. With little light to erase the darkness of night, he had to rely on his ears. He could hear the slithering and the hissing of snakes gathering around him, snakes he couldn't see—yet. It was very unnatural. The sounds got closer and louder, as if the snakes were actively seeking him out on purpose.

Avery softened her breath as she drew closer to the bed and the sleeping spirit. When she arrived beside the bed, she took a good look at the spirit. Its face was hazy and indistinguishable, like a photograph taken in thick fog, its chest rising and collapsing like rolling waves on the open sea. She could see the objects in the headboard more clearly now. Marble figurines— all nude—that glistened under the light of the thousand candles like wet stones in the moonlight. She could smell the stink of the spirit now, an odor reminiscent of a foul cheese, perfumed with the fragrance of the Muses. Avery squinted at the key, realizing there was no way to retrieve it but to climb into bed with the spirit. It would have to be retrieved by hand—a choice that would result in either success or certain death.

Ollie stepped forward into the darkness and saw a dozen snakes gliding across the rocks toward him. He turned around, and saw more. Their eyes were beyond that of nature. There was a presence in the snakes' eyes, that of a spell. They had been charmed, trained to protect the cave. Ollie waved his torch in front of him, sending bits of hot ash and sizzling embers across the rocks. The snakes disapproved, but remained dauntless. The hissing almost sounded like bloodthirsty laughter. "Avery, hurry up, oh, hurry up!" Ollie said nervously. All was still.

Avery held her breath and placed a hand on the soft bed. Her hand sank into the plushness. Her eyes locked on the spirit, her body amped with anxiety. All sound drained from the room until the only thing she could hear was the booming pulse of her heartbeat. She could feel it throbbing in her ears, like a thumb hit with a hammer. Her other hand sank into the bed as she hoisted her body onto the satin mounds and sat back on her heels. She watched in horror as the spirit's body shifted from her weight. Her eyes wide, her breath trapped inside her throat.

When what felt like an eternity had passed, Avery extended her leg and took her first step toward the key. Her foot descended into a pool of satin as though she were walking in quicksand. She could hear the spirit breathing. *I didn't know spirits needed to breathe.* Avery took another step forward, placing her foot on the opposite side of the spirit, straddling it. She looked down at its muddled and obscure face and waited for movement. There was none. Her eyes darted up to the key. It was almost within reach.

The snakes surrounded Ollie in every direction, even from above as they dangled from the top of the cave's entrance like poisonous vines. A large viper shot out from the crowd like lightning and slithered toward him. Ollie swung the torch back and forth wildly, sending specks of fire dancing through the air like tiny stars. There was nothing he could do, and the sudden pressure of imminent death clouded his judgment.

As if on instinct, he closed his eyes and asked for help as the snakes closed in around him. There was a wet, squishing sound. He opened his eyes and saw his totem, the bearded dragon, as large as a crocodile, before him with the snake in its mouth. The dragon's jaws opened and closed with determination as its throat fluttered. It swung around and took a ghastly bite out of the crowd of snakes. Ollie took a few steps back until he met

rock. A snake dropped down and surprised him with its venomous fangs like daggers. Ollie swung the torch and snuffed the
snake's bite with the flames. His eyes zoomed in every direction until he was certain there were no other threats. His dragon
was caught in the middle of a wild bloodbath, defending Ollie
against the bewitched snakes. It spun and twisted, its tail trail-
ing behind the whirling movements of its body. A deadly and
grotesque dance, poetic, mesmeric, and monstrous, yet necessary.

Avery reached as far as her arms allowed, her trembling fingers stretching like seedlings reaching for the sun. Her shadow
fell across the spirit as the tip of her middle finger landed on
the cold skeleton key. She lifted her finger, leaned forward ever
so slightly, and reached for the key once more. Her middle finger landed on the edge of the key, which slid from her grasp,
and the bow carouselled around and clinked into the bottom of
a nearby figurine. Avery's eyes dropped down to the spirit. Her
heart skipped a beat and continued to pound louder and louder.
The spirit remained still and asleep. Avery let out a silent sigh
that ruffled the hair that had fallen over her face. She was almost there; she almost had the key. Her fingers curled up like
the legs of a tarantula, and she drew the key closer to her palm.
The bone scrubbed across the wood as she seized the key and
clenched it safely in her sweaty palm. Avery wasn't in the clear
just yet. She had to somehow backtrack out of her unfortunate
position without waking the spirit.

Her eyes closed as she built up the nerve to remove herself
from the bed. She lifted her foot and her heel snagged a bit of
satin, tugging the piece that was under the spirit's arm. She
waited for half a heartbeat before proceeding quickly. Avery

slithered off the bed and crept away toward the cage. With haste, she slipped the key into the lock and turned it. The door unbolted with a heavy, metallic click that echoed throughout the room. She opened the door and ushered the Muses out of their prison. *Okay, now how do we get out?* she wondered. When Avery turned around to check on the spirit, her throat was met with ice cold hands. Her eyes went wide as her feet lifted off the ground. The spirit gripped her throat tighter as it effortlessly lifted her higher into the air and then slammed her body against the prison bars.

"Who are you? Where did you come from?" the spirit barked in a grisly tone, its face now suddenly crystal clear. Its eyes were like a swamp, its skin cold and blue. Avery couldn't have answered even if she'd wanted to; the grip was too tight. Yet the spirit's breath was so pungent, she could smell it without breathing in as it wafted up to her face. Wine and bile.

A Muse plucked a series of harp strings that resonated through the air. The grimacing spirit softened its face and loosened its grip on Avery's neck until she fell to the floor, gasping for breath. The spirit turned around and looked toward the harp as the Muse continued to play a hypnotizing cradlesong. The spirit smirked and revealed a mess of sharp and slimy teeth. The second Muse opened her mouth and released an operatic aria. Avery looked up to see the singing Muse approaching the spirit with confidence. The melodic plucking of harp strings and exquisite song echoed in the chamber like an intimate and preternatural concert held within a small venue. The spirit's eyelids grew heavy, and its eyes were dazzled with enchantment as it began to fall under the spell of the Muses, something that was impossible while they were within their cage. Avery rubbed her throat as she caught her breath. Until now, the

Muses' powers had been controlled and regulated, used for the spirit's pleasure and enjoyment only. The Muses could finally retaliate and use their power to ensnare the spirit instead of amuse it.

The third Muse spun toward the center of the room, her garments flowing in the air like ghostly wings. Another spell of enchantment. She danced and breezed across the floor like a beautiful daydream in shades of purple, blue and green. The air smelled sweet as she whirled through the room, breaking the spirit down through beauty. The three Muses worked together, creating a spell that would be irresistible. The dancing Muse hopped like wind across a meadow as the harp trailed behind the angelic voice. Avery watched the spirit fall to its knees as the dancing Muse drew closer, widening her steps. The Muse sailed through the air in a final spin and placed her hand on the spirit's head, like a crown. When she removed her hand, the spirit fell limp to the floor. In a delicate swing, the Muse removed a purple sheet from her robes and cast it into the air. It fluttered down toward the spirit's body until it landed upon it like a layer of freshly fallen snow. The Muse whipped the sheet away with a strong tug. Nothing but the scent of rosemary and lavender was left.

"Is it gone?" Avery asked.

"Yes," the Muses said together. "Thank you."

"I'd ask more about that, but we need to get out of here," Avery said.

The Muses grabbed hold of Avery and lifted her to her feet. When she was able to stand, they were no longer in the bottle but at the entrance to the cave. Ollie's dragon had left when the spirit was vanquished and the spell had been broken. Avery had nearly forgotten their whole mission for finding and releasing the Muses in the first place until Ollie brought it up. Only the Muses already knew.

The dancing Muse stepped forward. "We will gift you one request, as payment for releasing us," she said.

Ollie looked at Avery. They understood right at that moment, at the same time, what needed to be done. Neither of them questioned whether the Muses would be able to grant them their request; they just felt that they would.

"I ask…" Avery began, "for spiritual balance," she finished with confidence.

"As you wish. It would be our pleasure," the Muses said together. The singing Muse extended her hand toward Ollie and brushed the side of his cheek, filling his mind with exactly what they would do. As their skin began to glow like moonlight, they dissolved into the air.

The Muses retreated to three different spots around the world and began their spell—a spell for hope. The harpist in the middle of a busy city square, the dancer atop a rock formation in the desert, the singer near a snow-covered riverbed, invisible to all humans. They began to dance, a spell of the contagious kind. As they danced, their energy expanded throughout the world, spreading vibrations of hope that tipped the scales of spiritual balance with each light footstep. Their inspiration transcended every obstacle, slowly dissolving them with the carefree abandon of a luscious daydream. With the magic of the Muses, art begot change and encouraged balance. *It won't feel good, but what change does?* Ollie thought as he replayed the steps the Muses would take to carry out their wish. Everything they had done would function like pieces fitting into a puzzle, eventually leading to the full picture, mended and restored.

Shortly after the Muses departed the island, Ollie gave Avery a breakdown of all the details and brought her up to speed on the progress of their prophesied goal.

"That should have been it, I think," Ollie said. "We set everything in motion. Mental, emotional and spiritual balances should be *recalibrating*. If I remember what Nina said correctly, once those three are in the works, they will effect physical change as well. That should fulfill the prophecy. Or something like that."

"How will we know for sure?" Avery asked.

"I think the Advisory had some way of determining that. Some kind of device or something that would indicate when the energies have shifted. I think we just have hope at this point. Hope that we did it all right." Avery started thinking ahead to a point when they would know for sure and all the guessing would finally be over. She considered what that would actually look like, the rest of the journey. In her experience, change never felt great, and things often got worse before they got better. They had to. For a moment, she wished she had the Transcendent skills that Ollie did. She knew she would probably be powerful enough to see that future if she wasn't a Primordial.

Ollie knew that everything was just as it should be, and everything had worked out just as it had to, at least until now. There were no doors on the island for Rosemary's ring to enchant, so they drew one into the sand on the beach and fixed a rock for a handle. When they got back to the house, he was immediately reminded of how different everything already was and had been for quite some time. Nina, Leo and Mitch were gone. Bisa was possibly somewhere in limbo. He thought back to a time when he was interested in pursuing photography, and how he had broken his leg climbing a tree because he wanted to see what the fruit at top tasted like. Avery probably could've fixed his leg with a little magic. How wild was it to think that magic had always been around and he had never known about it? Would it have changed anything? he wondered. Would his family have stayed in Argentina if they had known he was going to be gifted with such amazing talents?

They had made it all the way home by the time he realized he didn't remember getting there because he was so lost in his own thoughts. He looked up at the house and fully understood something on a level he never had before: everything changes, everything ends; the only thing he knew didn't change was the fact that everything changes. One can't evolve without expecting, or even encouraging, change. Ollie took off Rosemary's ring and was placing it on the counter when he heard a sound.

"Avery," he said softly.

"What?" Avery looked at him.

"What was that?"

Avery shook her head. "I didn't hear anything."

Then again, a creak and a rustling. Both Ollie's and Avery's eyes were wild with confusion. Avery acted instinctively and followed the noise upstairs. The bathroom light was on and the door was open. Ollie followed closely behind her, grabbing a small bottle of defensive potion he'd left on the table in the hall, just in case. The faucet turned on briefly and was switched off a moment later.

"Someone's here," Avery whispered as blood rushed through her body, and she produced a small ball of whirling fire in her palm. They clung to the walls as they crept down the hall. Ollie could smell the sulfuric smell of Avery's fireball as the heat from it beat across his face as he trailed behind her. They reached the doorframe, and a few moments later, they both jumped into the bathroom. Avery lifted her hand up high, the fire blazing like a roaring sun. Smoke billowed up toward the ceiling and spilled out into the hall. Ollie bounced in beside her, potion retracted like a baseball ready to be thrown.

Leo dropped the bandages on the floor, cowered up near the counter and screamed, "Jesus, fuck!"

Ollie lowered the potion and rolled his eyes. Avery lowered her hand but held her fireball in her palm.

"Leo, what the fuck are you doing here?" Avery demanded.

"I live here!" Leo shouted as he grabbed at his chest to feel his beating heart.

"No you don't. You left. What are you doing here?" she repeated loudly.

Leo waved at her fireball, and a drop of blood fell from his wound and spattered on the floor. "You wanna relax that thing?" The realization that Avery could've burned him alive and he'd been caught off guard sank in pretty fast.

"This isn't a hotel. You left," Avery said sternly. "You *left!*" Finally she dismissed the fire in her hand.

"What happened?" Ollie asked as he nodded toward Leo's gash.

Leo waved it away like it was too exhausting to even dive into. "I had an accident."

"Yeah, no shit," Avery said sharply before she scoffed. "Your whole life is nothing but accidents. One accident after the other, one fuckup after the other."

"What the fuck is your problem?" Leo snapped back as he retrieved the bandages from the floor and continued to tend to his wound.

"I've known people like you." Avery rolled her eyes and laughed to herself. "My God, I even *dated* people like you before I learned to have more self-respect than that. You just waltz through life doing whatever the hell you want, leaving every single person you meet to drown in your wake."

"Oh, fuck you," Leo said, his face full of disgust.

"What? Like it isn't true? Do we need to count the number of people whose lives you've destroyed?" Avery held up her hands to count on her piping-hot fingers as tufts of smoke curled between them. "Nina? Dead. Bisa? Dead? Mitch? Gone! Rosemary, Per—*dead*. You're a corrosive serial killer!" Avery rested her tongue for a moment as she searched for the stinging sword that would cut deep. Then she found it. "Maybe your daughter would be alive if you hadn't been such a pathetic, piece-of-shit father."

Ollie's mouth dropped open in shock as Leo's whole body shook with rage. His chest puffed and his nostrils flared as he took a few steps toward Avery, letting his chest press into her and push her backward. He had never shown such restraint. He had never been so angry. Avery could feel his heavy, hot breath as though he were an ox that was seeing red. Leo stopped only when Avery's back hit the wall and he couldn't push her any farther.

"What are you gonna do? Huh? Nothing. You're not gonna do anything about it…"Avery said confidently.

Leo let out another heavy breath through his nose. "No? I could fucking kill you right now."

Avery ignored him and continued, "But you won't, even though you could…because you know it's true." Her voice was soft now, almost a whisper. "You're a fucking mess, a reckless, selfish piece of shit that sucks the life out of everyone around you. I see right through you, I always have. You're about as good at hiding it as a piece of plastic wrap."

Leo's eyes were bloodshot, and the bathroom lights flickered. A small river of red fell from his nose as he tried to control himself.

Ollie crossed his hands and chanted silently. He asked for help in the form of an incantation. He raised his hand in the air, and when he made a fist, Leo nodded and fell to the ground like a pile of dead weight. Ollie let out a breath of relief as Avery turned to him.

"What was that?" she asked.

"He's asleep. That was enough," Ollie said, looking directly into her eyes.

Avery looked at Leo on the floor and kneeled down beside him. "What is he doing here? Why'd he come back?"

"I don't know. Why'd he leave? Where'd he go?" Ollie asked.

Avery sighed and let her hand hover above Leo's wound until it started to heal. "I don't know. Can you figure that out? Are you able to do that kind of thing? Should be easy now that he's asleep." Avery healed him, simply because she could.

"Yeah. But I need a drink first."

CHAPTER 10

It didn't matter what choices Merlot made in her life; they were never actually her own. She would never know what her heart truly wanted or desired, because the blood that ran through her veins and pumped through her heart was infected. It had been that way for her mother, and her mother's mother, and all the women before them. They had all been robbed of a true life of choice because of the energy her blood carried. It had been accidentally defiled by one of her ancestors ages ago in a spell gone wrong, a Transcendent witch whose name was Perpetua.

The unvarnished truth was that she was the complete opposite of everyone around her, at nearly all times. Perpetua was the rebel, the outspoken, the unyielding, the uncompromising, a formidable woman to have in one's life in any regard. Those closest to her understood that she could never be broken, but she could be bent by love and friendship. And she was absolutely inflexible when it came to her own opinions, beliefs and perspectives. She was who she was, and people—whether they loved or hated her—thanked her for at least presenting herself truthfully.

It was exceptionally advantageous that she was exceedingly skilled when it came to influence, the most opportunistic power of a Transcendent witch. Perpetua prided herself on being incredibly talented and powerful when it came to magic, but she never actually needed to exercise her power because of her confidence. That shouldn't suggest she was cold and without heart. In fact, she had an enormous heart that could melt any frost, and an abundance of love to give.

Her greatest passion was a good fight, but her greatest love was not the man she married, but the woman she met after he passed. For months she had dreamed of a man who loved her for who she was and not for what he wanted her to be. She held full conversations with him while asleep and looked for him during the day. Perpetua found him in the spring. Before they met, his entire body ached, especially in the winter months, and when he met Perpetua, he became years younger. His body no longer ached, and he had more energy and appreciated the sunshine more than he ever had in his entire life. He called her his spring, which made for a delightful joke since his name was Invierno—Winter. He'd lost his entire family in a sudden and tragic fire, and the world had since burned a lot less brightly. Together they had one son, Augusto. Shortly after their son was born, Perpetua began a transformation into everything that she was not. She loved her family, but something was missing, a feeling of a life that was not yet finished.

When Winter died mysteriously of an illness no one could diagnose, many people pointed fingers at Perpetua, as if she were responsible for his death or had caused it intentionally. It didn't help that he had left everything—his successful bodega in the center of town as well as his entire estate—to her. She mourned the loss of her first real partner in life, and honored him by keeping a square of cloth from his favorite shirt in her pocket at all times. With his death came a certain level of relief, which came with its own load of guilt. It finally felt like she was given permission to be free of a life that wasn't everything it needed to be, everything that she knew it could be. She hadn't practiced her power of influence in the four years that they were together, and she had gotten so used to not using it that knowing she could was enough.

On the morning of the new moon, she awoke with tears in her eyes. It was then that she removed her late husband's clothing from her pocket. Perpetua suddenly had the urge to be near the water, and that was exactly where she went. That afternoon, she took her son for a walk along the water's edge, where the wind chased the waves toward the shore and tousled the leaves in the nearby trees. When they arrived at a patch of grass, they stopped to sit. Her son fell asleep under the rays of sun that broke through the clouds, pacified by the bird songs. Perpetua plucked a wildflower from the grass and cast it into the wind along with the wish to find whatever it was she was looking for. She sat for several minutes in quiet contemplation with her eyes closed, listening for voices in the ether, but there were none. When she opened her eyes, she saw a figure—a woman. Her clothes were simple and inexpensive, yet she had a way about her that made her seem glamorous even though everything about her suggested otherwise. The woman looked up and they locked eyes. Perpetua recognized her. The woman's name was Onofria, and she worked at her late husband's bodega, a place she hadn't stepped foot in since his death and had paid someone to run for her.

Onofria rose from her spot and approached slowly, very slowly, careful not to alarm or wake Augusto. "I'm very sorry about your husband," she said softly. She could have said anything and Perpetua wouldn't have heard it; the rush of blood to her head was too distracting. The voices in the ether didn't have to say much at all, because Perpetua felt it—instantly. It wasn't love; it was an attunement. There was a harmonious compatibility that she felt but didn't understand. Perpetua invited her to sit as she searched the chasms within the woman's eyes. She saw Onofria's life: previous work as a housemaid, an au pair, a prostitute, and, more recently, a barmaid. She saw her life, the losses she'd endured, the joys she valued, the exotic places she'd been to and the forceful way in which she'd justified all of it. It flashed before her like a series of paintings that filled a historical gallery.

Perpetua involuntarily began to read into the Onofria's likes and dislikes, learning her favorite thing to eat before she stopped herself. Perpetua could've learned everything anyone would ever dream of wanting to know about someone, but she didn't want that. She wanted to appreciate an elongated discovery of the woman. She saw a history with her, one that was by no means easy but was more genuine than anything she'd ever encountered in her life.

By the same time the following year, Onofria had moved in with Perpetua and her son. Perpetua had been so bewitched by love that she had entirely forgotten she was a witch. As close as the two women were, she never shared that part of her truth. She thought about it early on in their relationship, but it seemed less and less important over time.

Shortly afterward, when the seasons began to shift, a messenger in regal robes and with a groomed beard showed up at Perpetua's door. He brought with him word that the king was going to confiscate her land and her estate.

"Why? This is my land," Perpetua explained.

"Not anymore," the messenger said as he handed her an official document with the king's seal.

"What does he need my land for?" Perpetua shouted. "Where will we go? Why is the king doing something like this?"

"Because he's the king, and you—are a widow."

Perpetua narrowed her eyes and raised an eyebrow as she handed the document back to the messenger. "You tell your king that I will not give him my land. Tell him I refuse and that if he knows what is best for him, he will accept."

The rest of the day and much of the night passed without any further word from the king or his messenger. Perpetua put Augusto to bed and left Onofria to tell him a bedtime story. Perpetua then took a walk through the walled gardens under the dark moon as she did every night when everything was beginning to flower. The garden air was an ode to her senses, abundant with honeylike sweetness, rife with the seductive notes of rose and bougainvillea, walls covered in red, white and pink geranium that made for a breathtaking vision at all times of the day and night.

It was the disarming spell of the garden that made the sound of her lover's scream so horrific. Perpetua ran back toward the house. The screams that had sliced through the sweet garden air stopped as she climbed the stairs. All of her panic drained into her heart when she entered Augusto's bedroom. The sight of Onofria's body, limp and lifeless, with every limb broken, did what nothing else in the world had been able to do: it broke her. She couldn't breathe. All she could do was stand there.

"Courtesy of the king," the messenger said as the pack of soldiers dispersed throughout the room. "The bodega is no longer yours. It too belongs to the king. You seem to be confused about who can actually give anyone orders. When the king desires something of you, you give it willingly, or you have it taken. I suggest you be gone by morning or you will suffer the same fate." The messenger signaled to his soldiers, and they began to leave. "Now, if you'll excuse me, we are going to the bodega to celebrate and think of a new name for it. Perhaps the King of Cups?"

As they left, Perpetua looked around for Augusto, but he was nowhere. Her nose filled with the stench of pain. It was then she learned that the loss of love could break someone faster than any weapon could break a bone. She searched for Augusto and called out his name, but every call was left unanswered. Something switched inside her, and when the house was completely empty, she decided she had no reason to live. She had never experienced pain so deep and raw, all at once, so suddenly. An hour later, she reevaluated when she would end her life. The power that she held surged up like a roaring fire. And although there was nothing she could do to bring her son or Onofria back, she could do them justice.

Perpetua headed to town and stood across the street from the bodega where all the king's men had gathered to indulge in free wine. Through the window she could see the messenger, sloppily drinking from a cup. A single soldier was outside the door, polishing off a cup of wine. Perpetua sank her teeth into his mind and held him hostage. His mouth was energetically sealed shut, but his eyes were wide open so he could watch what she was about to do. She bit her quivering lip and pooled all of her rage behind her eyes, where she let it bleed out in the form of influence into the messenger.

He set down his cup, unsheathed a dagger from his side and stabbed a soldier in the throat. She had never seen so much blood, nor had she ever seen her power used in this way. The messenger stabbed another soldier in the side, and again in the chest. Perpetua found another soldier, immobile from shock, and she influenced him next. A sword ripped through a neighboring soldier's arm until it was left hanging by a mess of bloody cords of flesh. She swayed a few more men to secure the doors, locking them inside as another set fire to another. There was blood, and fire, and the unbearable screams that eased Perpetua's pain merged with the smoke pluming out of the windows like clouds of hell. When the bodega was wrapped in flames, she sent the single soldier back to the king to murder him.

It wasn't enough. Perpetua headed back home and drew herself a bath. The room was filled with candles, and her wet skin glistened like diamonds. It was time to die. For a moment she thought maybe she was being a little hasty, giving in to the feelings of despair and pain that would eventually become less raw. Only, she didn't care, not in that moment. Perpetua thought about how she was going to carry out the spell. She thought about chanting the words, an incantation that would allow her to die without pain and without the fear of death. The loss of everyone she loved was just too much.

"This body, this heart, this blood will never suffer again. It will never feel pain," she said softly to herself. She clenched her fists and looked down at them, surprised to find that she had already cut her wrists. The magic numbed her entirely so there would be no pain, but it also was muddled with a skewed and hazy intention. A spell made in the heat of the moment, riddled with pain and spiked with sorrow. As she faded from consciousness, she was completely unaware of the magical side effect that she had inadvertently germinated. That sorrow manifested into a blood curse that would darken the spirit of anyone with her blood in their veins. It would have ended with her, had Augusto not fled from the soldiers like a rat fleeing a trap and survived, carrying her blood—and with it, her curse.

Merlot was the full-bodied curse at the height of its prime. Her mind and spirit were tainted like a bottle of fine wine left to oxidize into a nose-wrinkling vinegar—undrinkable and spoiled. The color, odor and taste of her spirit had all been magically stained.

CHAPTER 11

There were many things that Merlot didn't have—a political background, a campaign manager, a colossal bankroll—but she did have a lot of power and ambition. With those two things together, almost anything was possible. And of course, if you threw in magic, especially the new kind of magic that Merlot had alchemized with Leo's blood, *impossible* would be a word of the past. The closer Merlot was to achieving her goal, the more heavily her foot pressed the gas pedal. She had a few years before the next presidential election, and that meant she had a great deal of time to make sure it worked out.

First, she had to choose someone to be her human golem. At best, there were a couple hundred people she could choose from the HelloMerlot payroll, but it was Austin Clay who fit the bill. The Co-COO of her marijuana company headquartered in New York. He was thirty-four, ridiculously ambitious and as confident as Merlot was conniving. Everyone loved him. He made a point of being an active face for the company, delivering the idea that running a successful business was accessible for all kinds of people, not just the wealthy, entitled and privileged, people who were born with a private chef and a free ride to an Ivy League school. When *HighAF* magazine ran an article about him, they called him "the COO next door." He was young and approachable, someone who wore colorful socks, someone who made an effort to connect with community—he inspired, and could roll a blunt while doing it.

Austin had an outstanding amount of energy and was always the first to give back, whether it was to a children's hospital or an LGBTQ+ youth center. He won over the hearts of everyone, even people who didn't agree with him or his beliefs. Merlot thought he was the perfect fit. He seemed the type who would actually enjoy the length of a taxing campaign because he would be so well received, so perhaps using him as her conduit wouldn't be all that bad. He might actually enjoy it, at least that was what she told herself.

When they met for dinner at the High Priestess, one of HelloMerlot's many wine bars, she had him completely within her control. It was the best fit; he would do all the heavy lifting and she could tell him where to put the boxes. By the time the ricotta cheesecake with passion fruit arrived, she had already laid out her entire plan: make him the CEO of HelloMerlot, arrange meetings with high-profile leaders in technology and influence them all with the same potion she slipped into Austin's wine, secure social media platforms, announce Austin's bid for political office and guarantee a win through any means necessary. She, of course, would cast a simple money spell; when it came to running a shady business, more was never enough. She was exceptionally gifted with abundance spells. By the time Pink Floyd's "Money" finished playing, stocks would have surged, donations would have been received and sales would be up. Money was easy.

For a moment she considered what life would look like once she reached the top and there was nowhere else to go. Would she be satisfied? Would she be bored? A slow global takeover would surely take some time to do well. She would have to do it slowly, savor the taste, enjoy the experience, like watching the full moon rise over the vast ocean. The best part was that no one would ever be the wiser with Austin at the helm. No human or witch would ever see it coming, and no one could stop her. How does one stop something they never saw coming?

CHAPTER 12

Ollie and Avery were on their third drink at Duncan Monday, the only cocktail bar with an internet jukebox. It was loud and full of people, but Ollie had enough bourbon to actually not be bothered by all the buzzing thoughts and energy. Alcohol seemed to dull it a bit instead of intensify it. It did, however, make auras a little more prominent, which added a lovely glow to the bar. There was something relaxing about the carefree energy that comes with a few cocktails, and Ollie was living for it.

"I still can't believe you told Leo off like that," Ollie said as he wiped up a small stream of bourbon that had spilled down the side of his glass.

"He deserved it. And it's all true," Avery said, and she tipped her head back to deliver the end of her cocktail to her throat. She licked her lips as they gazed at each other. "Well, it is!"

Ollie nodded. "Well…yeah…but, it was supremely cunty."

Avery waggled her head. "I hate that word. Look, I don't know what to tell you. I've always known he was trash. What kind of a sick joke is it that he's a Corporeal witch?"

Ollie shushed her.

Avery clucked her tongue. "Oh, stop it. No one cares! No one even knows what we're talking about." She ordered another round of drinks for each of them and looked at Ollie in a way that she had never looked at him before. "Oliver, I really like you. You are one of the best things to happen in the last year."

"You too!" Ollie said politely.

When the drinks arrived, Avery fingered the rim of hers for a moment as she thought about their friendship. "You're afraid of letting people in, aren't you?"

"What do you mean?"

"You know what I mean. I may not be a Transcendent, but I know people. I know people pretty well, and I can smell it."

Ollie shook his head, but hesitated before he spoke. "I don't know, I just, I dunno. Letting people in close isn't always easy for me."

"I mean, you're open with me, and you were with Nina. And you don't seem…shy, but, did something happen?"

"No," Ollie said quickly.

"I smelled that," Avery said with a smile.

Ollie took a sip from his cocktail and prepped himself with a deep breath. "If you must know, it's not a pretty story. Years ago, I went to pick my brother up from college. It was winter break. His dorm room door was partially open, and some Nirvana song was playing." He paused, lost in a memory, and his eyes fell to the bar. "I always knew he was sad—I mean, I knew something was wrong. I just didn't know what. I didn't know how bad it was, whatever it was. He was like that for so long that eventually I just stopped asking. Thought, *Maybe that's just…how he is.*

"It's funny, the things you remember and the things you forget. I remember the song playing over and over that day, but I don't know how long I was there once I found him. He'd hanged himself with some kind of rope. I remember it was brand new, like he'd just bought it. That's how I found him.

"Maybe he wasn't even sad, maybe he just had no hope. People always say that it's selfish, that suicide is selfish, like it's something done to the people who are still alive. People don't get that it has nothing to do with them, and maybe that's why sometimes they don't see it coming. They just don't understand it. They don't see the pain. They don't *understand* the pain. If they did, they wouldn't say something callous like, 'Killing yourself is selfish.' Suicide isn't selfish...it's lonely. Hopeless. He just wanted relief. I didn't know what to do, so I tried to cut him down with a knife from the dorm kitchen, but it didn't work. So I just sat there. I sat there until the paramedics came. Whenever that was."

Avery didn't need any further details and didn't push for more. Her hand went to Ollie's knee and caressed it. "I'm sorry," she said softly. "I didn't even know you had a brother."

"Well, no, I never talk about him." It was the one thing that Ollie hadn't healed from, the thing that prevented him from not only reaching his full potential, but also connecting with others.

They talked for another fifteen minutes before the conversation was abandoned per Ollie's request. They almost lost count of how many drinks they'd had, but they knew it had been enough to log in to the internet jukebox and fill it with all their favorites.

"I want everyone in here to hate us for putting in twenty dollars' worth of music," Avery said cheekily.

"I didn't know you were such a control freak," Ollie said with a smile.

"I'm not, I—"

Avery was interrupted by a screeching, obnoxious laugh that flew out of the mouth of a woman sitting next to her, a woman who somehow found everything unreasonably humorous. Avery began again. "I'm not a control freak, I just have better taste in music than everyone else here." She was kidding, but not really.

Somewhere between "Bam Bam" by Sister Nancy and Mark Farina's "Dream Machine," Avery decided it was time they had a little fun—not that they weren't having fun already, but some *tricksy* fun of the magical variety.

They each took a shot of tequila and turned around on their barstools to face the rest of the patrons.

"Okay! Illuminate me! Tell me something about…" Avery scanned the bar looking for someone interesting—anyone, really…"that guy." She pointed to a twentysomething man in a fluorescent yellow hat and a goatee.

Ollie smirked and focused as best he could through his drunkenness. "His last name is Benedetti, and he let his sister's boyfriend pee on him once."

"Oh get outta here," Avery said with a half smile. "You're making that up!"

"I guarantee I am *not* making that up. I can see it," Ollie said as he tapped his temples.

Avery lifted her hands in the air and shrugged. "Hey, I'm not gonna shame him. Benedetti!" she shouted. The head in the yellow hat turned to look. "You do you, boo boo!"

The man walked over, his eyes all a-puzzle. "Do I know you?"

"No, I'm sorry. I thought you were someone else," said Avery. The man scowled at her in confusion before he returned to his friends in the corner of the room.

"Okay, my turn!" Avery said excitedly.

"All right, all right. Umm…" Ollie's eyes scanned the bar and found a woman with long, straight hair and a massive cock-tail. "See that woman over there?"

"Which one? The one by the bathroom?"

"No, the one sitting at the table, with the black scarf."

"Yes!" Avery said.

"She's on a first date and she's really nervous. Lighten the mood a bit."

"I got you!" Avery said saucily as she readjusted herself in her seat. She watched in anticipation for the perfect moment. When the woman grabbed hold of her glass and lifted it to her lips, Avery blew gently. The woman's hair covered her mouth, and she took a sip through her hair before spitting it out in surprise. She giggled nervously and tried to take another sip. Avery blew again. The woman's hair blocked her cocktail again. She pulled impatiently at her hair, but Avery kept blowing it with the force of a mild storm.

The obnoxious laugh returned, and Avery turned around in her seat to shoot the woman next to her a nasty stare, which went unnoticed. As the woman lifted her drink in the middle of a laughing fit, Avery flicked her finger and the woman got a face full of cold negroni.

"Avery!" Ollie said.

"What?" Avery said innocently as she pointed to her drink. "I'm just having a drink!" A smile crept across her face. "Your turn, by the way."

"This entire bar needs a mood lift," Ollie observed. He influenced a few people to get up and dance, even though they hadn't a dancing bone in their body. The jukebox began to play "Pump Up the Jam." Before the end of the song, Ollie influenced three more people to dance—badly—and then swayed two other people to stand in the middle of the bar and shout out what they loved the most.

Me!

Dick!

Pancakes!

"Are we sure we are bringing things into balance? It doesn't sound like it from what they're saying!" Avery said. Right then, she noticed someone taking a big drag from their vape. It brought back all the times she would hear Leo sucking on it at all times of the day and night, and how much she hated the damn whooshing noise. The young man was reminiscent of Leo, but older, fatter and with a severely crooked nose with a gargoyle-like tip. The man took another drag of his vape and her patience shattered. As the coils inside his vape activated with his inhale, she amplified the combustion and made it explode in his hand. Ollie, on the other hand, had become distracted by a man near the front of the bar who was deaf. After he made sure no one was paying attention, not even Avery, he homed in on the man's body, feeling through his senses.

Ollie did something he never imagined he would be able to do. The man lifted his head, locked eyes with Ollie, and could suddenly feel the music. Ollie's intention filled the man's silence, and created the joyous emotions associated with hearing music through the combination of Ollie's compassion and the man's imagination—for the briefest of moments. Through the dancing bar patrons, Ollie glimpsed a look of shock and amazement on the man's face. And then it was over.

Avery turned to Ollie and grabbed hold of his arm; her ears perked up like a deer in the meadow on high alert. "Do you smell that?"

Ollie shook his head as he inhaled. "No, but I *feel* that," he said as he locked eyes with her.

Beyonce's "Partition" spilled out of the jukebox as Avery and Ollie turned toward the entrance to see Bisa rounding the corner. Avery choked a little on her tongue as Ollie's mouth fell open nearly halfway to the middle of his neck. Bisa smiled in a way that made them both immediately think of Nina. She walked like a stronger, more empowered version of her former self. Her eyes with a sheen of clout, her aura burning brighter than all of the lights in the bar combined. Bisa continued through the bar, patrons spilling out of her way as if brushed aside gently with a broom, her eyes fixed on Ollie and Avery, bringing their frivolous drinking games to a halt. As she drew closer, she almost looked younger, but her energy felt much older.

Avery tried to summon every word she could think of in the English language but was speechless.

Bisa leaned against the bar and watched their faces. When she tried to speak, a giggle came out first.

"It worked," Ollie said softly. "I can't believe it actually worked. How are you so clean?"

"I showered," Bisa said with a smile. She remembered everything, and memories came back at an alarming rate, like an electric shock. "I guess we have a lot to talk about. So let's get you two up to speed." She pulled up a barstool. "Bartender!"

CHAPTER 13

Ollie's revitalizing post-drink elixir allowed them to wake up without even the slightest hangover. The only person with a hangover was Leo. Ollie's narcoleptic spell came with a splitting headache. Leo walked into the kitchen clutching three ibuprofen in his palm. He downed them like candy and drank half a glass of water before the throbbing in his head stopped him. He looked over to Ollie and Avery at the kitchen table. Seeing Leo after hearing everything Bisa had to say made him look like a different person. It also made Ollie's stomach turn. He didn't know what to make of him anymore, and he certainly didn't feel safe with him around.

Leo cracked open his eyes and looked over at Avery. "What the fuck was that?"

"What was what?" Avery asked calmly.

"You know what," Leo snapped from underneath his magical hangover. "Last night. Knocking me out like that with some bitch-ass sleep spell."

"I did that," Ollie muttered faintly but firmly.

"What the hell, I thought we were cool," Leo said as he rubbed his forehead and sat on the counter. Leo knew that nothing he said would make any difference, not anymore. Something was different, many things were, and the one thing that remained the same was himself.

"It was necessary," Avery said. "And we can't trust you; you were about to get violent."

"But I didn't, did I?" Leo clapped back. "So you're allowed to just say whatever the hell you want?"

His question went unanswered as Avery stared him down, never intending to give him an answer, because he already knew it. Leo tried to magically alter the effects of his hangover with little success. It ended up giving him a slight nosebleed, which he doctored with a paper towel.

"Why'd you come back, Leo?" Ollie asked.

He wiped his nose clean and tilted his head back until the blood stopped running. "Well, you're right, I shouldn't have just dipped on y'all."

"So, what do you want?" Avery asked.

"I want back in. I want to be a part of the coven again," Leo said. He took a deep breath and chanced tilting his head back down. The blood had stopped. "It's what Nina would have wanted, right? That's why we were all here in the first place, right?"

Except Nina was gone. Mitch had left. Bisa was dead, and she was dead because of him, and they all knew it. But the thing that Leo wasn't sure of and hoped against was whether they knew it.

"Why?" Ollie asked.

"Why what?" Leo inquired, honestly confused.

"Why do you want back in the coven?" Ollie clarified. "It can't just be about Nina. That doesn't sound like you."

"Well, honestly, dude, I'm worried about Merlot," Leo said freely, feeling a little relief for the first time in a while. It didn't feel great to tell the truth, but it didn't exactly feel bad either.

He had lied enough for seventeen lifetimes, and told lies of every size and style: large, small, white, frequent, compulsive, exaggerated. But his specialty, the most common, was the bald-faced lie. Right there in that second as he told the truth, even he wondered if he was beyond saving. *Maybe coming here was the wrong decision,* he thought, although he didn't dare say it out loud.

Ollie heard it, though.

"So, that's where you went?" Avery said. "You went to Merlot? For what?" Her voice rose to a shout. "You do know she tried to kill us! You *saw* her kill Nina *and* Rosemary!"

Leo shook his head. There was so much conflict, and his headache blurred his thoughts so much that even thinking about thinking hurt. He cracked open his eyes and looked at them, only then fully realizing that Mitch was absent. "Where's Mitch? Is he here?"

Avery looked over at Ollie before she spoke. "Mitch left."

"Where?" Leo asked, clutching responsibility in secret.

"Back home, I think," Ollie answered.

Leo let out a sigh and found himself accepting all the blame for Mitch taking off. Maybe he would've stuck around if Leo hadn't been so self-centered—at least that was what Leo wanted to think. He liked Mitch, although sometimes he wondered if it was just in theory. But even he couldn't really explain why he cared about him. "If he's gone, and on his own, that means he's not safe. I mean like, for real for real not safe."

Ollie asked why as he leaned forward in his chair, sifting through Leo's muddled thoughts as best he could. Avery had her nose at the ready for the first lie she could smell. Leo had to concentrate hard to remember everything in detail. The throbbing aftereffects wouldn't wear off for some time. He told them all about Merlot, and what they were working on together, and finally about the spirit that he'd released, which would surely find Mitch and devour him and his powers whole.

Avery let out a sigh, leaned back in her chair and covered her eyes.

"I didn't mean to do it. I thought I could handle it," Leo said in the same way someone would say, *I thought the light was green, officer.*

"Well, we have to find him somehow," Avery said. "We need to get him back here. It's not safe."

"I can try to—" Leo started, but he stopped when he saw a figure enter the kitchen out of the corner of his eye.

A titter. "*You*...have done enough," Bisa said as she sashayed into the kitchen. The scent of assertion filled the air as she shot Leo a steely look that said *I'm serious.*

Leo's eyes widened. He couldn't tell if his heart was going to sink into his stomach or begin to sing. "You're alive. How are you alive?" he asked, dumbfounded. "Didn't you die?"

"Oh yes, I died," Bisa said as she narrowed her eyes ever so slightly. "But of course, you knew that. I died, and somehow I'm back." There was a tense silence before Bisa continued. "Resurrection is something that no witch has ever been able to do, and the truth is I don't really know how or why it worked. But it did."

The doorbell rang and interrupted their conversation. It was Ruby, and her face was filled with dread. Ollie welcomed her in, and when she saw Bisa, her face lost all color, like she was seeing a ghost. "Bisa?" she asked in disbelief.

Bisa nodded and gave her a smile. "Hi, Ruby."

"Is this real? How is this possible? Who did this?" Ruby asked suspiciously, although she was entirely grateful that someone had.

"That's a long story," Bisa said politely. "Apparently there are some exceptions to magical rules, but honestly, I couldn't articulate what they are or how I'm actually here. I left a spell, Avery and Ollie found it, carried it out and...here I am."

Ruby grabbed Bisa's arms and smiled. "I can't believe it."

Bisa nodded. "What's going on? Why are you here?"

The coven moved near the fireplace, and Ollie gave Ruby a cup of tea.

Ruby took a deep breath and, on her exhale, began giving the coven a recap of everything she had discovered about Merlot and the truth behind her Bacchanalia parties. "I only know all of this because an old friend who lives in Paris called me up out of the blue to invite me to a party. I hadn't heard about any kind of Bacchanalia party in ages, so it struck me as odd. She went on to tell me there had been several of them, all hosted by someone named Merlot. But I wasn't about to fly all the way to Paris for a party." Ruby found the rim of her mug and sipped nervously from it. The tea burned the back of her throat, causing her to jump and spill some onto her shoe.

"What do you think she's doing?" Ollie asked.

"I don't think—I know; I know what she's doing," Ruby said. "I called my friend back the next day to ask about the party, because it just didn't feel right. FaceTimed, actually. She was in the middle of lighting some candles, but she couldn't. Which is strange. She had always been a powerful Primordial witch. So, then her son tried, and he's always been just as good as her if not better. But he couldn't do it either."

"Did he go to the party too?" Ollie asked.

Ruby shook her head. "No."

A world of thoughts raced through Bisa's head until she arrived at the answer. "Contagious magic."

Ruby nodded. "I called and checked with other witches from all sorts of places, and everyone had been having reports of the same thing. They checked with others, and those witches checked, and so on, and everyone said the same thing: no one had powers. And it was getting worse too. Some witches caught on and tried to reverse it, but they couldn't. A couple people even died trying to reverse it, the spell had gotten so strong. It just kept getting stronger the more it spread. It was like it was mutating and spreading faster and faster. No one could predict it, or stop it, and it was just becoming more and more contagious."

"Why would she do something like that?" Ollie asked.

"She's preparing," Bisa said. "She's setting herself up for success by eliminating any threat."

"Success in what?" Avery asked.

"Considering how many parties she's hosted, I would assume she wants to host the largest party of all," Bisa said. "I would think she wants to control everyone and everything. She wants what all other powerful people want: more power. All of it. Over everyone and everything."

"But that's crazy," Avery said.

The conversation ended just as it had begun, with another surprise—Nina. Ollie, Bisa and Ruby turned their heads to see Nina standing opposite the fireplace, the amber light flickering off of her like a sheen of gold.

"You're right about Merlot," Nina said plainly. "She *is* going to try to dominate this entire planet, but that's not the only threat."

"Nina!" Ruby said.

Leo let out a breath and looked around, but saw nothing.

"What?" Avery asked of the group.

"A spirit is coming for you, for all of you," Nina said sternly.

"We know—Leo told us," Bisa said. "We can figure out how to protect ourselves in the meantime."

Nina's eyes turned to Leo and her gaze tightened. "You don't have a meantime. It's going to find you. All of you. It's attracted to the strongest magic—that's Leo and Merlot now. While he's around, you're all in danger."

"But if he's that strong, couldn't we use his power to help get rid of it? Or stop it?" Ollie asked.

"What about the rafkolite?" Bisa asked. "Maybe that could work?"

Then Nina was gone, just as quickly as she had arrived.

"What happened?" Avery asked.

"Nina," Bisa said. "The spirit is coming for us. For Leo and Merlot because they are the strongest. Everyone around or connected to them is at risk," she explained.

"What about the Union of Divine Dualities ritual?" Leo asked. "If we did that and found the rafkolite, maybe that could get rid of the spirit?"

"Oh, so now you want to try and fix this?" Bisa asked. "All of this is happening because of you. The only reason this spirit has its eye fixed on us is you. Merlot dissolving the world of witches and having power even greater than yours—is because of you. Even when you try to fix something, it ends up being more broken than it was before."

"I wanna do it," Leo said. His heart raced at the thought. "I wanna be the one to do the ritual."

Avery scoffed so hard that her whole body convulsed. "The fuck did you just say?"

"Think about it," Leo said as he tapped his forehead. "I'm the strongest one here. It makes the most sense."

"No way," Avery said. "You need to figure out what to do about this spirit you've released, and fast!"

"That's how I can stop it!" Leo shouted. "I have to do the ritual!"

Avery was on the verge of laughing with frustration. "Are you really that stupid? Or are you just a brain-dead warm body from all the fucking drugs? You *can't* be the one to do it!"

"Why not?"

"The person has to be incredibly close to Spirit. The circle that's cast for the ritual prevents *anyone* who isn't pure of heart from entering. I don't know if any one of us would be able to enter, except maybe Ollie or Bisa. You're a shitty person! You're a disease that no one wants and no one can get rid of! I couldn't tell you how much I can't stand you if I had three years to do it."

"You are preaching to the motherfucking choir, bitch!" Leo groaned. "Get in line behind me. Guess the fuck what, I can't stand me either, and I guaran-fuckin-tee you that you don't hate me as much as I hate myself!"

Avery and the rest of the coven were beginning to understand why Leo was the way he was. It should've been obvious, and it was clearly a discussion for another time. There was a heavy moment of silence.

"If you do it, and you fail, you won't have any power left at all," Bisa said.

"That true? Or are you just saying that?" Leo questioned.

"It's true," Ruby replied.

"I don't remember ever hearing that," Leo said as he shook his head in disbelief.

"Of course you don't, you don't care about anything if it doesn't serve you or thrill you," said Avery. "Maybe we should have a vote first? Then you'll really see how many people think this is a stupid idea that's going to get us all killed."

"You can't do it, Leo," Bisa said softly. "We may need your power. We have no idea what we are going to deal with between Merlot and the spirit."

Avery made good on the promised vote. Just as quickly as Leo fought to be the one to conduct the ritual, the entire coven voted against him.

Leo snorted. "Fine. Fine. I'll do it by myself. I have everything I need. I don't need any of you or any of your help."

"You'll fail," Bisa reminded him. "It has nothing to do with your power or your skill, which is extraordinary. It has to do with your character. You don't have the heart. Your spirit is dark, and it won't be allowed to enter the circle."

Leo stared at Bisa, torn in his feelings for her, but he remained unyielding in his position. "I'm doing this," he reiterated.

Bisa raised her voice in the calmest and most rational way possible. "No, you're *not!*"

Leo scoffed and knew that not even Bisa was going to stop him. For a brief moment, he wished he could get out of his own way, but he couldn't. The coven just couldn't compete with his phenomenally deep level of self-interest. "Yes, I am," he said as he turned around to leave.

"If you do this," Bisa said, "I'll crack your closet of skeletons wide open and make sure they haunt you."

"What does that even mean?" Leo asked, bristling. "You think I'm scared about some secrets? What is this, the fifth fuckin' grade?" His voice rose. "What are you gonna do, hack my iCloud and post my dick pics on the internet?"

"You know *exactly* what I mean," Bisa said as she bobbed her head.

"I don't care!" Leo shouted, shaking his raging hands so much that the air grew a little hot. "We don't even know what this ritual is actually going to do. Maybe I can enter the circle. No one has ever done it before. I'm the strongest one out of all of us, so *I'm doing it.*"

Leo turned around to leave but Avery jumped into his path. "You're *not* doing this!" she said, smoke brimming from her fingertips.

Leo looked down at Avery's smoking fingers and up into her eyes. "You're not gonna do shit and you're not gonna stop me. Move." His lips quivered.

"Oh, fuck off," Avery said as she whipped her hand back and filled it with smoke. Like an arrow snapping loose from a bow, her hand shot forward, and a bomb of smoke exploded against Leo's chest, knocking him back a few feet and filling his lungs with smoke.

When Leo finally stopped coughing and the smoke cleared, he couldn't see past his own ambitions. He had tunnel vision, and the only thing blocking his way was Avery. Leo needed only to look at Avery, and faster than any gun, he sent her flying through the air like a cat, but one that wouldn't land on all fours. She rolled and tumbled until she fell against the wall, ripping a painting straight off its hook on her way to the floor. When she was finally able to realize what had happened, the coven was rushing to her side—and Leo was gone.

CHAPTER 14

J ust before sunrise, when everyone else was asleep, Avery prepped for a spell. The ground was mostly covered in late winter frost, and what snow was left, Avery cleared away with her hands. The air was still, from the black house that was showcased by the abundance of white to the pines that surrounded Lake Peridot. *He's got another think coming,* Avery reflected in the blueness of the pre-dawn. *He's going to get us all killed; he's not the only one who can do something on their own.*

She took a sip from her thermos and set it down in a boulder of snow. Avery turned around and checked the house to make sure no one was watching. This was a secret, and certainly the coven wouldn't approve. They might even compare her to Leo and think she was just as careless and reckless. But this had to be done, she just felt it in her heart. Avery reached into her coat pocket, retrieved a piece of paper and read the title of the spell, *To Destroy and Dismantle a Powerful Enemy.* She had written the spell right before bed and planned to execute it as the sun rose into the sky. It was a *freezing* spell, one that would stop an enemy on their dangerous path. From her tote bag, she pulled out all the provisions she'd packed up in secret: dead wasps, wasps' nests, a wax figure she'd made of Leo from a candle in her bedroom, a mortar and pestle, a photo of Leo she'd found in her phone and printed out, Spanish moss, sulfur, black mustard seeds, black pepper, cayenne, Black Arts Oil, rum, vinegar and stormwater from Louisiana.

He'll never stop unless someone forces him to. Avery thought back to when she'd first met him and how repulsed she had been by him even then. Never did she think she'd get to the point of casting a spell like this, one with which she had very little experience and whose delicate nature she didn't truly understand. If Nina had been around, maybe Leo could've finally transformed into the better person he thought he wanted to be. A groomed and polite man, one with manners and a respect for others. With someone like that under Nina's guidance, the coven might have actually done far greater things than Volustina ever predicted. However, there was no use living in the past. They were where they were now, and there was no changing it. And however powerful Leo actually was, his power would never be able to equal Avery's cunning.

The early morning indigo was slowly becoming brighter, and so she began. Avery doused the Spanish moss with stormwater and vinegar. She placed the photo of Leo on a patch of frosty grass, dumped the rum on top and set it ablaze with a blow of her breath. When nothing was left but ashes, she gathered them and stuffed them into a hollow she'd carved out of the wax figure. Avery made a powder with the remaining ingredients and set it aside. She uncorked the Black Arts Oil and drizzled it over the doll as though dressing a salad, careful not to get any of it on her skin so she wouldn't accidentally absorb some of its dark energy.

Avery scooped the powder out of the mortar with her fingers and blew it onto the wax figure. Ashy wisps filled the space around her and were dispersed into the cold morning air. The wind began to pick up, and it whispered through the pines. Avery's nose had gone pink, and her fingers were blackened with ash and soot. She kneeled down beside the doll and glowered at it. This was it, there was no going back, everything would be different from this point on, and Leo, hot mess that he

was, would (she hoped) be done fucking up their lives and everyone else's too. The last bit of pure-heartedness drained out of
Avery as she tossed the dead wasps and wasps' nests onto the
doll. The wind blew across her lips, almost opening them for
her. She began to mutter the incantation.

*Find my enemy, seek him out, remove and block his escape
routes.*

*Destroy his power—sting, sting, sting, make him weak, dis-
mantle his wings.*

*May the guilty be tortured by the voices of the wronged,
bring justice and peace for which we have longed.*

*Remove his power, let it seek a new host, let it go where it is
needed most.*

*He is a dangerous, selfish, filthy liar, let him feel the sting
of my hellfire.*

Avery hesitated a moment and enjoyed the silence before
the war of the flames. As the sun brightened the sky, she waved
her hand over the doll and set fire to it. She stood there and
watched it burn to ash. The fire had burned hot, bright and fast,
and it smelled of success. There was almost a smile on her face
as she scooped up the mess from the ground and dumped it into
a small bowl. She climbed up the nearby boulders until she
reached the highest peak she could. She looked down the hill
toward the lake, the bowl full of ashes in her hand. The lake
had already begun to thaw under the suggestion of the approaching spring. When the wind picked up, she turned the
bowl over and cast the contents into the whipping breeze. The
ashes thinned out in the heavy Colorado wind, and she looked
toward the dawn. Sunrise was always her favorite time of day;
she had almost forgotten. She rubbed her hands together and

warmed them with her hot breath, the twinkle of triumph glistening in her eyes as she stared into the brilliant sun.

After a few minutes relishing the daybreak, she crawled down the rocks and cleaned up her mess. Once she was back inside, she washed her hands, drank a cup of peppermint tea and took a hot shower with witch hazel and rosewater.

When Avery dressed, she took a moment to face herself in the mirror. Sometimes she didn't recognize herself, so many things were different. A small voice in the back of her mind, one that kept her grounded, usually kept her in check, but right then, it had been asleep. Avery rummaged through her drawers of random objects and pulled out a few things to fashion a talisman out of. If by chance it came down to it, she wanted to be considered for the chance to conduct the ritual as well. The talisman, now around her neck, would protect her. Her confidence was growing wider, deeper, and darker.

CHAPTER 15

One major difference between Leo now and Leo then was that Leo now had a lot more money. One day, he'd really enjoy it, he thought. Right now, though, he had other pressing matters on his mind. The morning sun had dipped behind a few clouds, and the wind had stopped blowing. Fifteen miles away in the mountains, under a frost-tipped forest of pines, a determined Leo rented a small cabin through Airbnb. It was quiet, desolate, and bare bones—a cramped, two-room hut with a wood-burning stove, three windows and a bathroom that allowed one to use the toilet and the shower and nothing more.

It was so rustic that it almost seemed criminal to charge three hundred a night. Gone were the days when something like that would've pissed him off, when he would've had to budget to buy a bag of Voodoo Chips. Now it was almost kind of nice, knowing that he could spend so much on a drafty, wooden hut and not have to think twice about it. He almost wanted to do it, just because now—he could. It was nice being able to be so free because of money, and he imagined how free he would feel once he finally had the rafkolite. A shiver ran down his spine at the mere thought of something so exhilarating.

He didn't waste any time once he was inside the cabin; he got right to work. He studied his notes on the Union of the Divine Dualities and pulled from his pockets the provisions he had stolen earlier. He fashioned a talisman out of string, a single garnet and a feather he had found just outside the front door. He held it to his third eye, charged it with his intentions and draped it around his neck. Leo wasn't bothered by how cold the cabin was, not even when his fingers went stiff and his breath went opaque in the air.

The next few steps of the ritual went by quickly, in a bit of a blur. He mixed the stormwater with the fairy water and briefly challenged his actions. *Leo, what are you doing?* But the fleeting thought lasted no longer than it took to think it. He held his breath as he removed the powdered oak from one of his larger cargo pants pockets and dumped it into the water, praying for the first time in his life, to a God he didn't believe in, that it would combine. *Please, God, please work. Mix!* Leo dipped his finger into the mixture and swirled it around, encouraging it toward being a homogenous concoction. *I'm wearing the talisman, so it should mix*, he thought as he anxiously watched the contents swirl around. For a moment he considered that perhaps he wasn't the hot shit he thought he was, that maybe everyone was right. In fact, when he truly thought about it, he had to admit that the last time he had tried something major, Bisa had ended up dead. *But she's not dead now, so...whatever.*

Outside, the wind began to howl, and a stick snapped against the dirty window. An army of frost blew under the door and rushed along the floor. Leo never turned away from the task. His eyes were fixed on the mixture, and just like that, it blended together with a sharp crystalline sound like icicles breaking under the threat of warmer weather. The wind stopped, and the cabin was filled with a smell like baking bread. Leo smiled and chuckled as he relished his success. He grabbed hold of the bowl and poured the contents into a small measuring cup from the tiny collection of kitchen supplies next to the wood-burning stove. The mixture was pearlescent and ready to be used. Leo picked up his belongings on the floor and poured the liquid into an imperfect circle on the worn linoleum.

A realization of the most disappointing kind hit him so hard, he gasped: he'd forgotten the astral invisibility fluid that Bisa had taken from the magical drug dealer Evan's collection of rare potions so many months ago. He looked down at the circle of liquid, slowly spreading across the floor in tiny rivers. *Fuck it*, he thought. He had heard it so many times from so many people, witches, witches who knew a great deal more than him—he was a Corporeal, he was powerful. Corporeals were supposed to be able to do all sorts of things, like manipulate energy and matter. Leo was proud of the fact that after all the hard drugs, he had enough brainpower to consider that he could manipulate his aura too.

He didn't know how he could do it, but he just knew he could make himself invisible if he wanted to badly enough. He'd been able to do so many inconceivable things—why not that? Leo closed his eyes and thought back to when Nina was quizzing them on the ritual.

After he rehashed the fuzzy details to make sure he was ready to go, he took a deep breath and stepped a foot over the circle's edge and placed it flat on the floor. *All good so far.* Leo leaned forward and stepped inside to the middle of the circle. He looked around and saw that nothing had changed.

"Okay...invisible. Make myself invisible. Right," Leo said, trying to psyche himself up for something he had no idea how to do. He wiped his brow and stood up straight, something that actually felt uncomfortable after years of slouching. He took a few quick breaths, like a boxer getting ready to enter the ring. Then, he closed his eyes and began to turn inward. Leo slowed his breathing, controlling it, lowering his heart rate. A few meticulous breaths later, he felt a tingling all over his body and resisted the urge to open his eyes to look. He envisioned what it would look like to be standing there, totally invisible. Leo chuckled as he imagined himself completely transparent but still wearing clothes.

All of a sudden, the tingling sensation stopped. It didn't make any sense. *What happened?* He listened to his intuition and took off all his clothes until he was naked apart from the talisman around his neck. Leo removed all seven metals from his cargo pants, along with the written words he would never remember without a reference sheet. He tossed his clothes outside the circle and shivered as the cold assaulted his bare skin. He rubbed his arms to warm them, his toes curling away from the freezing floor. The hair on the back of his neck stood up as he tried to control his breathing again. His body trembling in the cold winter air.

After what felt like hours, his breathing was under control and the buzzing all over his body returned, but stronger this time, warmer, like he had been dipped into a hot spring. Leo continued breathing and removed every thought from his mind until nothing was left but the task at hand. He opened his eyes and looked down at his body, but couldn't see it. He lifted his arms, but he couldn't see anything. It felt like a ghost appendage. After a moment of panic, he reached down and grabbed his balls to make sure they were still there.

It worked. He was invisible; however, he hadn't anticipated not being able to see his own body. But at least he knew he was making progress, and no matter how many times he felt he should stop, he couldn't find a reason good enough to justify it, not when he had already accomplished what everyone thought was impossible.

Even the thought of losing his powers didn't scare him off. He just *knew* he was going to succeed.

Next came the voices, whispers from spirits that had arrived to aid him in the ritual, strengthening his intention, protecting him from outside forces. The breathy voices, like air escaping from a vent, filled the room. The power of their soft, unintelligible words was as entrancing as a piece of beautiful music, and Leo found his head tipping back and forth like a slow metronome to their rhythm. Moments later, he realized he'd almost automatically extended his arms out before him. Next, he cast the spell to create the cyclone of light, and as expected, it arrived. A blinding vortex of energy, white-hot and resplendent like the crux of a diamond. It began to dull to an aurora-like opacity and whirled gently in front of him before it disappeared completely. The voices grew louder, as if encouraging him to continue.

With each successful step forward, his heart boomed faster inside his chest. He confused excitement with happiness for a moment as he tasted the terrific flavor of accomplishment. But now was the real test. He had to conjure the esoteric alchemy fire, something that had to be manifested by the witch's sheer will. Leo had no idea how to differentiate between magic and will, or even if there was a difference; he just did things. He'd been able to make his entire body invisible through sheer will, so he thought it would be a piece of cake. He tried and tried, but there was no fire. The air grew colder and the voices fainter as the ritual almost became a misadventure.

The coven clearly didn't approve of his trying the ritual on his own, and they had warned him that if he failed, he would probably lose all of his power. *Theory*, Leo thought. They were all knowledge and no technique; they didn't know how to wing it and make it work like he did. But all his confidence came crashing down with the heaviness of the crushing hopelessness that his heart was stubbornly disinclined to ever be free of. The cold wind returned as all magic evaporated from the room and from his body. His chest heaving.

Leo could see himself again, and he now felt horrifically ordinary in ways that he'd never imagined, even in his darkest moments—like someone with no hope, no skills, no purpose, passion or value. The only sounds were of his own labored breathing as he realized he'd failed. It had happened so quickly, like a bullet to the brain. The ruthless humiliation was immediate, the anguish—relentless. His eyes glittered with tears as he realized the weight of what he'd done. His power was gone. Avery was right, his spirit wasn't pure, and no amount of arrogance could change that. Leo's overconfident naivete had proved to be the most terrible influence of them all. He had never been a good person, but he had been a witch, and now he was neither.

As the morning faded into a cold and dark afternoon, Leo could do nothing but stare at the collection of metals on the floor. His hubris had prevented him from seeing just how ill-equipped he was for the task. His power was great, but that's all it was—just power. There was nothing to breathe life into it, there was no heart, warm with blood. He was just a toxic vessel that had finally hit rock bottom, and he'd thought he'd hit rock bottom years ago.

When the cold seeped too far into his bones, he started a fire in the wood-burning stove and watched the flames, thinking about death. Witchcraft had been like the magic bullet for all his problems; he couldn't believe it was gone. The reality of that was more numbing and more bitter than the winter's chill. Maybe he wanted to die, for real this time. What was left for him? *Who* was left for him? What did he have to live for? Even after all these years, he'd still ended up right back where he started. He thought about his daughter, Krystal. He somehow was able to remember what her coos sounded like. *At least she never grew old enough to find out what a failure I really am.*

.

CHAPTER 16

The coven, what was left of it, sat around the fire discussing plans and imagining outcomes, their unspoken thoughts beset with worry and uncertainty. Ollie turned Rosemary's ring around in his hand as he tried to calm his fevered mind. After a few uninspired ideas, he suggested that their first line of action had to be putting a stop to Merlot. He knew the power-eating spirit was hungry, it was always hungry, but that wasn't half as dangerous as a world under the reign of someone like Merlot. Finally, after everyone agreed, he and Bisa retreated to the sun-room for some focused meditation. They clasped hands and opened their inner eyes to the ether. Merlot's resistance was strong, and all they met were blocks and protective barriers, like the trance of a deep sleep without dreams. Ruby joined them for a Transcendent triple threat, but they still couldn't penetrate Merlot's magical shields.

"What if we ask Leo?" Ollie suggested.

Bisa scoffed. "Absolutely not," she said sternly.

"He could know something, though," Ruby said. "Maybe he knows where she is! He might even be able to connect to her and bypass all her enchantments."

Bisa shook her head. "If she's gone to all this trouble, she's not going to leave the back door open for someone like him. She's covered her bases from every angle. We need to find an-other way." *Then, I need to figure out what to do about Leo*, she told herself, even though she knew she'd already decided what to do. "If we can get to her next Bacchanalia party, we can stop her before she takes anyone else's powers. We just need to find out where it is. If we know where it is, we can crash her party with Rosemary's ring. The ring will sidestep most enchantments. Maybe we'll get lucky and find a key to the back door."

Ruby nodded. "How are we going to find out where her next party is?"

"It could be anywhere. Literally anywhere."

Avery entered the room with a large paper map of the world and a bowl of water. "Why don't we try a scrying spell?"

The coven tried method after method, hoping for a little luck. They lit candles, stared into flames and into bowls of water, swung crystal pendulums over the map, and read tea leaves and even a scattering of runes and bones, but nothing worked. Avery even tried a new kind of locating spell where she rubbed her fingers raw against a panel of wood and asked the wood spirits for answers. Nothing.

"I don't know what else to do," Avery said, completely frustrated.

Bisa glanced over at her by the window. She could hear the soft sound of Avery's running thoughts. "Would you be able to stop her?" Bisa asked gently.

Avery turned to Bisa. "What do you mean?"

"If it came down to you and her, to you having to end her life—would you be able to do it?"

The room fell silent and all eyes were on Avery. Her powers were the most active, powers that could actually do physical harm, but she hadn't realized that with Leo and Mitch out of the picture, she might have to do a lot of the dirty work. The question stung. She'd never fully considered the possibility that she might have to actually kill someone, not subdue or restrain, but kill. Avery had a fierce respect for life, even if that life scared her, like snakes or documentaries about serial killers. She immediately thought about the deer in her father's barn, and how their dead bodies had haunted her ever since. She hated that he hunted, but she was the one with the gun now, and Merlot was the deer. Only Merlot was no deer, she was dangerous, unpredictable and lethal. She might as well be a snake.

"I'll do what I have to do," Avery said sharply. She looked around the room and walked over to the chair to sit. "We just need to make sure it doesn't come to that. Stop her before anyone else dies. Including her."

Ollie was suddenly struck with an idea. "Ruby, what about asking your friend? The one in Paris who told you about the Bacchanalia party?"

Ruby furrowed her brow. "What about her?"

Bisa linked up with Ollie's thoughts and said, "She might know where the next party is!"

She wasn't wrong. Ruby called her friend and woke her up. After quickly apologizing, Ruby got right to the point and asked about other parties. A smile formed on her face, one filled with hope. There was a lengthy pause before she closed her eyes. Her eyelids fluttered, and when they snapped open again, she cleared her throat. "It's under the bowl near the front door. By your protection jar." Another few moments passed. Ruby looked at the coven, who were all staring back at her. "Yes! When is the next party and where is it?" She nodded. "Thank you! Okay, bye—"

She sighed and glanced back at the coven out of the corner of her eye. "Can we do this another time? It's not convenient right now." She laughed bashfully. An eye roll. A sigh. "You're going to hang up the phone and go back to sleep, and when you do, you're going to dream the best dream. You're going to be surrounded by croissants and sushi in a room with a ceiling as high as the sky, and servants will bring you golden forks and glasses of wine while you eat and watch the snow fall over the mountains below. And Guillaume Canet is there, and there are three hundred puppies all with sweet puppy breath, and you'll be—"

"What is this? What's going on?" Bisa said as she motioned for her to hang up the phone.

Ruby nodded. "Okay, thank you, good night!" She gathered the confused stares from everyone and smiled. "She likes me to influence her to sleep with all her favorites."

Bisa shook her head. "So you found out when the next party is?"

Ruby stood. "Yes! Three days from now. At seven."

"Where?" Avery asked.

Ruby opened her mouth to speak, but Bisa stole the words off her tongue. "Boulder," she said, shocked.

"What? Like Boulder, Colorado?" Ollie asked. Ruby and Bisa nodded in confirmation.

"She said it was the last date on the flyer. The last party," Ruby said.

"Then we have to stop her. This is the last chance we have," Avery said. "Where in Boulder?"

Ruby looked up to the ceiling as she tried to recall the details. "The Grand Oriana Hotel, on Pearl Street."

"Good," Bisa said. "Now that we know where and when, we can prepare. When the time comes, we use the ring, and stop Merlot."

Just as the group felt a wave of relief now that a plan was made, the front door opened. Avery could hear the shuffling of footsteps, and with them came the scent of something familiar. The coven exchanged glances as they listened to the door shut and the footsteps continue, drumming slowly across the floor. Bisa smiled, eyes full of pleasure, as if she were the only one in on a private joke. Avery dashed abruptly toward the stairs as soon as she identified the familiar scent.

"Mitch?" Avery shouted down the steps, but she knew it was him.

A few moments later, Mitch appeared at the bottom of the stairs, his bulging backpack slung over one shoulder. The expression he wore on his face was brand new, something Avery had never seen before, the look of someone who had finally found their power.

Mitch smiled a strong smile. "Hey!" he said with a gentle wave of his hand. He took off his hat, a crocheted identity piece that was truly the only thing that made Mitch look like Mitch, at least the one Avery remembered. It hadn't even been that long, but she was looking at someone very different from the person who had left.

Bisa took a few steps forward. She could sense him perfectly now. "Mitch?"

"Yeah," Mitch answered as he ascended the stairs. When he reached the top, the entire coven was staring at him like he was a stranger, but a familiar one, like someone you see on the train platform every morning on the way to work.

Avery reached out and tousled his hair. "You came back," she said happily.

Mitch nodded. It was no easy task, to return. No—the return was the easy part, the growth experienced before his return was the challenging bit.

Bisa walked up to him, her eyes absorbing his shining aura. "You're glowing," she said softly. Mitch smiled uncomfortably. Hearing compliments would still take a little getting used to.

Bisa wet her lips and shook her head, proud of what was now before her. "Mitch Wickleby, back with the coven, with a fire I've never seen." She could feel it all, everything that had shifted and changed for him. She saw it both in his eyes and in his aura. "We were just talking about some plans, so we'll need to get you up to speed. Have you eaten?" She sounded almost like Nina.

They caught him up over a plate of Ollie's vegan mac and cheese* and a side of Kale and Brussels Sprouts Salad with Green Goddess Dressing*.

Avery forked the last cavatappi noodle in her bowl and used it to wipe around the bowl to collect the cheesy cream. "I've already made the talisman for the Union of the Divine Dualities," she said, "but we haven't decided who is going to do it."

They debated over who should attempt it and why right up until Ollie brought out a plate of vegan brownies* that no one knew he had stashed away in the fridge. Ruby's phone rang. She licked her fudgy fingers and wiped them clean.

"Grace?" Ruby answered.

The mood changed as soon as Ruby hung up the phone a few minutes later. "Grace ran into a witch she knew from Phoenix while out shopping. They asked her if she was going to the Bacchanalia event later tonight."

"Tonight?" Avery asked.

"Maybe she just had the date wrong?" Ollie suggested as he dropped his brownie.

Ruby shook her head. "No, she specifically said tonight at seven. The woman showed Grace the flyer."

Ollie lost himself in thought for a moment. "Could she have read it wrong?"

"Well, someone read it wrong, but if there is one thing that Grace can do, it's pay attention to detail," Ruby said.

"We have to think of something—" Ollie said heatedly.

Bisa closed her eyes softly. "I know…"

"We don't have time to prepare. We have to do this tonight! Now!" Ollie said.

Bisa opened her eyes. "*I know*." She looked at the clock. "We have an hour."

The coven prepped as best they could. They grabbed amulets, talismans, potions and powders. They sped-read through all the books with defensive spells and incantations as Avery warmed up her lightning and fire magic like a runner stretching before a marathon. It was seven o'clock exactly when Bisa called everyone together. Ollie had cast a small protection spell for the coven moments before. There was hope in that, amidst a really uncertain and unnerving time. No one knew what was going to happen. After so much trauma, so many deaths, several crises, a power-killing spirit on the loose, and a dangerous megalomaniac with a global empire set to take over everything and everyone—there was only so much more they could take. Ollie felt they had tipped the scales of balance and that that would surely work in their favor, but no one knew how long it would take for results to show, or how great they would be when they did.

"All right, this is it," Bisa announced as she took a head count of the coven. "Everybody ready?"

A sea of nods.

"What do we do when we get there?" Mitch asked. "Do we just look for Merlot? What do we do if we find her?"

"I have a feeling she'll know we're there to stop her. Do what you can—don't hesitate. All that we've accomplished so far will be undone if she continues."

Avery pushed forward. "What about Leo? What about the spirit he unleashed?"

"We can deal with both of those later," Bisa said calmly.

"But what if it shows up?" Avery continued. "Isn't the spirit attracted to power? Doesn't it sense it? With all those witches under one roof, surely it'll be drawn there."

"It's possible," said Bisa. "If Merlot is as strong as Leo says she is, then the spirit is already seeking her out."

"Could that be a way to stop her?" Ollie suggested. "Just, let it take her power?"

Bisa sat with the idea for a moment. "We have to go," she said. She was in no mood for questions she didn't have the answers to, and there was no way to articulate the feeling she had in her gut—a feeling of a wrong being set right. "Ollie, take us there."

Ollie pulled out Rosemary's ring and opened a door to the Grand Oriana Hotel.

CHAPTER 17

Mitch walked toward the door like an introvert hesitantly approaching a party where they knew absolutely no one.

Ollie was waiting by the newly made door, ushering everyone through with whispery words of haste. Mitch stopped in his tracks, his index finger stroking the scar tissue on his thumb that was finally beginning to heal. He licked his lips as he thought about saying what was on his mind.

"I'm gonna start the Union of the Divine Dualities," Mitch said assertively.

The coven turned around to face him, and Mitch just stared right back with confidence.

"Mitch, no, come on," Avery said. "You're not going to try that on your own, not right now. We can talk about this later."

"You could lose *all* your power," Ollie reminded him.

Mitch nodded. "I know, I think—"

"No!" Avery interrupted. "You're not ready! We need to sit down together and figure out which one of us is the best candidate for it. Who is the most...*pure.*"

Bisa was standing on the other side of the door, now inside the Grand Oriana Hotel, when she felt a new presence, a new energy. It was such a strong presence that she instantly recognized it wasn't Merlot, even though she could feel her energy too. The energy was so intense that Bisa had trouble feeling much else for a moment. It was the spirit that Leo had foolishly manifested and unleashed. Bisa's eyes glazed over for a moment as she lost herself in the ether. Then she spoke. "The spirit is here."

Everyone turned to look at Bisa.

"It's here…looking for us. All of us," Bisa said. "It knows we're close. I don't know how close or where it is, but it's not far." She looked into Mitch's aura, and his energy was so bold that she felt with complete certainty that he *should* stay behind. Mitch had a part to play, and it was not with them at the hotel.

"And what happens if we all go, and we fail, and then there is no one left to perform the ritual at all?" Mitch said.

Avery waggled her head a little, knowing that Mitch had a point. She pulled a piece of hair back from her face and ran her eyes over him from head to foot. "You really want to do this?"

Mitch nodded and rubbed the rough skin of his thumb once more with his finger. "I can do it," he said reassuringly.

Bisa nodded. "Start the ritual. We'll be back when we're back."

"Good luck," Mitch said as he signaled to Ollie to let the door close.

If anyone needs luck, it's you. "You too," Avery said, a ring of uncertainty in her tone.

When the door finally closed, Bisa grabbed hold of Ollie's arm, her gaze locked into an unknown area of space.

"What is it?" Ollie asked.

"I can see it," Bisa said. "Not just feel it, but I can actually make it out, the spirit. I can see where it is."

Never before had Bisa had this kind of reaction with the spirit realm. Her skill and the sheer might of it took her by surprise. There was a special fascination with the level of power, and for a moment she thought about the idea that it had always been with her; she just hadn't tapped into it before. She rubbed her hands together, building up energy, and turned her palms outward—sensing where to go. Then she turned to Avery and Ruby. "You two, try to find Merlot. Ollie and I will take care of the spirit."

"On your own?" Avery asked.

"Yes. We have two threats, we should split up," Ruby said.

Avery didn't seem to fully support their plan of attack. "All right, let's do this, I guess."

Bisa and Ollie walked down the long hallway, with its cream-colored damask walls and dimly lit wrought-iron lanterns along the ceiling. A hallway that was both soothing and eerily haunting. Their footsteps muffled by the rich, deep burgundy carpet that chased into the cherry molding along the hall.

Avery turned to Ruby. "Where do we start? Do you feel anything?"

Ruby closed her eyes and focused on Merlot's energy. When she found it a moment later, she shrugged. "I can feel her." Ruby began walking before she opened her eyes, and she led them to a marble staircase with sturdy wooden banisters. "I can feel the energy of the Bacchanalia. I think it's all happening in the rooftop ballroom. Multiple ballrooms or event rooms, maybe." She peeked up and down the stairwell to the end of what she could see.

Beyond that, more hallways. Ruby rubbed her temples a little and dropped into her heart space, where she could often pick up on people's energy. Behind them, a hotel door opened and a woman exited the room. Ruby clenched her eyes tighter and tilted forward, like someone about to be sick. "I can feel it! I can hear her." She grabbed hold of the banister just as the stranger passed beside them to descend the stairs. Ruby, completely oblivious to the stranger near her side, straightened her back, tilted her head and said, "I can feel it, oh, I can feel it!"

Avery rubbed Ruby's back as she smiled innocently at the stranger, who looked at them as if they had four heads.

"She owns this place; this is her hotel!" Ruby exclaimed.

Avery ran her finger in a circle, urging Ruby to get on with it. "Where is she? We need to find out where she is."

"I'm trying! There are a *lot* of witches here. Just…give me a minute." Her eyes were still shut.

Avery looked around the hotel. She had never been in such a nice place before. She had always stayed in hostels, or cheap hotels, never somewhere like where she stood now. It looked expensive and historical, like the kind of luxury experience people eat up when something is old but has a ton of modern conveniences. The kind of place that defines its luxury by the bathroom alone, rooms with a slew of bespoke comforts and amenities, room service with moody and arcane dishes designed to inspire and amaze, and a cocktail lounge where all handcrafted drinks are called elixirs. Half the beauty was the exclusivity, a place and a concept that Avery never had much time for, not when all the world's wonders, beauties and idiosyncrasies were far more luxurious than any five-star hotel. The richness of an experience held more magic for her. However, now that she could smell the inside of a hotel she'd never have stepped foot in, she almost felt bewitched by the temptation of private extravagance. She looked around at the console table along the wall, with two antique brass lamps, a lit candle, and a nonfunctioning, enigmatic, black rotary-dial phone.

Just before Avery figured out the candle's scent, Ruby let out a tiny gasp. "This way," she said as she began to ascend the stairs. They took the stairwell up to the twentieth floor, where they could hear the party happening. When they arrived, they took a moment to catch their breath, wondering why they hadn't just taken the elevator. As they drew nearer to the ball-room, the liveliness became more apparent. Balloons, balloons and more balloons, like a thousand red grapes, decorated the hallway. A table of glittering candelabras rested right alongside the large double doors to the ballroom. Witches were spilling out into the hallway, blissfully unaware of all that was happening, downing drinks, dancing and just having fun.

Avery clung to the wall, careful not to get too close. "Remember, we can't risk catching whatever it is that Merlot cast on them. It'll leave us powerless, and then we'll have no way to stop her—or anything else, for that matter."

Avery spied a large four-tiered cake inside the ballroom, the kind of cake specifically for frosting lovers, where there was more frosting than actual cake. As they hovered at a safe distance from the entrance to the ballroom, they took a closer look inside. A live DJ was spinning from a glitzed-out booth in the far corner of the room, and beautiful floor-to-ceiling windows offered panoramic views of the city.

They scurried to the opposite wall, hid behind a large potted palm and peered into the other ballroom. It was darker, more mysterious, with large crystal chandeliers, moody red lighting, and a set of doors that opened out to a large terrace where witches spread out under the sky, warmed by torchlike heating lamps.

The magic in the air was thin, as Merlot's contagious magic spell was draining all the power there was to be drained. The witches didn't seem to notice. Normally a drunk witch who was surrounded only by witches would never turn down the chance to have a little fun with their powers. But not a single spell was being cast, not even a little innocent fire magic, which would be irresistible to someone like Avery after a few dark and stormies. One thing was positively certain, though: Merlot knew how to throw a party. It made the little solstice parties back at the house look like a toddler's birthday party in some obscure suburb in Wisconsin. Even with the pounding, deep, funky house music, the endless cocktails, the cake with all the frosting and an entire floor full of laughter and smiles, it was really a sad sight. *None of them even know what's happening. They're just normal people now*, Avery thought as she considered what that would feel like after having tasted the deliciousness of power.

"Come on," Ruby encouraged. "Merlot is this way." She pulled Avery down a hallway. Each floor of the hotel was nothing but a square-shaped hallway, which made for an easy search. Through the frivolous laughter and blaring music, Ruby heard delicate and rhythmic mutterings on the air, the kind of special speech that holds as much magnificence as crashing waves on the beach, the chants of a witch—Merlot. Ruby stopped in midstep and listened to the energy from beyond the door in front of her. "She's here," Ruby said as she fingered the door handle gently.

Avery nodded. She could feel Merlot but couldn't hear her. There was a loud pop of laughter coming from down the hall, followed by the crash of dozens of champagne glasses, then even louder laughter. "Ready?" Avery asked, cracking her knuckles.

Ruby nodded as her hand twisted the door handle ever so slowly. A sliver of light. She peered inside, her eye searching through a thin line for any sight of Merlot. There was no movement, but there was sound. Ruby listened harder and pushed the door open a little more. The candlelight of the room splashed onto her face. Then she saw her. Merlot was standing at the opposite end of the room, facing a large window. Ruby pushed the door open, and she and Avery slipped inside with the stealth of a cat hunting its prey.

Avery narrowed her eyes and rubbed her fingers together, warming them up. Merlot continued to chant, ever so faintly, like the memory of a dream upon waking.

Avery knew that this was it, this was their only chance to stop Merlot, and it might be the time for her to kill. She straightened her spine and held her breath as she felt the heat pool in her fingertips. The hair on the back of her neck began to stand up.

Merlot stopped chanting, and there was nothing but silence and the pounding heartbeat of anticipation.

"You're too late," Merlot said softly through a satisfied smirk, her back to the witches.

Avery's fingers twitched a little as she continued to call forth lightning in a way that she never had before. Her hands tingled, and the sensation quickly spread to the rest of her body. Her entire body felt electric, from her bones to the tips of her hair. A light warm breeze filled the room, ruffling the flames of the candles that lit the arched ceiling above them. Before them, Merlot stood very still for an uncomfortably long time. Avery didn't like that kind of stillness. It suggested future carnage, not peace. Merlot turned around to face them, her eyes all aglow with wild wickedness.

"This has to stop," Ruby said firmly. "You're not like any witch hunter in the history of witch hunters—you're worse."

"I'm just better at business. That's all this is. Cutthroat killer instinct. You don't get to the top without eliminating the competition."

"We're not competition," Ruby said.

"No, you're not!" Merlot said sharply. "Competition is for people on the same level. I'm smarter, more patient, and more powerful than all of your coven put together and multiplied by ten thousand."

Avery mumbled something vicious under her breath as her heart beat faster and faster. She whipped her hand forward and launched a ball of roaring fire at Merlot. It rumbled through the air, leaving bubbling droplets of magma on the ground. Merlot raised her hand, and the fireball dissolved into thin air, leaving a thin wisp of smoke behind. The two women stared at each other, like battling rams about to charge. Avery launched another ball of fire, and another, and another, all of which were dismissed with only a look from Merlot. Avery took a deep breath and then let out a scream that echoed throughout the smoky room. The lit candles in the room exploded all around Merlot, and when the boom subsided, a breathy laugh came sneaking out through the smoke, playful and amused.

Merlot was a few steps closer when the smoke cleared. She walked slowly toward Avery, like some kind of ridiculous, invincible villain that could never be killed. Avery continued to build up her lightning, pulling from her teachings with Volustina, hoping, knowing that she could call forth lightning in a way she had never done before.

Ruby muttered a small enchantment, asking the spirits to slow and bewitch Merlot, but Merlot kept walking, quickening her pace. For a moment, it looked like Merlot was going to lunge at them like some kind of roided-out quarterback, but Avery shook her arms out beside her, and a flash of forked lightning shot out from her fingertips and ran toward Merlot. Avery swung a balled fist, white with energy, into Merlot's stomach and discharged a cloud of lightning. A cloud of energy, blue with tiny veins of lightning, spilled out around them. Merlot stepped back, surprised by the power, but not harmed. Avery struck again with her other hand, and a violent thunderclap roared through the room. Merlot's eyes widened as her pupils shrank away from the bright display of lightning.

Avery summoned up a furious, almost godlike storm of buzzing cords of energy, opened her fists and shoved her fingers straight into Merlot's core. A flash of white sparks, plumes of hot volcanic ash, a blaze of bright orange fire gleamed like a hundred candles, and shards of ice ejected from her palms, along her fingers and discharging into Merlot. Sheets of white light pulsed from Avery as ribbons of curling fire spilled out into the room like party streamers. Orbs of light and thundersnow surrounded Merlot and popped like lightbulbs as she launched from the ground under Avery's fingers. The sulfuric smell of fireworks blasted across Ruby as she watched in awe, her hair blowing free in the stormy wind.

Avery released her hold on Merlot and recoiled back toward her chest. The aurora-like particles of energy around her froze in place. Avery released her arms, and a shockwave with a vein of lightning bolted from her hands. Merlot soared through the air as the lightning washed over her like a helpless victim caught in a river's current. She landed on her hands and knees like a cat, only she had more lives. Avery stood strong, her nose a little bloody, her cheeks flushed with red. Sweat covered the backs of her hands. She breathed heavily over a faint sizzling sound, like freshly cooked meat just removed from a fiery grill. She watched Merlot stand up, unscathed. Now there was a level of shock and disbelief, and the feelings rushed in and immediately replaced those of triumph and success. Avery held her breath as she watched Merlot stand on two feet and smile back at her.

"You can't stop me," Merlot said. "None of you can," she sniggered, and then with the flick of her wrist, she sent Avery and Ruby into a wall, where they fell to the floor.

The sound of footsteps. Under the door, shadows could be seen. The footsteps stopped just outside the door, and a hand poked through the open space between the door and the frame. *Who is this now?* Merlot wondered as she tried to detect what witch was coming for her by their smell. She had only a few enemies left, and they wouldn't be any harder to deal with than Avery on her best day. The smell of witch wafted into the room. *I know that smell, I think.* The door opened, and Bisa and Ollie entered the room.

A look of puzzlement covered Merlot's face as she watched Bisa enter, a new and mesmeric aura surrounding her, in metallic shades of purple, green and white. *This has to be some sort of trick,* thought Merlot. *No one can bring the dead back, not even me.*

The three of them stared at one another for a moment, having a conversation with only the expressions on their faces.

Merlot clicked her tongue and shook her head. "Bisa?"

Bisa raised her head proudly. "In the flesh."

A guffaw. *Impossible*, Merlot thought.

"Clearly, it *is* possible," Bisa answered telepathically.

Merlot grinned, her lips like the waxing moon. "I thought you were *dead* dead," she said, confused. "Leo said you were. I felt it."

"You couldn't feel half of what I do even if you were listening to Adele on 'shrooms," Bisa said sharply with a sense of humor that was so new, it almost made her question her own identity.

Merlot laughed and looked to the heavens, lost in the music playing in her head. "No one sells heartbreak like Adele," she said. "I do wonder if she really just wants to sing about happiness but her label keeps saying, 'No, no, no, you sell pain and suffering! Cry—but make it a song. Suffer—but make it marketable.'"

"This is over, Merlot," Bisa said gently as she narrowed her eyes and looked into Merlot's aura. There, in the delicate space between spirit and body, Bisa saw something she'd never seen before—on anyone. A curse. It was plain as day. Her powers had grown so much, she intuitively knew what it was. She could see it coursing around her, inside her, flowing through her veins, bright as dawn's first light, old like a family tree. A curse that was so old, it was part of her spiritual and physical makeup. Removing it would be like a sort of spiritual gene therapy. Bisa could read the energy in ways she'd never been able to before. She felt it, knew it, understood it—without even the temptation of trying to intellectualize it. She blended with the energy and was able to psychically interpret it.

The next thing she felt was sadness, a deep sadness that didn't belong to Merlot any more than the heart of the curse itself did. It was inherited, passed down from Merlot's ancestors, and now she had to bear its weight and suffer the consequences. Bisa felt the urge to cure her of it, or at least try. Maybe with a heavy wave of psychic energy, or dissolving it with some kind of incantation. There was no way to be sure if she could, no matter how much she wanted to try. The time for trying was over. She just had to stop Merlot, not fix her. Bisa found herself staring into Merlot's aura so deeply that she almost felt hypnotized.

"Is that it?" Merlot asked. "How exactly are you going to stop me? Look at those two over there. Poor thing, she really has that nature magic down." She closed her eyes, tilted her head back and inhaled the leftover smoky fumes through her nose. "Mmmmm, what a delicious smell. The only other scent that makes my heart melt is saffron, but it pales in comparison to good, old-fashioned Primordial magic. It's just so, visceral, so…well—primal. You should've seen it in here moments ago. I haven't seen a spectacle like that that *wasn't* CGI. Really, she's got a gift—well, had."

"Before I end this—" Bisa started.

"No," Merlot snapped. "It's already over. So, tell me, Bisa…do you want to die slowly, or do you want to watch me kill your coven in front of you? Or is that too nostalgic? Too close to home?"

"Before I end this, you should know the last thing I want to do is kill you, but I will if I have to," Bisa said.

"So, slowly, then?"

"The only slow death I'm going to suffer is the one standing here listening to delusional threats from a megalomaniac trying to *take over the world*. Did you get that idea from a Marvel movie?" Bisa lifted a single finger in the air. "However, I agree with you about Adele's label controlling what she sings about."

Merlot nodded and looked over at Ollie. "So, are you going to tell me? How did she come back?"

Bisa walked toward Merlot, her footsteps breaking through the smoke that lingered along the floor. Ollie's hand slipped into his pocket, and his fingers felt the tip of a tiny potion vial that he always kept on his person specifically for times like this.

A strong stunning potion that he had developed a while ago with angel's trumpet, belladonna and black henbane. Just toxic enough to disorient, nauseate and knock out, but not exactly kill. It was worth a shot if he could actually get some of it on Merlot's skin, but he had no idea if it would affect her if she was as strong as she seemed.

There was a tiny *pop* as Ollie uncorked the tiny vial in his pocket. All he had to do was get a little closer without seeming like a threat, and without being attacked. There was nothing he could do if she used any sort of magic on him. All the hoping, wishing and ancestral begging he could do in a day wouldn't protect him from whatever Merlot could unleash. But he had to try.

Merlot's eyes snapped down to Ollie's pocket. "I wouldn't do that if I were you. The last person who tried something is unconscious on the floor over there."

Ollie retracted his hand from his pocket. His palms were sweaty, and his heart was beginning to race.

Bisa continued farther, only a few paces away from Merlot.

Merlot unsheathed a beautiful knife from her side. "So, come on, tell me, how'd you do it? How'd you come back? Who did it?"

Bisa stopped a few feet from Merlot.

"Bisa..." Ollie said from behind her, worried.

Bisa took one final step closer and closed the gap between them. She could see the curse much more clearly now, with all its strange detail, like a blizzard of a hundred shades of red. The air was colder standing in front of Merlot. She may not have been able to detect that in the recent past, but Bisa's senses were wide open, her third eye full of sight, absorbing, feeling. She realized the strength of Merlot's power, but her power was drowned in arrogance. Bisa had seen this kind of thing before, felt it, been around it, even kissed it—someone so blind that all the eyes in the world wouldn't allow them to see.

Merlot shook her head and raised her eyebrow. "No?" she asked. "I suppose it doesn't matter if you tell me or not, you're still going to die."

(bitch, please)

Bisa heard the faint echo of Nina's voice from the ether. *Exactly that*, she thought as she stared deep into Merlot's blind eyes. "I've already died once, and I've seen Death itself," Bisa said. "Dying doesn't scare me. There are things worse than death." Bisa was never one to beat around the bush; she had always been very frank and truthful. But in that moment, what she said was half true. She wasn't afraid of death, but she was afraid of any pain that might precede it. However, the new Bisa was more accepting of it than she had been, if only because she knew what was inevitable for all of mankind, regardless of whether balance was restored. There was a sort of peace in that knowledge, peace with a devil-may-care attitude.

"Yes," Merlot said with a sinister nod. "There are things much, much, much worse than death." She lifted her fingers from the handle of the knife and curled them back around it tightly, ready to strike. She could think of a dozen things off the top of her head: being a Taurus or a Gemini, being weak or ordinary, or without power or ambition; living a life without power and rife with failure and regret would be the greatest tragedy of all.

Bisa began to chant an incantation in her mind as she watched Merlot's eyes twitch wildly like the flickering tongue of a cornered serpent about to strike. She opened her mouth ever so slightly as if to take a small breath, and energy flowed in from her crown and cocooned her body. She felt heavy, as if she were underwater in all her clothes.

Ollie didn't know what to do or how to intervene or if he should or even *could*. He called out to Bisa once more, but no one noticed. He knew the language of the Transcendents, their magic and their connection to Spirit, but he had never felt Bisa so distant before, so blended into the cosmos. He couldn't see her aura anymore, but she was standing there, without question, vulnerable and about to be killed. Right as he took a step forward to intercede—or mediate, he wasn't sure which—a soft, warm hand grabbed hold of his wrist. He turned his head to see Nina. She shook her head gently, urging him to do nothing. Ollie looked over at Avery and Ruby in a pile on the floor, just starting to rise, their faces a likeness of someone waking from a dream. They wiped the confusion from their eyes and then locked eyes with Ollie. There wasn't a sign of hope in either of their stares, but the amount of uneasiness could have swallowed him whole.

Avery looked over toward Bisa and Merlot, fearing the worst, watching the silver blade in Merlot's hand pull back to strike. Avery was quick, but she wasn't that quick. *Why is Ollie just standing there?* is what she would've thought had she had time to process what was happening in front of her at seemingly lightning speed.

Ollie turned back to Bisa and blinked back stress tears.

Merlot had used so much magic that it only seemed a test of her power and might to use something as banal and ordinary as a knife. If she could do that, she could do anything—truly. The metal caught the light and glimmered like a bolt of lightning as she swung it directly into Bisa's chest. The last thing Merlot saw was the light in Bisa's eyes. Merlot almost felt embarrassed for her. Whatever she'd planned...just hadn't worked. Bisa wasn't witch enough for her. She hadn't learned any secrets or tricks or gained special powers—she was just a witch, after all, one who thought they could challenge her—and win.

Bisa let out a whimper as she felt the stab of bamboozlement. Her eyes wide with fascination as she stared into Merlot's face—through it, past her eyes, behind her mind, beyond the curse—and into her spirit. There was a tightness in her chest, but there was no wound. She could feel it all, all that wasn't hers.

Merlot let out a horrified scream, slow at first, like a deeply buried trauma only now coming to light, as she lowered her head and brought her eyes to the knife pressed deep into her own heart. All of her ambitions and goals shattered before her in an instant like a dropped clay pot.

It worked, Bisa thought as she stared at the knife Merlot had unknowingly stabbed herself with under Bisa's stellar influence. Merlot's hands shook as she reached up to the knife, bewildered and confused about how she had allowed space, time and her mind to be twisted enough by influence.

Merlot shrieked again, but this time the sound was deep and guttural. She took a few steps back before all the life drained from her face, and she slumped to her knees and fell to the side like a discarded puppet.

Bisa caught her breath and grabbed hold of her chest, still in disbelief of the amount of influence she was able to have over Merlot. She was flushed and a little nauseated. A wave of dizziness captured her and dropped her to her knees. Ollie rushed to her side as Avery and Ruby watched in amazement. Bisa lifted her head and looked over at Merlot on the ground, the knife in her chest, blood seeping out around the wound, staining her already crimson top. The curse faded and dissolved from her aura like a sky full of stars in the dawn. Merlot was finished, her reign was over, and the curse—broken, but with a price. There is always a price, and Bisa knew it. She felt it. Her power of influence was gone—forever.

CHAPTER 18

For as long as he could remember, Mitch had had a very complicated relationship with self-improvement—a love/hate relationship, in simple terms. He had always shown up in the battle for self-improvement with all the best intentions, but he lost every fight, and the war felt eternal. He couldn't figure out how to stop being at war with himself. Being at war with himself *was* his personality; that was his identity. Mitch couldn't figure out how to change any more than he could figure out why he acted and thought the way he did. He was caught in an endless, spiraling loop of realizing he wanted to change but not being able to figure out how.

Even when he knew what one of his particular problems was, he didn't know how to change it, and he couldn't accept it any more than he could accept that he couldn't change it. The feelings only festered in a cavern of self-hate that he lived in like some gangly creature who never saw the sunlight and fed on the disaster of the cavern collapsing on him time and time again, cursed to never die and always feel. Once he realized he was capable of practicing magic, he had always hoped it would allow him to break free of all the patterns that felt more a part of him than his blood type, had always hoped that magic would give him exultation.

When Mitch fell into the water and met his totem, something shifted, an entire mental perspective. It wasn't just the conversation; everything he knew but hadn't paid attention to suddenly made sense. A level of acceptance allowed him to transmute his negative thought patterns and traits into something that worked for him rather than against him. Mitch, at his core, had very little light, but all he had to do was fall in love with that darkness, embrace it, accept it, alchemize it into gold. That gold was sweeter than honey lemonade made from the sourest lemons.

(what is gray can be gold)

Mitch approached his ritual space with an internal gold, scuffed and tarnished by the wounds and traumas of his past, but nevertheless—gold. He removed his clothes and along with them all of his doubt, cynicism and secret hopes for epic failure. In truth, Mitch was ill-equipped for the ritual, and he knew it. But people had done great things with far less, he told himself as he prepared all the ritual tools he would need for the Union of the Divine Dualities.

"Pure of heart," Mitch said aloud as he remembered what the text of the ritual said was necessary for it to be successful. He repeated it again and again, each time more quietly, until he heard it only in his head. *That could mean so many things*, he thought as he repeated *pure of heart* over and over, until it didn't even begin to sound like English. He had another thought: *Maybe I'm taking this too literally. Maybe all that means is that someone believes in themselves. Right? That's pure, accepting one's self, in all their darkness and light.*

He took a deep breath and cracked his neck. He would've been lying if he'd said he didn't feel any different. He did, he really did. His spirit felt electric in ways that he'd never felt before. At first, he figured it was just the excitement of the experience, like the rush a bunch of junior high kids feel while using a Ouija board at midnight during a sleepover when the candles go out. Only he knew there was something more, something extra, he could feel it, and it was more than just confidence.

Mitch draped the talisman around his neck and proceeded to mix the ingredients for the circle. When he was finished casting the circle across the floor, he took one final look at it in its entirety and stepped inside. His lungs felt a stab of tightness whenever he tried to take a deep breath, something to do with the ritual space, he assumed. It was heavy magic he was performing, magic that came with a risk greater than that of failure. His powers could be gone entirely. *That's the cost of accepting the darkness, I* guess, he thought. His heart was beating fast, sweat was beginning to bead up around his hairline, there was no turning back now. He was half surprised that he didn't have the army of thoughts that normally accompanied an attempt at, well—anything. He was determined in a way that he didn't even recognize, and it felt good. He had a feeling that even if he failed, it would still all be worth it somehow.

He fingered the bottle of astral fluid and realized he had no idea how he was supposed to use it to make himself invisible. There was no one to ask; he had to rely solely on his intuition. *Drink it*, he thought. And he did, all of it. There would be no second chances if he failed. Then came the first punch of doubt, as if it had snuck back inside the circle and crawled up his leg like some kind of sneaky ant. He accepted the thought and let it go. After a few breaths, he licked his lips to get all the astral fluid he could into his system. He looked down at his feet, but they weren't there. None of him was there. He was invisible. It had worked.

Mitch cleared his throat and picked up the paper with the next part of the spell from the floor. "Okay, cyclone of light," he said to himself in a breathy whisper. His nerves caused the paper to rattle in his hands as he continued to read. He cast the spell, saw the blinding bright vortex before him before it faded away. More success. Now came the true test, the power to summon the esoteric alchemy fire through sheer will and not through the use of magic. *How the hell am I gonna do that?* he thought. *How will I know that it wasn't magic that did it? That doesn't even make sense. No, stop. Stop trying to intellectualize it. Just...do it.*

Mitch took a few deep breaths and wiped the invisible sweat from his brow. He found it incredibly freeing to be naked. He thought about all the layers he wore, all the crocheted items that covered him up. Even while he was in bed, he kept himself in some kind of shield. It was hard to find the truth about someone under all those layers. They would've probably caught fire anyway with how hot he felt. Mitch held out his left hand and spread his fingers wide, palm down, the back of his hand covered in sweat he couldn't see but could feel dripping onto the floor. His eyes fixed on the hardwood before him. There was nothing. He turned his head and looked over at the collection of metals he needed to use in the fire, hoping he'd be able to use them. *Not hope—know*, Mitch thought.

As he closed his eyes and concentrated on his heartbeat, he found himself remembering when he had first arrived in Louisiana. It had been a strange time in his life, and turned out to be stranger than anything he had ever thought possible. He then thought about his parents, his brother, and everyone else who never really understood him. Mitch thought about himself and who he wanted to be—knew himself to be. His eyelids flickered lightly as his mind traveled through all the times he'd spent with Nina that had made an impact: the moment she taught him about crystals, when she caught him off guard and told him about his perfect eyesight, when she revealed that she knew he could communicate with animals, when she said he'd never experienced success because he hadn't yet explored the one area that would allow him success—because it hadn't been available to him yet. Mitch's racing heart skipped a beat.

(there you go...)

Mitch had always assumed that Nina was talking about magic, that magic had never been available to him but would ultimately lead to his experiencing success and feeling successful. He shook his head slightly, and the corners of his mouth turned up into a smile. *She meant me. She meant believing in myself.* Magic was only the catalyst.

In that moment, he truly found acceptance. When he opened his eyes, a fire burned before him under his hand. Flames danced freely in the air in fingers of purple and blue, tipped with green. He felt neither heat nor cold on his palm above the flames. He could smell it but couldn't articulate what it actually smelled like. He might as well try to describe what the interior of another galaxy was like. There was no question: he knew the fire had arrived without magic. He let out a breath, rubbed his hands on his knees, and stared into the fire, mesmerized by its beauty. There was nothing hidden in the flames. There were no secret messages, no mystic odes wrapped in riddles. There was just flame. He was hot, so hot.

On his next breath, he scooped up the metals into both hands. They clinked around in his palms. He held his hands over the fire and for some reason instantly thought about Isildur in *The Lord of the Rings*, who fails to destroy the evil ring and instead keeps it for himself. He heard Hugo Weaving's voice ring out in his head: "Cast it into the fire!" There was an oddly cinematic quality to the ritual, so it made sense to him. With a quick turn of his wrist, Mitch dumped the seven metals into the fire and watched them sink into the flames. They melted instantly as if made of butter and flooded together on the floor in a beautiful mess. The fire burned until all that was left was a molten pool of metals.

Another wave of heat rushed through his body. The whiskers on his cheeks were soaked with sweat, and his armpits were sticky and swampy like an August afternoon in the South. The racing in his chest grew faster and faster, like only two hundred cups of sugary coffees could do. He adjusted his knees on the floor and sat back on his heels. *Summon the celestial and infernal spirits*, he reminded himself. He ran his fingers through his sopping wet hair where it slicked back and held place.

"To the celestial spirits high and above, and the infernal spirits low and below, I invoke thee," Mitch said softly. "I thank you for growth, for guidance, for lessons learned, and for the gift of a golden egg." He looked down at the pool of metal and listened for their presence. There was no sound, but there was a feeling. It was the kind of communication that he felt aware of, like when he understood the feelings of animals. They had arrived. The pool of metal began to form a perfect circle on the floor, still as death. A few moments of wonder passed, and then the pool rose from the center, slowly, like a heavy quilt being pulled from the floor.

Mitch's mouth twisted into a smile, releasing more beads of sweat from his upper lip. The metal, like rolling waves of mercury, began to take shape. The shiny surface, like freshly polished jewelry, glittered in the light of the room as it formed into a solid gold egg. It was larger than he expected, even though he hadn't truly thought about what size it would be until that very second. It somehow looked both delicate and weighty at the same time. So gold that it almost hurt to look at it. He stared at it for a few moments, hesitant to touch it before completing the rest of the ritual. A strange urge to lick the egg overwhelmed him, as though the gold were a thin foil wrapper and inside was solid milk chocolate. Easter candy was always his favorite, after all.

Even with an entirely invisible body, he knew he still looked like someone who was powerless over a Cadbury Creme Egg, or a bag of Mini Eggs, or a family-size bag of malted milk eggs. The hypnotic glazy look in his eyes, the captivated fascination all over his face.

Finally, Mitch blinked himself back to the task at hand and chanted the final incantation.

"*Cogitatio, communicationis, stadium, completionem, defensionis, misericordia, disciplinam, patientia, intuitio.*"

A few nightmarishly long seconds passed during which nothing happened. Radio silence. He dared not even close his eyes, for fear of it somehow breaking the spell and causing the egg to shatter, melt or disappear. Inside him was a world of certainty, one that had always been there, but he wouldn't have valued his achievement nearly as much had he not been through so much in the past. It all seemed like it was almost supposed to be that way. He would've hated thinking something like that earlier in life, when things were exceptionally shitty for what seemed to be no reason at all other than things were just supposed to be shitty. *They were supposed to be that way*, Mitch thought, *which sucks, but I am where I am now, doing what I'm doing now because of that shit.*

Mitch leaned in a little toward the egg, like it was going to hatch something ridiculous like a million-dollar bill or a velociraptor, or even more appropriately—a black hen. There was some sort of pleasure to be had in the anticipation before the hatching. It was almost soothing, like a warm bath or a deep massage. He could've sat there with that feeling forever had he actually had the power to make time stand still. It was like a fabulous birthday party that begins to end as soon as it starts, so it was better to wait for it to arrive, for the joy of it hadn't begun to expire yet. *What if it doesn't hatch?* He thought for a second. It was hard to tell if it was pessimism or realism in that moment, and to be fair, he truly didn't know what would happen. No one did. He'd had moments of hope like this (not quite like this…) in the past. He could see there being at least a sliver of a chance that it might turn out unfortunately.

Mitch's heart finally caught a normal rhythm and his body began to cool. His mouth was dry, and he had never been so thirsty in his entire life. He realized just how thirsty he was for toxicity when Leo was around. *My God, never again.* He wiped the sweat from around his eyes and waited.

Crack!

Mitch's eyes blinked as his ears perked up. He was too focused on the egg to realize that he was no longer invisible. It didn't matter. The only thing that mattered was the egg—or, rather, what was inside it. The egg wobbled violently for a moment, and then a crack appeared in the shell like a bolt of lightning. There was a tapping, like someone with a tiny pick was inside, desperate to get out. Shards of shell began to break away in the same fashion as pieces of popcorn popping in a pan. The egg cracked straight through the center and vaporized to reveal a tiny black hen. Mitch laughed. Birth had always kind of freaked him out, but this was a little different, something he could get behind without being weirded out. The black hen was cute, and he instantly felt a bond with it.

Mitch licked his lips. "*Crescere, locate*," he said assertively.

The hen chirped a few times before waddling around in circles.

He had done it. Somehow, Mitch had been able to pull off something that no one in a million years ever thought he would be able to accomplish with complete success. He grabbed his clothes and got dressed, but was too fascinated to bother with his socks. He sat staring at the chirping new addition to the house. All they had to do now was wait three full days. In three days, it would be full grown and lead them to the rafkolite. Somehow.

CHAPTER 19

It was close to the turn of the hour when Bisa felt the presence of the spirit they had been looking for. Actually, it found *them*. Bisa glanced at the members of her coven: Avery, Ollie, and now, unofficially—Ruby. All the other witches in the hotel had lost their power under Merlot's spell, and they were the only ones left. A shiver ran up her back. The spirit was close. There was no more time. She had to act now.

"It's here," Bisa said gently. "The spirit, it's here."

The coven looked around for signs of its presence, but there were none they could see.

Ollie was the second to pick up on its energy. "It's going to come for us, all of us—first the most powerful one here, then the rest," he told the coven.

Bisa glanced at Ollie and saw a wave of panic flood his face. He knew what she was going to do.

This is no time for a gambit, Ollie said mentally. "Bisa, no."

Bisa felt the spirit coming for her. It was almost in her aura, close enough to feel her essence. She closed her eyes, tilted her head back and opened her palms. Her heart raced for a moment before her whole body collapsed to the floor.

Merlot's eyes snapped open, and she rose up with a ghastly wheeze. She looked around, but she was no longer in the room. She was somewhere else, a long stone hallway that she didn't recognize. She couldn't see an end to it, no matter which direction she turned. The coven was gone. There was no noise, only a heavy sense of dread. A pocket of black was in the distance, so far that it could've been miles away. She looked above her, and there was sky, the dense type of blue of the hour and a half before dawn.

She took her first step forward into the stone hallway. Her footstep echoed into the chasm of the limitless. Another step. Another.

"Come to me," an ominous voice said from the ether.

She looked all around but saw nothing. Her face darkened at the sound of the voice. "Where am I?" she asked. "Who are you?"

Her voice reverberated off the enchanted milieu like a rock plummeting into the deepest, darkest well.

"Come. Come to me," the voice beckoned again.

She took a few more steps, listening, watching, waiting. Then, ahead of her, she caught sight of the spirit. First it was the eyes, two blazing yellow eyes that burned through all space and time. She proceeded forward, as requested.

The eyes gave way to a shadowy shape as she moved closer and closer. How obedient and helpless she must have seemed to the calling spirit and its vicious hunger. There was no denying its power. It was frightening, but she was anything but a coward, even in the face of something so unknown, so dangerous and so ravenous for all of her. She stopped in her tracks and stood still, holding the gaze of the eyes in the darkness that were wickedness incarnate. She found herself thinking of the Land of Perpetual Midnight. She had faced Death itself. *Is that why I'm not afraid?*

The two of them stood there in the hallway of nowhere, as though about to duel in an old western, moments before someone drew their pistol. But she knew something the spirit did not. The moment was short-lived, because the spirit turned to mist and surrounded her with the speed of a viper's bite. She opened her mouth to let the spirit in willingly, offering herself up freely to it. She could feel it everywhere, in every fiber of her being, in every atom of her energy, like being in a vise that was slowly but constantly tightening. She could feel the spirit's insane pleasure as if reading its very own thoughts, experiencing its very own emotions.

"So much power. So delicious," she heard in the air, although she couldn't be certain it was actually said aloud.

"Take me, all of me," she told the spirit. For a moment, she was so thoroughly blended with the spirit that she couldn't tell if she was being consumed or she was consuming it. Next came the pain. A searing pain like being stabbed with a million knives all at once. And then, the spirit was inside. Feeding. All she had to do now was return. If she could.

Bisa reemerged from the spirit realm in her own body, the coven hovering above her in a state of panic. "It's okay, I'm okay!" she said as she caught her breath. She was right: she had emerged unscathed. The spirit, however, was not okay.

"What happened?" Avery asked as she grabbed hold of Bisa to make sure she hadn't been harmed.

"I trapped the spirit. It'll be gone soon," Bisa said.

"How did you do that?" Ruby asked.

"I possessed Merlot's body," she said plainly, as if it were common practice for someone to do such a thing. "I could feel it coming for me, and before I let it take hold, I projected myself into Merlot's body, allowing it to feed on her instead."

"But how? She's dead," Ollie said.

"Right," Bisa said as she clutched her forehead, feeling a little light-headed from the heavy burden of the transference of energy. "The spirit can't pull power from a dead witch. The power it felt was mine, but I wasn't really there. It was more

like the…essence of me, the perfume of me, not *actually* me."
She took a deep breath and rose to her feet. "The one thing a
spirit can't do is feed from the dead. Well, a dead body."

"How did you know that would work?" Avery asked.

Bisa shook her head, allowing the question to wobble in her
uncertainty. "I didn't."

"So what happened to it?" Avery asked.

Bisa looked into Avery's eyes and had an intuitive vision of
the spirit. She was aware that it had been tricked into feeding
from the body of a dead witch, where there was no power at all.
It hadn't realized it was all an elaborate ruse until Bisa had vanished completely and returned to her own body. The spirit had
bonded so tightly to the body and mind of Merlot that it was
impossible for it to escape. Like a mouse entering a trap where
there was no cheese, only the illusion of it, the scent of it. The
windows to the soul and all its power were closed, there was no
lifeblood to sail in and out of, there was no escape. It would
never again be able to savor the taste of another witch. Instead,
it would be confined in the body of the deceased, where it had
no power. Trapped in the lifeless cells until they decayed into
oblivion.

"It's gone," Bisa said simply.

They spent the next hour relocating Merlot's body to the
middle of nowhere via Rosemary's ring, where they burned it
with Avery's scorching fire. Afterward, they made a pit stop at
Ruby's to grab a few provisions before they spent a little time
working out an elixir that they could administer to the witches
at the party who were now powerless. With Ollie's expert and
obsessive knowledge of plants, Ruby's experience in potion
making and Bisa's connection to the divine, they had found the
right recipe to stop the spread while also making sure they were

fully protected against her contagious spell. Avery charged the elixir with healing energy before they poured a little into a small spray bottle and dosed themselves with a single spray.

"So, this is, like, a magical vaccine, then?" Avery asked.

Bisa nodded. "After a fashion, yes. Have you ever seen the Poo-Pourri commercials? It's kind of like that. Once the elixir is atomized, it sticks to their aura, traps the spell, envelops and neutralizes it. It won't cure anyone or reverse the effects of the spell; those unfortunately are permanent. But it will stop the spread and create a sort of herd immunity in case any one of them comes in contact with another witch in their lifetime. It pains me to say that these witches are no longer witches, physically. In spirit, they will always be. What is a witch anyway?" she asked rhetorically.

"Aren't they all going to lose their shit, though?" Avery asked. "I can't imagine this is going to be an easy thing for some of them to swallow, especially the Primordial ones or, my God, if there are actually any Corporeal witches out there."

Bisa looked over at Ollie and they spoke to each other telepathically for a few moments.

Ollie shifted his weight and a smile appeared on his face.

A phone call to the front desk later, they had two large standing fans in their possession. They rolled them into the hallway between the two rooms of the Bacchanalia party, and turned them on high. They sprayed the elixir into the path of the high-powered fans and dosed every witch at the party. It wafted through the air and no one was ever the wiser.

"I do feel kinda bad, though," Avery said.

"Why?" Bisa asked.

"Well, none of them know what happened. Or why. Doesn't that bother you?"

Bisa shrugged. "Well," she said, choosing her words with extreme care, "It's not that it doesn't bother me—it does—but there's also nothing I can do about it, besides this. It is what it is, so we have to accept it. Maybe we can figure something out later, when the time is right. But that's not now. Besides, think about how many people around the globe Merlot has affected with this spell."

"Well, that too! I mean, surely not every witch in the world is here at this party. What about all the other ones we can't dose?"

"I'll work something out," Ruby butted in. "I have a few ideas."

"What do we think happened with Mitch?" Ollie asked as he squirted several sprays into the fan. "Think he pulled off the ritual?"

"Let's finish this up here and get back to the house," Bisa said.

They had done the best they could with what they had in a short time. It was more of a temporary bandage than a solid cure to the problem that Merlot had created. They intended to stop the spread, but it would undoubtedly continue to advance a little further into the witch community before it declined. There had been far too many Bacchanalia parties in far too many locations; it would prove nearly impossible to treat all of them. So many witches had been afflicted: witches from North America, South America, Europe, Africa, Asia and even Australia. The best they could hope for was that Ruby had something to curb the magical spread so that no more witches would fall victim to the infection. Their numbers were already few to begin with.

Twenty-some minutes later, the whole floor of the hotel was thick with the scent of the elixir.

"All right, that'll have to do. Let's get back to the house," Bisa said.

Moments later, they arrived back at the house, eager to check in with Mitch and find out whether he had succeeded.

CHAPTER 20

He did it, Avery thought as she picked her gaping jaw up from the floor, her eyes fixed on the tiny black hen.

I knew you could do it, Bisa thought, loud enough for Ollie to hear.

"That's it?" Ollie asked.

"Yeah! It worked!" Mitch said excitedly.

"It's really small," Ollie said.

"Well, yeah, *now*," Mitch said as he started to put on his socks. "We have to wait for three days for it to grow to full size. Then it'll be able to show us where the rafkolite is. How, well…I have no idea."

Bisa smiled and rubbed Mitch's back. "You did it, Mitch!"

"Do we have to feed her?" Avery asked.

Mitch shook his head. "No. She doesn't need food."

"Are you sure? She looks so skinny," Avery asked as she leaned in closer.

Mitch nodded and smiled, still enamored with the tiny hen and his ability to produce her.

He broke his gaze and turned toward Bisa. "So is it done? Is it over?"

"Merlot?" Bisa asked.

Mitch nodded.

"It's over," Bisa said. Two words was all she offered, but they said a lot more when he looked at the expression on her face.

"Maybe we should find the hen a bed?" Avery suggested. "Or a nest? Or something like that? I'll get one of my shipping boxes, it'll be fine."

"I think we can relax for now," Bisa said as she finally started to settle into the fact that they no longer had reason to be on edge.

"Anyone hungry?" Ollie asked. There was a unanimous *yes*. All their success and achievements called for a celebratory meal, something out of the ordinary, something from scratch that didn't come from a package, something that was more common when Nina was around. Ollie and Avery took to the kitchen, where they split the tasks of the late meal, Avery handling the panzanella* and Ollie preparing a roasted carrot soup*, something he'd been wanting to try for a while. After the carrots had been roasted, he decided to make a juicy sangria* on the fly. They were celebrating, after all. He found himself thinking of Nina, and how proud she would be of them right now. Only he didn't have to imagine much: he could feel her, and he could see her from time to time as she hovered behind him in the kitchen, micromanaging how he seasoned the soup.

"Careful, that might be a little too much salt," Nina said from over his shoulder.

Ollie smirked, rolled his third eye and dipped his pinkie into the soup to taste. *It needs more salt*, he thought, trying his best to hide the thought from the ether, where Nina could pick up on it. He looked back to see her hovering over Avery fiddling around with the panzanella. He seized his chance, and with his eyes locked on Nina, he added more salt to the soup before taking a sip from his red sangria. The extra salt paid off, because everyone felt the soup was borderline addictive, almost suspiciously so, as if it had been enchanted in some way. Ollie just knew his way around herbs—and salt.

Before long, they were all having the best dinner party they'd ever had in their entire lives and were all drunk and wobbly on sangria. The only thing that would've made it a little better would have been having Nina there, actually there. There was laughter in the house again, something that had been absent for quite a while. The house itself had missed the sound of it, too. Even when Mitch somehow cut himself in the kitchen without knowing, he didn't mind, even though it would probably leave a scar. He had lots of scars already, and he didn't mind that so much anymore.

It was Bisa who started dancing first, after she changed the music and added a few songs of her own to the playlist Mitch had been guarding. Bisa looked like a different person, partially because she was. She wasn't much of a drinker, and when she did drink, it was never to get drunk; it was an accident that she happened to drink more than normal tonight. Ollie was not just a wizard with potions but also quite the talented mixologist, as it turned out. She probably would never have admitted it, but it was exhausting always having to be the lucid, logical and clear-headed one. The moment the sangria touched her lips, she finally realized no one was giving her that job but herself. She was allowed to unwind just like everyone else.

Avery made sure to take a few videos on her phone in case they needed help remembering anything once they crawled out of bed from underneath a possible hangover late the next afternoon.

Ollie felt a tickle in his pocket and pulled out his phone. He swiped his lock screen away to see a text notification from an app for his fancy, bladeless, four-hundred-dollar designer fan that was also an air purifier.

Something is wrong with your fan.

His eyes shot up from his phone to the fan at the other end of the room, where Avery had her head in the long and narrow, rounded rectangular cavity where the blades of a normal fan would be. Her face was nestled tight, nearly stuck, between the two sides, with laughter pouring out of her mouth.

Things were getting wild, and they deserved every minute of it.

Soon after Ollie gave a stunning impersonation of Bisa, one that made Avery laugh so hard that she spilled the orange slice in her drink, the mood shifted as a darkness approached their happy place. There was a series of knocks at the front door. Bisa might have felt that energy coming had she not been too busy finally letting loose a little. She scurried over and shut off the music. After everyone hushed, they all heard it—another set of knocks from a heavy fist. Then Bisa knew.

The coven gathered and headed toward the door.

"Hey, can y'all hear me?" Leo shouted politely from outside. "The door is deadbolted."

Bisa didn't even bother looking at anyone else—she made a mad rush to the door and opened it wide. "It's to keep you out," she said sharply.

"Look, I know y'all are pissed," Leo said as he glanced around at everyone's faces. "But—"

"Leo, I don't want to hear it," Bisa said. "No one here wants to hear whatever it is that you have to say."

"Just, wait," Leo pleaded.

Everyone was silent, and waited, but Leo didn't actually know what he wanted to say now that he had the chance. He struggled with the words he couldn't find and finally let out a sigh. "Look, I know I don't deserve anything, or another chance," he said gently.

"You left *us!*" Bisa said. "Not the other way around. And now, you're back." *I know exactly why you're here.* "You left to try to carry out the ritual on your own. And it didn't work, did it? You lost your powers, didn't you?"

Leo's shoulders dropped a little. "You were right. Is that what you wanna hear? I fucked up, and you were right."

"Yes," Avery said. "That is what we wanted to hear. Now leave."

"You guys need me just as much as I need you," Leo said.

Bisa scoffed. "I don't remember you saying anything like that before when you left us, against our wishes, against better judgment. I don't care what you think we need, all I care about is fulfilling the prophecy, and you're not a part of that. Not anymore."

"I have to be," Leo said. "The prophecy said that *this* coven, which I'm a part of, would find the rafkolite. And I'm a Corporeal, which may be something that we need."

Bisa shook her head and laughed. "What 'we'? There isn't any 'we.' And you're not a Corporeal anymore—are you?"

Avery clicked her tongue, and everyone else let out heavy, impatient sighs.

Bisa's eyes tightened as she listened to the energy in the air. "Maybe the coven would like to know exactly who you really are. Maybe they'd like to know how many people you murdered back in New Orleans. Or maybe they'd want to know what you did to Mitch. Or what vision you cowered in front of that caused the talisman to break." Bisa kept going and going, listing all the things that she now knew, things that were supposed to be secrets, things that Leo had purposely forgotten to avoid any sort of accountability or change.

Leo didn't like anything Bisa said, but he hated that all of it was true even more. It sounded so horrible when she said everything consecutively. He had almost forgotten some of the things and was impressed at how much she was able to reveal. But he had to stop her.

"Okay, okay!" he said sharply.

"You aren't a part of this coven anymore," Bisa said. "You're not a witch. And none of us even like you enough to care."

Leo glanced over to Mitch, who wasn't mourning over the twisted thing they had had between them that was already gone.

"Not even him," Bisa said quickly.

"You're not a good person, Leo," Mitch said. "I wish you were."

Avery let out a small laugh as she noticed how pathetic Leo looked. "What are you laughing at?" Leo asked.

"Just your bad karma," Avery replied.

Leo looked down at his shoes, to the trees on the side of the house, and anywhere that wasn't at Bisa directly. "Maybe there's a way to bring my powers back. If you can come back, then maybe my powers can come back too."

"They won't," Avery said. *I made sure of that.* She was repulsed by the very sight of Leo. Her eyes had daggers that could've cut straight through him if she stared long enough. She stepped forward, and Leo could feel the heat as she approached Bisa's side.

"Oh yeah? Says who, you?" Leo said mockingly.

"Says the spell that I cast to rid us of an enemy," Avery said.

The entire coven gaped at her in surprise, and when no one said anything, Avery took another step forward. "You, Leo. You're the enemy. And it worked. So leave."

Hearing Avery tell him to leave and then not having anyone stop her only made him more desperate. He brought his hands together and turned to Bisa. "I understand so much now, and I *want* this all to be different. Please, just, help me be better," he begged, realizing that he might truly be on his own again.

Bisa sighed deeply. A Transcendent's sigh was always a heavy one—it could sink ships. She crossed her arms and spoke briefly about her feelings for Leo, illuminating that she had once felt *something* for him, even though she couldn't truly figure out why. Bisa had never felt the kind of feelings that she had had for Leo, and had certainly not felt feelings for someone *like* Leo. Being brought back to life in such a way gave her a stinging sense of clarity. Almost too much clarity. It would take a little getting used to, having that much information. Her mind had always been a little tuned in without having to reemerge into her body completely rewired for full transmission.

She looked Leo straight in the eye. "I had a dream that we were happy once, in a way that made no sense, and we watched the sunrise together from the window in my room. That dream is long gone and you can have the memory of it too." Bisa frowned. "You're not a part of this coven anymore. You don't live here anymore. This isn't your home. *Go home.*"

It took the better part of a minute for Leo to realize that he didn't know where home was, and it was another few moments before it sank in that nowhere had ever really felt like home. The place where he'd spent the most time was Louisiana, but he wasn't sure if that was actually home. By the time he understood that he was homeless, he was horribly sad and distraught.

Now what would he do? Where would he go? He couldn't just go back to being a line cook, not after everything that had happened. What kind of sick joke was that? He had money now, but that was about all he had. Clearly, money wasn't everything.

"What about the ritual?" Leo asked.

"It's done. Mitch did it earlier," Bisa said.

Leo looked over at Mitch in complete shock. "Mitch?"

"Did you really think it was going to be you?" Avery asked.

"Well, I thought the person had to be like a saint," Leo quipped.

"And you thought that was *you*?" Avery said loudly.

Leo suddenly had all sorts of ideas. He just wouldn't quit. "Well, what about the rafkolite? If you guys find it, maybe I can get my powers back and maybe it can fuse my soul back to me too."

"I guess we'll never know," Bisa said as she began to close the door.

Leo shook his head, half in disbelief, half in disgust. "None of you know what it's like. None of you know how it feels to live like this! You just can't find any way to be understanding, can you?"

"You just want us to condone everything?" Avery asked.

"I want you guys to be sympathetic! Or empathetic," Leo said, recognizing that he didn't actually understand the difference between the two. His voice rose to a shout. "You can't just kick me out. I have nowhere to go! What about all my stuff?"

Bisa grabbed hold of the door again and closed it just enough to signal that the conversation was over and there wouldn't be another one. It was the last time he would see them. "I will pack up your dirty socks and your vape cartridges and you can pick them up tomorrow at noon," she said. She started to turn around, but quickly stopped herself. "Oh, and just re-member, all I have to do is call up that officer in New Orleans and ask him to do anything I want, so don't even bother trying to come back. I never want to see you again."

Now that her power of influence was gone, it was the only card she had left to play, one of the benefits of a spell cast with a sort of time-delay, extended-relief benefit. The seed of influ-ence had already been planted. All she had left to do was water it with her voice and it would blossom into whatever she de-sired. She turned around without even a second glance or a second thought, and the coven followed, all but Mitch.

Mitch grabbed hold of the door, ready to close it. When he saw that Leo was finally realizing that what he did to people actually mattered, he almost felt sorry for him. It was hard not to, with Leo standing there with his janky shoes full of holes, and his disheveled hair. *Has he always looked this dirty and I just never noticed? What does that say about me? What does that say about who I was?* Mitch knew Leo had potential; he was just too much of an asshole to get out of his own way and realize that potential in any sort of decent way. *You never cared until everyone decided to give up on you.* Mitch didn't know what would happen to him now that he truly had nowhere to be and nothing to do. If he wasn't destined to become a street punk, he was certainly the closest thing to it.

"Mitch," said Leo, "I want you to know that I'm sorry for all that happened. I know that I totally took advantage of you, and then I made you feel disgusting about it and blamed you for it and tried to make you feel shitty about it. That was on me."

Mitch nodded, accepting the apology, or whatever it was. He had no desire to hold on to any sort of grudge; it took too much energy. "Thanks," he said. He looked into space for a moment and then back to Leo. "It's just a little too late. I can't take any more chances with you; I don't have any chances left to give. You're not good for me, you're not good for us. You're not even good for yourself." Mitch turned around to see the coven lingering in the distance, waiting, watching. "You need to go."

Fuck, this is really it, isn't it? Leo thought. *I'm screwed.* "Wait," he said, his voice dripping with desperation.

"Bye, dude," Mitch said with a kindness Leo didn't deserve as he gently shut the door.

The lock clicking was the last thing Leo heard. He'd been evicted—from the coven, from the house, from everything he had taken for granted. Outside, where Leo now stood, completely alone, the wind picked up, making the idea of having nowhere to go incredibly uncomfortable. He couldn't experience happiness. His soul would forever be detached from his body, and he would never be able to perform any sort of magic again. His body was a cage, one that would imprison him with himself forever. It would've been so easy to just manipulate a little energy and project himself somewhere, anywhere—but he couldn't. He looked up to the sky, but even the moonlight was hiding from him behind the clouds. Leo turned to walk away, taking one last look at the house and hoping to find someone looking out a window, but all of them were obscured by drawn curtains.

Inside, Bisa called the coven together to renounce Leo's ties to the coven and dissolve his connection to them. It was something that would have bothered Mitch in the past, but that wasn't the case now. He didn't like it, but he didn't have to. He didn't have to like things that were for the greater good of everyone involved—including himself. He figured that in a few years, the changes that he made now would finally begin to pay off in ways that he couldn't even imagine.

Once they finished severing Leo from the coven, Bisa cast another spell to prevent him from coming onto the grounds, no farther than the end of the driveway. There would be no way around it now that he had not a drop of magic inside him. He wouldn't even be able to find another witch to do it for him if he wanted.

It wasn't until much later, just before the sun rose, that Ollie found himself alone with Avery in the kitchen. They were the only ones still awake.

"Can I ask you something?" Ollie asked quietly before he reached his hand up to cover a yawn.

"What's up?" Avery replied. Her eyes getting a little heavy with sleep, still a little tipsy, but ready to answer any of Ollie's questions just as much as she was ready for bed.

"Did you really cast a spell on Leo? You know, to destroy an enemy?" Ollie rested his head on his hand, cupping his cheek.

Avery looked Ollie straight in his sleepy eyes. "No," she lied. She wasn't sure why she lied, but she did. It felt justified for reasons she couldn't explain.

Ollie couldn't smell a lie like she could, but he could feel the vibes as much as he could read it on her face. Although Avery was a talented witch, she wasn't an actress. He thought it must've been the first time she had lied, and he was right.

Nina leaned down and rested her elbows on the counter next to Ollie. "She did," she said. "She just lied."

Ollie turned his eyes to the side but not his head, acknowledging Nina's presence that only he could see and feel. *I'm sure she has her reasons.*

"I just wanted us to be done with him," Avery said. "He tried the ritual, it didn't work, he lost his powers, just like everyone said."

Maybe she just wants to avoid a fight, or maybe she just cared more about Leo being gone than she did about lying about it, Ollie thought. "Okay," he said. *Covens are like families, right? We don't always have to agree, or get along, or like every decision someone makes. Living with Leo was evidence of that, so maybe this just isn't the fight that needs to be picked. The damage has already been done. It's over.*

CHAPTER 21

Leo grabbed the large, empty duffel bag and hopped out of the Lyft car. He checked the time on his phone: a little past one in the afternoon. He watched the car pull away through the cloud of his steamy breath. Something felt a little different, but he couldn't articulate what. *Maybe this is what they are always talking about, how growth never feels good. Maybe I finally am changing, for the better.* He turned to look at 444 Smoky Quartz Drive. He couldn't even remember what he'd left behind in his room besides some dirty clothes, but that wasn't the point.

He hoped maybe everyone had calmed down and would be a little more receptive to him now that they'd all slept. It took being right back at square one, powerless, exactly who he was before any of his powers developed, to open his eyes. He thought about all the things he was able to do as a witch: he could move things, set things on fire, project himself to other places. As a witch, it didn't matter what kind of person he was or what kind of things he did, he was always the one on top, the superstar, the hotshot, crackerjack whiz kid. But only as a witch. Standing on the edge of the property in the wintry air, he was slapped with cold, hard reality: he was just a man, a gigantic man-child.

He saw a box at the end of the driveway with his name written across it in black permanent marker, which Avery had crossed out and replaced with the word "TRASH" in big bold letters. Leo walked up to it, peeked inside and looked up at the house. He decided he had the right to check the house for himself, so he continued straight past the box. But he made it just a few feet before he was unable to walk farther. He'd felt a sensation like this once before, a sort of magnetic force, repelling him so that he couldn't proceed. *Magic*, he thought. *Magic to keep me out. Those bitches. Avery, probably.*

Leo tried with all his might and all his will and all the magic he no longer had but wished he did, but he still couldn't get any closer to the house. It didn't matter which angle he tried to enter from; it was like the entire property was surrounded with some kind of enchantment that he could never break. He turned around and kneeled down next to his box of belongings. It was depressing to realize that everything fit into a small cardboard box. Was that all life was? Was that how little he'd accomplished? People his age were buying houses and getting promoted, and here he was with a cardboard box, like some kind of vagrant squatter. He poked through his belongings: some clothes, dirty mismatched socks, three old vapes, random keys, pens, a journal, and a lighter. He didn't want any of it any more than they did. He picked up the box, took it to the trash bin and dropped it inside. *I'll give Avery that one.*

Leo ordered another Lyft and waited for it to arrive, casually lurking on the outskirts of the property like someone with a restraining order who wanted to push the limits of what they could get away with before actually getting arrested. When it came, he took it to a hotel in Denver, where he checked in with no plans for checking out anytime soon. He decided he was at least going to enjoy a nice hotel, since he could afford it now. But when he closed his eyes, it didn't make any difference. He didn't care about the luxuries, they weren't even his. He had nothing and no one.

He drew himself a bath, something he'd done only two or three times in his adult life. He didn't mind the stray hairs from a previous guest floating around on the top of the water. Leo grabbed the bottle of complimentary body wash and poured it under the running faucet. A compilation of floral and woody influences created an illusion of a forest in spring. The scent made his nose tingle as he hopped into the bath and broke through the bubbles on the surface. He soaked until the water turned tepid. He might be a little cleaner, but no amount of soap or bubbles was going to cleanse him to his core. Nothing was going to erase his past or make him any happier. He'd learned that the hard way.

When he got out of the bath, he looked at himself in the mirror. He stood there in the bright light of the moderately opulent bathroom and realized he'd never felt so vulnerable—and it wasn't just because he was naked. There were so many ways to experience the world, not only as a witch but also as a human being, and he didn't know how to do either. If he were really going to be completely honest with himself, he had to admit he was the common factor in pretty much every single problem in his life. It was the first time he understood that it was a painfully long road to unfucking himself, and he was standing at the very beginning of that road with no idea how to start walking.

CHAPTER 22

It had been three days since the black hen had hatched from the egg, and she was now fully grown. When Mitch went to check on her, he let out a gasp that could be heard in the farthest reaches of the house. "She's full size!" he shouted.

The coven stopped whatever they were doing and ran to the room. There was the hen, pacing around on the floor in front of them. Her thick feathers, black like a dark secret, glistened in the light.

"Oh, look, the chicken's full size!" Avery said pleasantly.

"Now what do we do?" Ollie asked the group. "She's supposed to find where the rafkolite is, right?" He bit into an apple. No one answered him. They all pondered his question as they listened to the sound of his chewing. Finally he swallowed. "Do we take the hen on a walk or something? What if the rafkolite's nowhere near us? I don't get how this is supposed to work."

"There has to be something we're not thinking of," Bisa said. "Because you're right. What if the rafkolite is in Greenland or something? I don't know how we're supposed to get there for the chicken to find it for us."

I wonder if we just ask her directly, Avery almost said, but she thought that would be a stupid thing to say, so she kept her mouth shut and waited for something that made sense. Only nothing came. She was completely out of ideas, as if none were to be had anywhere in the entire universe.

Mitch clicked his tongue as he tried to think about what to do, if there was something that needed to be done.

Ollie paced around the hen in a circle, hoping something would come to him, or that Nina would just flat out tell him what to do and how to do it. No ideas came to him, but a sudden craving for a green juice hit him instead. He headed to the kitchen, gathered up some fruits and vegetables and the high-powered juicer, and made a quick batch of his Green Fire* juice. He tossed it back, hoping that maybe the sudden urge was a sign from the universe that it would encourage the answer to come to him. He poured a glass each for the rest of the coven and brought it to them where they sipped and watched the hen sit.

Mitch had forgotten how good Ollie's juices were and soon found his mind wandering after the spicy notes of jalapeño hit the back of his throat. It was spicier than any of his previous batches, and even though the burn was slightly uncomfortable in the best kind of way, he drank the entire cup in less than a minute. *How long are we supposed to just sit here and wait for you to do your thing? Do we have to force you to do it?* Mitch thought. Right then, he found himself randomly mentally singing *creature of the night...touch-a, touch-a, touch-a, touch ME!* He didn't even like the *Rocky Horror Picture Show*—in fact, he hated it, and he didn't understand why anyone liked it; being a cult classic wasn't a good enough excuse.

Touch-a, touch-a, touch-a, touch ME! Ugh! Why is that stupid song in my head? Mitch thought as he chewed on his lip to stop himself from mouthing the words. He thought about it. It was a message, in some sort of crazy way. It was telling him what he needed to know. The arrival of the message in a form he could recognize, understand and interpret was his first introduction to becoming more psychic, the first of more than he would ever be able to remember.

"Has anyone actually held it?" Mitch asked the group as he wiped a little green juice from the side of his mouth.

Not a single one of them said yes.

"Really? No one? Not even picked her up?" Mitch asked again. He scooted over to the hen and kneeled down on the floor. The hen cocked her head and looked directly at him as if she were saying, *Took you long enough.* Mitch reached out and placed his hand on her back.

There was a flash of light, and his stomach sank like the first drop on a tall roller coaster.

When he could see again, the hen was in front of him, but they were both somewhere else entirely. It was cloudy and underneath him was a beach, more of a gallery of rough rocks than a sandy shore. He released his hand from the hen and rose to his feet. There was nothing and no one, just ocean and a strange rocky shoreline. *Where the hell am I?* he thought as he looked around for anything familiar. Colorado was nowhere near the ocean, so he could be anywhere. The better part of a minute passed before he realized that the hen had begun to wander off without him.

"Wait!" Mitch shouted at the hen as he chased after her. He wondered if she would answer him, like in *Return to Oz,* where Dorothy's chicken can talk when transported to Oz. *Mitch, get a grip. This isn't Oz.* He refrained from touching the hen again out of fear that she would transport him somewhere else—or worse, that she wouldn't transport him back home. Instead he let the hen scamper over the rocks as he followed. They continued along the beach, stumbling over the uneven rocks and pebbles under the gray skies.

After five minutes or so, Mitch wondered if there was any point to any of this. Was he just randomly following a chicken around for no reason? *Is this what my life is now?* Without knowing anything about anything, the whole situation seemed terribly ridiculous. He had made some pretty silly choices in the past, but nothing like this. Ten minutes later, the beach hadn't become any easier to walk on. Even after he chose to walk closer to the water where the pebbles weren't as large, it wasn't any easier, because the tide was washing in and moving them practically right under his feet. He had no choice but to keep going.

The hen stopped in her tracks, and her head bopped left and right before she darted off the beach to a small patch of sand and grass. Mitch stubbed his toe on a large rock that caught him off guard, and he hobbled his way over to the hen. Suddenly, he could hear something he had never been able to hear before, a buzzing that sounded almost like a voice. *Is that the hen? Is she trying to talk to me?*

The hen clucked about in circles, then pecked violently at a patch of ground. She left V-shaped dents in the dirt, bringing some of it back up in the air as she peck peck pecked. Just as suddenly as she had started, she stopped. The hen took a few steps away from him and then rested upon the rocks like she was ready for a nap.

"That's it?" Mitch said aloud.

He looked back at the patch of ground with the peck marks. He stepped closer, until it was at his feet. The voicelike buzzing returned. It wasn't the hen at all, or a voice, it was something else. He could almost smell it when he closed his eyes. Mitch inhaled deeply through his nose, and the scent of something unknown almost made his eyes water, like cutting onions. Being a Primordial, he felt a presence. For a Transcendent witch or even the rarer Corporeal witch, the feeling wouldn't have been so intense; they would've been used to that sort of feeling, he thought. He kneeled down and ran his fingers through the dirt loosened by the hen. He traced his finger through it, pushing the bits of black earth out of the way, like removing debris from a rising spring sprout. He wondered what he felt, what presence it was. Was it finally what they had been looking for?

He rose to his feet, stood beside the patch of dirt, and let his heart guide him on what to do. He closed his eyes and held out his hands. He hadn't worked with earth magic much, but when he finally did, it felt incredibly natural, like hearing a song that hadn't crossed his mind in twenty years but that he still knew the lyrics to even though he'd never bothered to learn them.

With all his heart, and all his Primordial strength, he asked the ground for answers. His magical reach penetrated the dirt and went deep into the earth, like roots seeking nutrients and water. As he concentrated harder, images flashed through his mind, images that made no sense and were gone faster than they arrived, so fast it was hard to determine what they were, besides old, very old—ancient. He broke through time and traveled through it all as he connected to something deep within the earth. Like a shovel hitting rock, his magic met resistance. He introduced himself, asked for it to come to the surface, had a conversation with it in the type of way that Ollie had with his plants. Everything was about communication, Mitch realized.

Mitch felt a bond between his magic and the unknown. He curled his fingers into a fist and twisted his wrist. There was a quaking. A storm of dirt and rock shot up and showered down upon him, spraying his face. Unearthed rock rapped against beach rock. Mitch locked his eyes shut. His mouth tightened, gripping tiny bits of dirt and sand between his lips. There was a loud thud in front of him. When the clacking of the rocks stopped, he opened his eyes. At first, it was cloudy and hard to see much at all. He wiped the flecks of dirt and debris still resting on his eyelashes and then looked down to the ground. There was a giant hole where the patch of dirt had been, and beside that, something that took his breath away.

It was beautiful in ways that only poets know. It was more than a rock from the earth—silvery green and rippled with smoky and mosslike violet bubbles. It was the rafkolite. The sight of it instantly sent a wave of warm joy through Mitch's entire body.

"That's it, that's the rafkolite," Mitch said aloud. He spit out a few chunks of dirt that had entered his mouth. "Well, *nigrum pullum*, you delivered."

The beauty of it could almost be heard, like a room full of diamond wind chimes. The sound he heard humming inside his head was the rafkolite. It was plain as day now that he could see it and was close enough to touch it. He almost didn't want to. It just seemed too precious, even under all the dirt and debris. Nothing could snuff its splendor.

To the side of him, the hen clucked. Mitch looked over and smiled before he reached down to pick up the oddly shaped rock. He brushed off its surface, cleaning away all the dirt until it shone back at him, even under the gray skies, like it was the only rock that should ever be seen again. When he held it, he instantly felt relief, and joy, and creativity, but most of all—an inspired sense of happiness that felt infectious, like the laugh of someone charismatic and kindhearted. It was entrancing in the best possible way, a warm blanket on the cold, rocky beach.

It was amazing that he had found it on his own, but he had no one to share it with. Not to mention he hadn't the first idea about where he was or how to get back. There was no ring to create a door to go back home, there were no spells he could use, there was only the hen, who clucked at him once more.

"All right. Let's see if you work both ways," Mitch said as he stepped over to the hen and reached out his free hand. When his finger touched her beak, the flash of light returned, and before he knew it, he was back at the house among the coven and the hen was not, she had stayed. His feet were filthy and the bottoms of his pants were soaked through. Bits of dirt were still falling from the folds in his clothing when he opened his hand to show them what he had brought back before they could even ask where he had gone.

"You found it," Bisa said with a smile.

As Mitch rehashed the entire story with dramatic detail like a fevered pitch from a newbie screenwriter, the rest of the coven fell under the spell of the rafkolite's beauty. It was almost too stunning to see, and nearly unbelievable that it was there in the first place. It was like watching someone's dreams finally come true when no one actually thought they would ever be realized.

After Mitch cleaned himself up, the coven finally realized that finding the rafkolite was the easy part. Using it without instructions was going to be an even greater challenge.

CHAPTER 23

The next afternoon, the coven gathered together to discuss what to do about the rafkolite.

They placed it on the dining room table, as if it were a centerpiece to be admired, a fancy bouquet of summer flowers, or a cornucopia with an overabundance of fruit. Mitch could tell that the coven's disposition had grown a little sweeter, cheerier, and more joyful, simply because of all the smiles and laughter. A deeper level of understanding within the group had been reached; they were open, euphorically so, accepting of one another in a tremendously empathic way they had never experienced before. Even Mitch, the most socially awkward and opposed to touch, found himself needing to hug, touch and be close to the others.

They had meant to discuss all things rafkolite, but shortly after they gathered around it, they felt an overwhelming urge to discuss anything but. Ollie brought up Nina, and they reminisced about all the wonderful things they loved about her, sharing their favorite stories and personal interactions with her that they wanted everyone to know about. As the time ticked on, they moved from the dining room to the kitchen, where Avery and Ollie began making a honey cheesecake* for later while Bisa and Mitch sat on the couch and asked questions of each other, questions that no one had bothered to ask either of them in what felt like years.

When the cheesecake was finally baked and fully chilled, they each enjoyed a slice, apart from Ollie, who wouldn't eat it because it wasn't vegan. When the stars were shining in the sky, Mitch lit an incense and wafted the smoke throughout the house. As he passed by the dining room, he was reminded of the rafkolite. *I feel like now is the time to talk about it*, he thought. *You're all in the right frame of mind for it now.*

They brought the rafkolite to their meeting space and discussed how to access its magic.

"Maybe we can connect with it, like it's a spirit," Mitch said.

"Right, good idea," Ollie said. "Treat it like a natural element, like a plant." He was no stranger to talking to plants, so the idea seemed completely normal. It had become more than a quirky habit, like some sort of old recluse with forty-three houseplants. He had a bond with the plant world.

"So, what do you think we should do, Mitch?" Bisa asked as she kneeled down on the floor and motioned for everyone to join her around the rafkolite.

Mitch scratched his head and adjusted his neon-orange knit cap. He thought about how he had managed to find it in the first place and what it felt like. It was something he felt on a cellular level, something that couldn't be described in any book or magical text. He knew what to do. "Here, gimme your hand," he said as he offered his hands out to the coven. "All of us, join hands."

Their hands formed a circle and they could feel the flow. "Focus on the rafkolite. Feel it. Connect with it," Mitch said softly. He waited for a few moments. A few heavy breaths filled theair. Their communal meditative state was a place of quiet contemplation and discovery, a place filled with unspoken visions and the warmth of closeness. Mitch could see it, the essence of the rafkolite in his mind's eye, his witch eye. He could hear it as one would hear the sound of traffic through an open window, only to him, it was much prettier, like the rustle of delicate silk and lace. Had this happened a few months ago, maybe even a few weeks ago, he wouldn't have had the connection he did now, he oh so loved to obsess over his ineptitude. Now the insides of his eyelids were glowing, rife with sight. It was almost as if everything, even the most horrible things, had shaped him to be where he was at this exact moment, leading everyone and connecting to Spirit. And the coven was there to support him.

Some twenty minutes later, the bond had been formed. Mitch was soon too tuned in to lead or instruct them any further. The rest of the coven held the connection and listened to Mitch narrate what he saw and felt.

"It can only be used once," Mitch said aloud, his brow furrowing slightly as if trying to understand a whisper. Time seemed to stand still in an effortless silence as he lingered in meditation, connected to the rafkolite's essence. Even though its vibes were far too faint for the rest of the coven to hear, Mitch was bonded to it, and he heard and felt them all. He saw all the ways that it could be used and how, and he was left with one very important choice: what would *they* use it for? Oh, the things they could do. *It's like a genie offering a single wish*, Mitch thought, acknowledging his grief over Robin Williams's passing when it intruded into his mind. He released it back to the ether. He even asked the rafkolite for a suggestion, but there were no more answers, none that it could give. Only they were able to decide.

What does one do with such a power? They could experiment, give themselves something, something beneficial that would be long lasting, something that would make a difference, whatever that thing would be. Or, the more seemingly *right* thing to do—use it to help reestablish balance, like they had been destined, prophesied, to do. And then the connection to the rafkolite slowly faded, and the rest of the coven felt it as their hands gradually slipped from one another's grasp.

"What next?" Bisa asked.

A few moments passed, and Mitch sat in silence with his eyes closed and his hands in his lap. When he opened his eyes, he was ready to answer.

"I know what we have to do," Mitch said with total certainty, as if he'd known the answer all along. He could've done so many things if he were someone like Leo. But he wasn't Leo, and he wasn't the Mitch from a few months ago either. His thumbs were healed, his soul was strong and his eyes were open. It would've been so easy to fall into the temptation of using it for something selfish—Volustina had refused to erase his traumatic memories, and the rafkolite surely had the power to do that. Only he didn't want that, he didn't *need* that. "I'm going to need Rosemary's ring."

"To go where?" Avery asked, desperately ready to be filled in on the knowledge he had that she didn't.

"It has the ability to perform one magical task, yes, but it's also, basically, like, contagious magic. It's contagious magic in physical form." He was smiling now. "It's how we're going to reestablish balance like we were told we were going to do."

Bisa tilted her head back and felt Mitch's energy. "You want to use it as a beacon of positivity, radiating its energy and influence and essentially balance out into the world," she said with certainty.

"Exactly that," Mitch said. "The rafkolite is, like, the metronome keeping things in order, in time, instead of a bunch of witches witching their way to balance."

"What does that even look like?" Avery asked as she shook her head as if trying to comprehend the infinity of outer space. "We kept hearing about establishing balance, but what does that look like? What do we look like...as a world...you know, what does that mean for our species?" She lifted herself off her heels and sat cross-legged. "But seriously, guys. What *is* balance? I mean, is it here on earth? Or balance in the universe?" She waved her hands in the air in circles. "Is it balance within all of the infinite universe?"

"I don't think we can really think about it in micro or macro terms," Bisa said. "I think we just have to accept whatever it is that is. Maybe it means something that we truly don't understand yet. We're just a small part of a larger plan. Individually, we mean very little in the large scheme of things. Maybe it's just not up to us to know *that.*"

Avery struggled to make sense of everything and was lost in thought.

"So, Mitch," Bisa said, "where are you going to go?"

"I think I know, but not right now," Mitch said. "I feel like it's gonna, like, come to me. Maybe if I sleep on it."

"I wonder if it will affect other planes or timelines, if there really is such a thing," Ollie asked the air.

"What do you mean?" Bisa asked.

Ollie blinked and looked up, almost surprised that someone was listening to him, or that he was actually saying his thoughts out loud. Sometimes he forgot. It was tricky being a Transcendent. "I mean, establishing balance. Is that just here, for us, in this plane? Will doing that here affect something in another plane or timeline, if there is that?"

Bisa shrugged and pursed her lips. "Hmmf! I have *no* idea," she said as he got up and sat in a chair. "But, I bet that's something you and I could figure out. Or at least...dabble in. Just something for a rainy day, maybe!"

CHAPTER 24

Mitch did the first thing that anyone who got their groove back would do—he went shopping. Several clicks later, he found himself with a new wardrobe. He even paid for the expedited shipping, now that he could afford it. Mitch wanted to dress for the occasion. After all, they—whoever they was—always said dress for the job you want, and Mitch wanted to be the witch who helped put the world back in balance but did it with style. A sheer floral Dries van Noten shirt hung loosely on his thin torso, and he wore a pair of slacks from some shop on Etsy, gemstone rings on seven of his fingers, also from Etsy, and a hat and scarf—his own. A kind of elevated bohemian only someone who felt the confidence to wear a brimmed hat could pull off. Someone who stood up straight and looked confident. And he was.

The next evening, after a serious slice of honey cheesecake, Mitch checked the world clock on his phone to see what time it was in Tokyo. *Noon.* For a brief moment, he considered something deeper (literally) and more esoteric, like the Mariana Trench. Thinking that it would sink into the depths and radiate outward to the whole world. In the end, he opted for what made the most sense, a practice that he wasn't very familiar with. Only now wasn't the time, his gut told him. He received the information while he was making adjustments to reopen his online shop on Etsy. A vision of cherry blossoms under the new moon. He could wait—he should wait. Mitch scrolled through the moon app on his phone, found out when the new moon was in April and made a mental note.

The coven continued to meet every morning and every night, practicing ritual magic whenever it seemed fit. They made an altar near the window and prepared it for the new season. Only the altar wasn't the only thing changing with the seasons: each of them was changing as well.

Bisa contemplated writing a book as she placed a few magical textbooks back in the house library during cleaning day, but a story really worth telling, something unlike she'd ever written before. She wanted to write stories that filled a gap she believed existed, stories that needed and had an audience that had been waiting long enough. The spark of her spiritual revolution ignited when she opened the window on the first warm day. After years of living in Chicago, where the cold and merciless winter lasted far longer than even the most die-hard winter fan would ever desire, making a permanent home out of Colorado just didn't feel quite right. She needed more. Her heart and soul craved a new community, a hunger for people who felt and saw things like she did, people who understood her in ways that the coven couldn't. She had grown to care for the coven, a great deal more than she could've ever anticipated, only there was something calling her, another layer of her soul's desire.

Her room had remnants of paint here and there, like some kind of historical site kept intact for tours in the future. She needed to make art again. It wasn't just the weather that had been cold; the warmth she felt from making art had also frozen. When Bisa opened a tube of cobalt blue and squeezed a little out, she choked up a little because it had been so long since she'd painted something besides her self-portrait, which was now burned to ash.

All the cold and snow had Avery longing for spring, mostly because she missed the apiary and her bees. As she looked out over the hills and the mountains during her morning meditation, she felt that she was being pulled somewhere else, to do something different. Avery had always been a wandering spirit, and the winds of wander had begun to blow. *Maybe I need to be more like the bees, maybe I need to seek out new pollen.*

Ollie could feel emotions bubbling to the surface, feelings of grief that he'd never fully processed. It was like the chat with Avery in the bar had unearthed them in a way that he wasn't prepared for. Suddenly, he found himself at a crossroads as he clipped datura blossoms from his indoor garden. His thumb was far too green for it to be a hallucinogenic brought on from his clippings. He knew there was another path just down the road a bit, one he could take if he wanted to, one that would really do the world a bit of good—if he processed a little of his own trauma first. *What does that road look like?* Ollie thought as he took a light sniff of the white flower. *How could I help others with my gifts? Is that what I want to do? Is that what I should do?* The spontaneous meditations were the ones that had always worked best for him.

On the new moon in April, they made a dinner of sweet pea and tomato ravioli with mint pesto and fresh rosemary focaccia, which was really just a vessel for crunchy, flaky salt, something Ollie had become obsessed with after Avery's chocolate chip cookies that he pretended were vegan. He couldn't help it: Muscovado sugar and brown butter do strange things to your brain. They had their own power of influence that could rival any Transcendent.

"You know," Avery said as she took the last bite of her ravioli, "you might just make a vegan out of me yet."

"How are you feeling about going?" Bisa asked Mitch as she sipped red wine.

"Tonight's the night," he replied. "Well, today, I suppose, as it'll be daytime over there."

"Should we all go?" Avery asked as Mitch slipped on Rosemary's ring.

"We don't need to, Mitch can do it," Bisa said.

"You sure you want to go now?" Ollie asked. "You feel confident about where you're headed?"

Mitch nodded. Every word the coven spoke almost made him think they were trying to keep him from going. *But why would they do that? Why would they want that?* Mitch was far more self-assured than he used to be. He was a gemstone that had finally been cut, and he was able to see its beauty and splendor from the outside for the first time. It just might take a little more effort on the coven's part to allow him to be that gem. If he were to wait any longer, he might second-guess himself, and he wanted to make trusting his vibes a more regular practice.

Once everyone finished dinner, Mitch took one final gulp of water and rose from his seat. He used the ring and opened a door to a maze of flowering branches somewhere in Japan, wherever the ring had decided he needed to be based on the intention he'd set in his mind. The coven smiled and waved as he proceeded to enter the bushes.

"See you soon!" Bisa said.

In Japan, the wind was cool and whirling the scent of cherry blossoms, oddly green with subtle honeylike notes. Mitch clawed his way through the branches with the rafkolite in hand, all the way to the light. When he emerged, he found himself in the middle of a large park filled with hundreds and hundreds of people. Mitch looked around, almost wanting to be a tourist for a hot minute. He'd never been anywhere in Asia before. The grounds were covered with people, almost as many people as there were trees. *Okay, now where do I go?* he wondered. He walked, half touristing, half searching for a place for the rafkolite.

He strolled through the beautiful, prim and proper French garden first, and then explored the grounds of the English countryside landscape, where the cherry trees blew in the afternoon winds. He strolled the lawns before finding a large tree surrounded by rocks within the Japanese garden. Without having to think about it, he approached it and instantly knew it was what he was looking for. He'd found the right spot. Mitch took one last look at the rafkolite in his hand and mentally recited his wish to the mineral. After a moment of silence, he decided to speak aloud.

"This is where you're going to be. You'll rest here by this tree, and as Bisa put it, act as a beacon, radiating positive energy out into the world. And your contagious nature will, like, catch on and spread, like a pop song. Then, the whole world will feel it and it'll be part of everyone and everything."

The rafkolite vibrated in his hands, and thoughts that were not his own entered his mind.

...Until of course my power wanes, and the need for balance is necessary once more. But it is still up to mankind to make better choices. It is always about choice and what one chooses to do with the gifts one has...

Mitch was so shocked that he looked like he'd walked in on his own surprise party. *The spell...to become the highest and best version of myself. Gold.* It all seemed to make sense in ways that it never had before. He remembered many things that he'd said recently. They were all true, but one thing stuck out more than the rest. *You're not good for me, you're not good for us. You're not even good for yourself.* Mitch had said that to Leo, and it was as much about Mitch as it was about Leo, maybe even a little more. A certain awareness had accompanied his words in that moment.

Let me speak the truth... Mitch thought as he recalled the incantation of the spell. Parts of the recent past filled his mind as he thought about the next portion of the spell: *let me see the truth.* Mitch remembered the time he had spent with his totem animal, the inexplicable Australian frog who refused to sugarcoat anything, not because the frog wanted to hurt Mitch's feelings or make him feel worse than he already did, but because it was a necessary step in his growth, a catalyst for the change he so desperately needed. *What kind of person are you?...A fucking good one,* the frog had told him. *Do you believe that?*

I don't know, Mitch said. And he didn't. But at that moment, he saw the truth about himself, right there in that very lie. He did know, and the answer was no...he didn't believe it. Everything began to look a little clearer, as if a dense fog had finally evaporated. His soul was running short on patience. He was lucky it had happened when it had. *Are you going to wait your entire life to think differently?* his soul would ask, but Mitch had never heard it—until recently. He thought about the final part of the incantation—*hear the truth of others*—and clicked his tongue as he evoked all the incidents where he had waded through the haze of uncertainty and ambiguity, and all the times he just hadn't heard the truth when it was so blatantly obvious.

The strongest memory was of Bisa when he returned to the coven.

You're glowing, she had said. *Mitch Wickleby, back with the coven, with a fire I've never seen.* He wasn't deaf, he was always listening, but he just hadn't been hearing things. He needed to hear, really hear, using more than just his ears. He needed to hear with his heart, his soul and his spirit. And now he could. Because of this new kind of hearing, he was able to hear what Leo was really saying to him on the doorstep. When he finally heard the truth, he saw the truth as he looked at Leo, and in that truth, he saw something that he hadn't in the past— despair, sadness and even a little fondness for that kind of hopelessness. Maybe it was because Leo reminded him too much of himself that it was hard to acknowledge and easy to overlook. But when that shift finally happened, and he finally emerged from his self-made cave, his anxious habits and coping mechanisms began to collapse under the weight of his new self. It was heavier, more substantial, harder to knock down and much more valuable.

If Mitch had had the choice, he absolutely would have chosen not to go through more than half the things he'd gone through, especially the traumas he'd experienced since joining the coven. But life is funny that way. When he'd finally hit rock bottom, there was no one to help him out but himself, and all the horrible experiences that he would've liked to not endure had trained him, given him the foundation and the strength to get where he was now. His spiritual growth was always going to happen whether he liked it or not, and it had no plans to stop. It couldn't be smothered with more trauma or gaslit away by some psychic vampire, it was there for the long haul, and now that he could see it, he wouldn't let it go.

With so much clarity flooding his mind, it was inevitable that he began to question and reevaluate everything else in his life, even his journey as a witch. *Why did I even attempt the ritual? For what purpose? What did I really care about? Why did I decide to use the rafkolite for the greater good rather than for myself? Maybe I'm just a good person. I didn't have much of a life...Wouldn't anyone who was as bored and uninspired as I was decide to use it for themselves? Wouldn't most people? What makes me different?*

Mitch returned his attention to the rafkolite on the ground before taking a cursory look around to see if anyone had been watching him. His eyes lowered to the spot where he had placed the rafkolite and took notice of the fact that it had begun to melt like molten lava, only at a rapid pace. It split into small streams, gliding into the rocks like roots until it was completely gone. The rafkolite had been used; the magic had been cast.

Mitch stood there next to the tree in the middle of the park and took a few moments to himself. With the uncountable number of people, the cool breeze blowing the subtle green scent of flowers, the damp spring ground, the sound of children, laughter and life, there was no doubt that he had found the right spot and made the right choice.

It was over, it was all finally over. The coven had completed their mission, fulfilled the prophecy, and moved energies back towards a state of balance. And it seemed like it had only begun. So much had happened in such a short time that he wondered how his brain had been able to keep up. Mitch finally understood that all his traumas reminded him that life is a wonderful, great and irreplaceable privilege.

Mitch walked around the park aimlessly until he noticed a group of tourists eating some kind of food from a shop across the street. He bought himself some red bean taiyaki and ate it as he strolled through the busy streets.

He finished quickly, thinking that the coven was surely waiting for him to return. He was just there to leave the rafko-lite, not become a tourist. The wind had picked up, and clouds began to cloud the sky. He found himself in the middle of a large group of people that practically carried him down the street like a branch caught in a riptide. It was busy. He took it as a sign that it was time to return. He found a place where it was safe to use the ring, and made it back to the coven a few minutes later.

Mitch took off the ring and set it on the table next to the couch.

"How'd it go?" Bisa asked, knowing full well that everything was fine and it was finished.

"It's done. It melted right in front of me right after I stated my intention," Mitch said as he reached up to scratch his head. "I guess that means we did it, right? Everything Nina and Volustina said that we were supposed to do, we actually did?"

"I guess so," Bisa answered.

"Wow," Avery said as she contemplated the whole idea of it being over. "It's all gonna change, ideally for the better."

"So, what do we do now? I mean now that we're finished?" Ollie asked.

Bisa shrugged. "I guess we keep doing what we're doing— that is, if we want to."

"What do you mean?" Avery asked.

Bisa took a deep breath. "Well, we were brought together for a reason, and that reason has been satisfied. The coven wasn't meant to be our *identity*, or our *permanent state of be-ing*, and if it isn't, what does our future look like? Do we return to the world we left behind with the gifts that we have? Do we meet like old friends, only for events or special tasks? Are there special tasks? Will there be? Imagine…What do we want? Each of us? I guess we're all going to have to ask ourselves that, and then also figure out what that looks like together. Do we remain a coven?"

"Shouldn't we?" Avery asked. "I mean, there are lots of other covens, right? They're all doing their thing somewhere, right?"

Bisa nodded and took a seat and crossed her legs. "Yes, that's true. But, from what I understand, they all function however they want to function. There is no right or wrong way. We were a very special case, given a very special task, one that has been fulfilled. So, yes—we are a coven, and we can continue. But we can decide what that looks like."

Bisa was lost in thought for a moment, and her eyes drifted out into space. When she returned, she rose from her seat. "It's not something we have to decide right now. Why don't we talk about it after dinner tomorrow night?" she suggested. "If you'll excuse me, I'm going to go meditate for a little bit."

Bisa returned to her room and shut the door, where she was alone with her thoughts. The thoughts that she had no answers to and new thoughts that made her a little melancholy. She lit a pile of incense and wafted it around her to prime her space. She reached up to the blue kyanite necklace that hung at her chest and rubbed it gently between her fingers. She lowered her head as she focused on deeper meditation, a state that seemed to be calling to her. Bisa knew by now that when feelings like that arose, it was best to pay attention to them. So she did. She parted her lips and began to breathe in through her nose and out through her mouth.

Then there were visions—circumambient.

A rush of hot and cold and all the small variants in between. Like a movie with a hundred different plots and genres with thousands of story lines that seemed to play all at once, they flashed before her and seemed to burn deep inside her, past her physical body, and her mind, and everything beyond. Bisa shivered in a way that one would in the silence before a scare.

Visions from Source itself straight to Bisa, displayed in full-color geometry of spirit.

Massive light flares and plumes of streaming magma hurling out into space. Melting ice caps. The death of a star. Debris. Matter. Energy. Movement. Earthquakes. Laughter. Ego. Riots.

Cake. Surfing. Harpists. Permanent, irreversible, inevitable change. Universal change—from the places in space where mystery is abundant.

Suddenly, it all made sense. *We don't end…but we will. That is the change…that is the prophesied balance we achieved.* Everything looked and felt different, and her perspective on the world shifted. Never had things seemed so…manufactured, so man-made, from the construct of time to norms, values, countries, roles, class, money, economics, beauty, fashion, law, worthiness, work and the hustle culture that is built on a sense of urgency. All the things that humans recognize as part of being human, even *art*…all of it—invented. All of it alive because humans had agreed that they have life and a place in the world. But that, of course, was the world's heartbeat, a system of values that benefited the ones obsessed with establishing and expanding a colony with a system of insurance that benefited some, but not all. The system, with all its anachronisms, and its thirst for power, greed and survival, was easy to control through the archetype of the Emperor. Structure. Ideas. Systems.

The banished, ostracized and oppressed members of the world who struggle...are forced to stay that way, their beautiful, creative and Empress-like minds deemed too wild for the system...are whittled down to exist in the only place suitable within the construct: the bottom, where ideas, imagination and creativity are never fully realized because there is no opportunity, no way through the gate lined with gatekeepers who decide what is what, and why, based on nothing other than *it has always been this way*. The richness that exists within the energy of that fertile ingenuity is often denied by the order and fixed authority who above all else...dislike change and condemn liberation.

What good are social constructs if they don't promote the peaceful union of all? They have a place, but are they meant to be absolutes? Are they meant to never be challenged? If they are alive, are they not allowed to change as all human beings on this place do from the moment they are born? In all the countless years of life on earth, humans have yet to find a way to marry the Empress and the Emperor, give structure as well as nurture. And who are we but pieces of stardust in the vast cosmos, insignificant grains of sand in a universe that has no boundaries?

Right as the complete realization of our absolute inconsequentiality became as clear as air, Bisa heard the sound of her own heartbeat throbbing in her chest. She opened her eyes and caught her breath. She raised her hand to her heart as if she'd been pierced straight through it.

What is the point? a small whisper came trickling in from the back of her mind. It didn't matter to her, though. She knew the point. To give life value. Rich with all the things that actually matter, the things everyone had lost touch with, or weren't able to achieve, or were prevented from doing, the things that were lost in the dark, or hidden by their ghost-filled traumas. Life was meant to be lived. She almost wanted to laugh because it sounded so generic and borderline commercial. It was also one of the truest things she knew. A life lived is not one without pain or loss, but one that includes them.

They don't know what I know, Bisa thought as she rose to her feet and looked out the window. The balance…was the end. But it wasn't for anyone to know. She could do no more than what they had already done…and it was exactly what they were supposed to do.

April 30th, 2022

It was just before dawn, and the energy of the new moon in Taurus was in the air. The new moon was also in Aries, if one followed sidereal astrology instead of the tropical system, but Leo didn't know the difference, nor did he care, nor could he feel it. When he arrived at the end of the driveway to 444 Smoky Quartz Drive, he did feel something that had nothing to do with the astrological energy of the universe. He listened to the stillness of the grounds and studied the empty windows for signs of any early risers. If he hadn't known who owned the house, and hadn't once lived there with an entire coven of witches from whom he was now estranged, he could've easily believed it was vacant.

Maybe it's some sort of trick. An enchantment or whatever, Leo thought as he noticed the bare windows without any curtains. There was a curiousness to it, like seeing a conch shell abandoned on the beach. He looked down at the ground and realized he was standing in the same spot he had been two years ago. Then, there was a box of his things they'd left out for him to come by and collect, things he'd tossed into the trash. He could smell spring in the air, with winter's chill riding on puffs of cool wind.

Leo took a step forward and felt no resistance. His eyes darted up to the house to see if he had triggered any sort of magical alarms they might have set for him. But there was only silence and a brightening sky. A few more steps forward and he knew for certain that there were no enchantments, he was free to access the property. Whatever spell they had cast had been removed, or its defenses had eventually worn thin.

The closer Leo got to the house, the more aware of his appearance he became. He was dressed far more adult than he'd ever been in his entire life. It had been that way for a while now. His closet no longer had worn sneakers full of holes where his toes broke through, or oversized tie-dye T-shirts that fell to the top of his thighs. He was even wearing matching socks. His face was clean shaven, but with a little scruff, since he hadn't shaved since the day before. He wasn't entirely fresh, but it was a considerable difference from how anyone would have remembered him.

When he arrived at the front door, all he heard was the song of the morning birds on the crisp breeze. He lifted his hand to knock, even though it was so early that it was likely no one was awake. *Do I just go inside?* Leo wrestled with the idea of inviting himself in, still feeling a little entitled to do so, even though he knew deep down it was completely unjustified. He didn't even have a key. Nevertheless, he knocked three times. The longest minute passed.

Leo knocked a few more times, harder—*Thud! Thud! Thud! Thud!*

After the second set of rappings, he reached down and grabbed the door handle. He gave it a good twist. It turned. His hand squeezed the handle a little tighter before he gently pushed the door open. The cool morning breeze rustled through the doorway and tousled his hair. There was nothing but an empty hallway. There were no shoes, or coats, or muddy footprints from whatever Ollie had tracked in from the garden. He looked back over his shoulder. Nothing but nature. There were no bikes by the door, there were no vehicles outside.

Maybe they just moved things around. It's been two years, Leo thought as he entered and shut the door behind him. He proceeded upstairs quietly, respectfully, only to realize the only one he was respecting was the house itself. It was empty.

"Hello?" Leo uttered softly.

No one answered. They were gone.

Leo searched the house. He searched every room, looking for something, anything, but there wasn't as much as a note. His face puckered and his throat tightened. It took him by surprise more than anything else; he hadn't expected that kind of reaction at all. He rested in the living room for a moment as he tried to make sense of the last couple of years and how he had gotten to be where he was now, standing in an empty house with a life void of all things that make life worth living.

Without even realizing where he was going, he found himself in Mitch's old room. Oddly enough, it smelled familiar. If Leo closed his eyes and breathed in slowly, he could still smell all the yarn that smelled undeniably like Mitch. He stood there in the middle of the room, watching all the memories that filled his head. Then, he felt it before he saw it: a tiny crocheted hat in the corner of the closet. Leo walked over and retrieved it, slowly and full of discomfort.

He sighed as his fingers ran over the yarn, but that was all he could do. He didn't know what he was feeling, he just knew he didn't like it. He picked at the frizzy edges of the yarn as he thought back to when he'd first met the coven, when his biggest accomplishment was being able to hold down a job long enough to cover rent. He sighed again, and as the breath left his lungs, he realized just how alone he really was. *What am I gonna do with this?* Leo asked himself, feeling silly and sentimental that he was already stuffing the hat into his back pocket. It didn't stop him.

Leo looked out the window and into the periwinkle-blue sky. The sun was about to rise. He found his way to Bisa's door, the only closed door in the entire home—house—as if even her room somehow didn't want anything to do with him. He scratched his chin and debated whether he should enter. *She's not in there…You know that, right?* he asked himself as he opened the door. As expected, more emptiness. Although her room seemed to be the most barren of them all. There wasn't even dust. It was as if everything, down to the last trace of a memory, had been cleansed into oblivion. Without Bisa, the room was unrecognizable. He crossed his arms in front of him and approached the window, where he watched the sky grow more orange with every passing second.

A swatch of green fabric jutted out from the closed window where it met the windowsill. When he inspected it more closely, he realized there was more. It was a shroud, and it spilled down the side of the house and billowed in the morning air. *The shroud spell.* The only other evidence in the house besides the hat that the coven had ever lived there. Leo pressed his forehead to the glass and looked down at the shroud, his fingertips pressed into the windowsill supporting his weight. His thoughts rushed back to the shroud that Nina had placed in the window at the Barrow House in Louisiana. It was red. He wondered for a moment what the significance of the green was.

Perhaps if he had paid a little more attention, he'd have known. Only…what did any of it matter now?

Leo closed his eyes, and his eyelids were met with warmth. The sun had peeked over the hills, and it splashed across his face. He opened his eyes and stared directly into the sun. He didn't care how many sunspots his vision would suffer as a result. His eyes were fixed on the morning sun, radiant and brand new, something he so desired to be, so much that it left him with nothing and no one. He looked into the auric glow of the shimmering sun. Leo knew what that was: *something I will never, ever be.* He scoffed as he remembered how Bisa had told him she'd had a dream where they watched the sunrise together. His breath fogged up the glass. As he waited for the fog to vanish under the gentle, delicate heat of the morning sun, he knew it was too late. It had been too late, probably for quite some time.

His selfishness had cost him every bit of hope he'd had and didn't truly deserve. *I wonder if they'll ever come back here*, he thought as his eyes dropped from the rising sun to the floor. Maybe he could wait, find a place close by in Denver. He'd be ready for them when they came back. It finally hit him: it was an awfully, wearisomely, exhaustingly long road to unfucking himself, and the end was a place he would never be. At least not anytime soon.

Ten minutes later, he was finally ready to leave. Only he had no idea where he was going or what he was going to do. He thought about returning to Louisiana, even though there was nothing for him there. The gas station wouldn't miss him if he just up and quit and moved out of state. He squinted at the thought of returning, but it seemed to make the most sense. It was what he knew. He didn't care whether Bisa had called in a favor with the police like she'd threatened to do. Maybe that would be for the good of everyone if she did.

As he left the house, he saw memory after memory, even of things he'd never paid attention to in the first place. He shivered in the cold air and set out to endure the life he'd made, so carelessly, without hope and without happiness.

Ollie fell in love with the interesting seasonal changes in Colorado and never wanted to leave. He had returned home for a short while after the coven parted officially. He didn't fully understand how much he liked it in Colorado until he was ascending into the air on a plane and watching it disappear from his window seat. He wasn't looking forward to returning home. This wouldn't be a visit for pleasure, or for business, but for work. Not the kind of work that pays the bills, but the kind of spiritual work that allows someone to grow.

It was time he did a little work on grief. He needed to deal with the death of his brother. Ignoring it until it didn't exist wasn't going to work anymore, nor would it do anyone any favors—not if he was going to enter the business of helping other people, which he suddenly felt compelled to do, although he didn't know how. He just knew that by exploring grief, he would find the answer by the time he had to check in for his return flight.

Somewhere around 40,000 feet, he started to pick up on someone's thoughts, but they were more like a foreign energetic language than actual thoughts. The person turned out to be the one sitting next to him in 15B. He had been so focused on what his healing would look like that he hadn't even noticed that the person had been trying to get his attention in the cleverest ways possible—well, clever to them. Interestingly enough, it wasn't one of the many attempts to get his attention that drew him in, it was when they picked up their book on psychism and pretended to read it that Ollie noticed.

"You know, everyone's a little psychic," Ollie said right as the fasten seatbelt sign chimed above them.

They folded their book over their lap and turned to Ollie. "I'm sorry, what did you say?"

"I was talking about your book. I just said that everyone is a little psychic." Ollie looked over the features of their face and saw himself getting to know them throughout life. *That can't be right. They're a passing acquaintance on a plane. I'll never see this person again.*

A look of interest washed over their face. "That's kind of what this book is all about. It has a lot of exercises to help you learn how to develop that sort of thing. Have you heard about the Akashic records?"

Ollie smiled a little. *They're not even a witch.* "I have…" He saw visions of himself with the person in all sorts of places doing a variety of different things. It was like being haunted by the future instead of the past, but by a friendly ghost. Ollie adjusted himself in his seat to make chatting more comfortable. That chat lasted the entire flight, and the two of them learned a lot: they'd both moved to California when they were three, they both had a love for photography and had nearly abandoned it for something new—Ollie for gardening, them for electronic music production. There was as much in common as there were things that were different, which was something that Ollie always enjoyed about anyone he was interested in, as few people as that had been. He didn't want a carbon copy of himself. Some things were okay, but not everything.

Ollie chose not to try to read their thoughts or influence them in any way. In fact, that never even occurred to him, at least not until the moment they deboarded the plane and said goodbye. He was able to get a phone number by the sheer fact that he no longer had social media, deeming it as primarily marketing for toxicity with rose-colored filters. Fortunately they had a 303 area code, which meant they didn't live far.

He thought about the plane ride straight up until he decided to go to the cemetery to visit his brother's grave. He hadn't been there since the funeral, and the last funeral he had attended was for Nina. It wasn't something he wanted to experience on a regular basis, not even in remembrance. Being a Transcendent didn't mean you were impervious to pain sometimes—you just got more of it, or got better at hiding it. He didn't really want either.

When he started down the pebble path, with its immaculately trimmed hedges, he wondered if he would be able to connect with his brother, Hugo. *What if I don't want to? What if I don't want him to come through?* He might not have a choice. He couldn't always control his connection to the spirit world, although he was getting better at it.

He was able to find Hugo's grave without even having to double-check the location. He remembered. It looked just as he'd remembered it, even though he hadn't been able to really remember until he set eyes on it. There was a deafening silence in the air, and the cemetery was empty, apart from Ollie and the other lingering spirits that knew better than to show up at a time like this. He whispered something under his breath and lost himself in the memory of their youth. He wished things had been different, but they weren't.

Ollie wanted to cry, so he did. It didn't last as long as he thought it would, and he immediately felt much better afterward. He sat down on the freshly mown grass next to the grave and invited Hugo into the space. He never appeared, not like everyone else had. Ollie didn't really know why. But he felt him, and could even hear him, in a subtle kind of way, like one would hear an echo in a canyon.

He spent an hour there at the grave. And he experienced a new kind of communication, one beyond physical, psychic and everywhere in between, and from that communication, he found his peace, and Hugo was there for it.

Ollie had a lot to think about as he left the cemetery sometime in the early twilight. Things just looked a little different, and they felt even more different. Whether it was feeling someone's pain from across the street or getting a juice, his life had shifted.

When he returned to Colorado, he had planned out what he was going to do by the time he got out of the Lyft and back to his apartment. Maybe it was the luck of having a driver who said nothing other than to ask for his name to make sure he had the right patron. He'd stared out the window the entire time, watching the world go by as they cruised into town. The truth was that while he sat in the back seat, he had an explosion of ideas, some that made no sense and some that seemed wildly exciting but weren't practical. Once they zoomed out of the fast lane and took the exit off the highway, he crossed off considering going back to school for a degree in mental health counseling. It would take far too much money and way too much time—there were better options for what he was best suited for.

Ollie ended up wearing many hats. His most profound role was in the North American Advisory, reorganized with and revised for the new age, something he wished the States would do to their democracy and constitution. It was just a supporting role, much like that of Per, or Nix, or even Nina. Bisa assumed the role as the leader, with Grace by her side and Ruby occupying the last final seat. But it would be open for more witches to have an active participation. There wouldn't be just a small group deciding things for a large mass of people.

They might have to make unpopular decisions from time to time—what leadership doesn't?—but the Advisory would always be invested in the witches for whom it was meant to serve the greatest good.

Their new Symposium room was on the ground floor of an old bakery with white tiled walls, exposed wooden rafters and a colorful mosaic floor. Ollie first thought about turning it into a vegan bakery, but decided that would be a little too ambitious to take on along with everything else he wanted to do.

Ollie had a tremendous gift. He was a spiritual healer, and he felt truly fulfilled only when he was able to share that with people in pain. So, when he applied for a part-time job as office assistant at a funeral home in Denver, it seemed like a good idea. It wasn't—it was a great idea. It didn't matter that he had to do the banal, tedious paperwork and data entry every now and then; what he found was that he knew just what to say and when to say it when people came in for whatever loss brought them in. It didn't last forever. Nothing does. Everything ends.

He'd been at his job nearly seven months when he realized he had his own client list of people who were seeing him privately for mediumship and spiritual readings. He avoided trying to build his business via social media because he couldn't figure out a way to make it work without a scam account being made, like he'd heard from so many other people. The clients found him. He went to yoga classes, art classes, garden stores, bookstores, coffeehouses and all the places where regular people exist, and he just found a way to connect, in the most nonintrusive way. He opened up to them with a word of wisdom that resonated with them. He quit his part-time job once he couldn't juggle both anymore. He saw his partner in the off times, the one he'd met on the plane, and slowly but surely, he saw all the visions come true.

It was a Thursday, one of the days when he for some reason had the strongest intuition, when he received a text from Mitch. He sat in the plush gray chair he had nestled into a collection of plants next to the sunny corner window of his apartment. It was a jungle, and it was as soothing and rejuvenating as it looked. *I knew I'd hear from him today!* Ollie thought as he opened the text message, something that he never did while he was in the chair, but did just this one time.

Hey Ollie! How've you been? Guess what I did today? I had my first day of classes! It went really well!

Ollie smiled the widest smile. Mitch always assumed and expected that everyone was as unorganized and forgetful as he was, the same way that not everyone can keep track of the dozens upon dozens of passwords modern life makes one keep track of. Only, Ollie remembered. Ollie even knew that Mitch's last class ended at seven, and he wanted to give Mitch a little time to wrap up.

Mitch actually had finished an hour earlier, because he was now on California time. He had moved out to Idyllwild and used the money he'd received to pursue what he was most passionate about, and it had nothing to do with being a witch. No magic was involved at all, other than the magic of art, which allowed Mitch to not only grow even more than he had already but also to heal on deeper levels than he expected. If one isn't healing in some way, is it even art? There was even some symmetry between the Symposium and Mitch's school. Mitch bought an old printing house and turned it into an art studio. It had everything he needed and wanted and all the things he wanted to share with others, including a full course on knitting and needlework as well as his signature course on mixed-media knitwork. He went into the school a bit naively, thinking he would be doing all the teaching, but it was a fantastically romanticized version of what it actually was. Soon enough, he had a staff of four, all teaching a variety of mediums.

Mitch was happy now that he had found his power. That power was not magic, but that shouldn't suggest that he didn't use it—he did, as much as any artist would use elemental magic. It was a lot. He just no longer felt the pressure and anxiety that came along with it when it arrived in his life. It was now more of an accent, like a cocktail at the end of a long week or the bottle of champagne to celebrate an event. He would always be a witch, and there wasn't a day that went by that he didn't think about the time he had received tough love from an Australian frog. He carried that memory around with him for the times when he felt his mood starting to shift. It always managed to remind him who he was and where he was.

A scant few months later, he secured a show at a small gallery on the outskirts of L.A. It was something to celebrate, because he had spent every waking day since his arrival back in California trying to convince the art world that his art needed to be seen. It was the outrageous amount of rejection from the galleries that caused him to feel a little guilty about giving Bisa such a hard time about her writing. He had no idea if it was his talent or the spell he did for a little success that secured him the show at the gallery; it was probably a little bit of both. Magic, he learned, likes it when you do the work and meet it halfway.

Near the entrance by the large floor-to-ceiling windows, Mitch was browsing the conversations of the guests in the gallery, all giving their opinions about the art, when he noticed a familiar face: Jace, the random stranger from that weird party he had gone to when he was in the middle of a mental break. He instantly felt a rush of excitement and scurried over to meet him.

"What are you doing here?" Mitch asked with a large grin.

"I work across the street," Jace said. "I stop by the café next door for lunch sometimes, saw your name in the window and figured I had to come by and at least say hi." He was older than Mitch remembered, with a little more gray, and he was wearing the ring Mitch accidentally left in his car, but the only thing Mitch cared about was whether he wanted to go out sometime. Mitch had learned that he needed to give himself more credit, accept that he had flaws, that he was not just what had happened to him, that things take time, that no one has it easy, and there are no shortcuts, even with magic—not really. Only with the eyes that he had now was he able to see how low his self-esteem had been and yet how he'd had such an enormous ego at the same time. What a strange and difficult life that had made for.

Jace and Mitch were officially dating before Mitch finished out his first month teaching art. He thought, *This has to be the real deal—we bought an aquarium together*. It was more of a mutual gift, one that they shared the expense for. Jace seemed amused that Mitch wanted to get saltwater fish, even though they both knew that it was far too much upkeep for Mitch to handle without waking up to dead fish. Mitch loved how amiable Jace's eyes were when they had disagreements. It didn't matter what kind of nonsense Mitch was perpetuating, Jace always had a way of grounding him. It was a good match, one without expectations or demands, and the sex was good too.

Bisa found her way to the desert—Santa Fe, to be exact—but it was never meant to be forever. A pull would eventually lead her to the south of Spain (on some evenings she felt it might be northern Italy), but for where she was in life now, New Mexico was where she needed to be. Near the edge of town, in her Spanish-style house built with and around the natural environment, Bisa ensconced herself in her garden of cacti, sunflowers and colorful wildflowers with a clear and meditative mind. She would meditate there every morning and every evening, when the air was cooler. It felt complete, but neither her home nor her garden were ever truly finished. The moment something is finished or complete, its life is done and there can be no more growth, no more expansion. Bisa needed her home to reflect her ever-changing state of being. After all, the journey is always more fun than the destination.

Before she knew it, her garden was filled with more than decorative plants. It was soon populated with people once she found something she hadn't even known she needed in her life—community. The coven was like family, but as she grew, her soul craved something extra, something the coven alone would never be able to fill. She introduced herself to the few witches who lived within driving distance, but oddly enough, they weren't the ones she connected with the most. Her community was mostly women, all of them artists in some form or another. It was completely by accident that two of them

happened to be from Nigeria, which was both unexpectedly re-
freshing and comforting. They loved the heat, and exploring
desert trails was one of Bisa's forms of therapy. While hiking
the dusty paths she often let her mind wander, which was a welcome experience for someone with such psychic talent,
someone who was naturally *on*. It allowed her to unplug, much
like painting and writing, which she never abandoned again.

Her home was old, and drenched in sun, and although it had
natural beauty, it was she who gave it life. Lavender and tall
wispy desert grass crowded the front door in beautiful bundles,
and sharp juniper bushes lined the walls. Her entryway was
filled with large amethyst geodes and chunks of kyanite, and
the backyard overlooked the vast array of magnificent landscapes: staggering foothills, deep canyons and even patches of
forest here and there, with too-good-to-be-true views of the
Sangre de Cristo Mountains even on days without plentiful sun.
It was a place that made people who passed down her quiet
street stop and wonder, *Who lives in that magical place?*

And there was magic, a great deal of it, as she pursued the
career path of a professional reader and medium, something she
and Ollie shared. She limited herself to only a few days a week,
canceling when she needed to, something clients never understood. She imagined it was similar to not knowing how your
life is going to change after you've had children until you actually have children. Self-care was highest on her list, and her
community understood that, being sensitive artists themselves,
artists beyond paint and the spirit of brush and pen. They made
art out of the way they lived.

Every Sunday she had dinner with her Nigerian friends,
where they all brought dishes they knew and loved and always
had dessert. Bisa became incredibly skilled at making esquites

after introducing it to her dinner menu one evening, and it was all they asked about from that point on. With practice comes perfection. She found that the secret to elevating it from good to great was really just copious amounts of lime.

But Monday was her most introspective and sequestered day; from noon to five she did nothing but write. When she sat down at her desk, her keyboard knew that it was in for a workout. Her writing habit was sacrosanct, and it was that very attitude that allowed her to complete a few books within a few years' time. Some were novels, some were nonfiction books on psychism and magic, all of them were inspired—and all were self-published. The person she always thanked first in her acknowledgments was Nina.

"Damn, that's good" was the last thing the man said as he left Avery's Apiary in Portland, Maine, a wooden sample spoon full of blueberry cinnamon honey in his hand. It had to be good, for fourteen dollars a jar, and it wasn't the fact that it was enchanted—of course it was—Avery just had a way with the bees.

"It's the bees! I just take what they gift to me and share it," she said with a wink.

Avery was always guided by Spirit and had trusted it her entire life, but when she felt her spirit darkening, she knew that when the opportunity to split from the coven arrived, she needed to take it. If she were to be completely honest, she had no idea how she'd ended up in Portland. It all seemed like kind of a blur, like when you wake up from a vivid dream and your entire world seems upside down. She took a few beekeeping classes, found herself a business manager and opened Avery's Apiary. They did the books and boring things, and Avery managed the bees and did the creative production.

People started to take notice of her raw, unfiltered honey (with a little help from the enchantment), but it was her blueberry cinnamon honey they kept coming back for—ironically, the only product that wasn't enchanted. It was hard work, busy work, but she loved it. She treated the jars of honey like dressed candles, each with their own recipe and intended purpose, and each one crafted with care with her own magical process. It was delicious spread on toast. It was raw and packed with healthy enzymes, so it was a health food, right?

At the beginning of every month, she woke up extra early, prepared a special batch of enchanted honey and mailed one jar to each member of her former coven, custom-made and tailored to their needs. Whenever a bee would cross their path and land on their hand, they knew Avery's package would arrive soon.

Everything changed for her when she got to Maine, even her physical appearance. The unnatural colors were absent from her hair, and she wore the same clothes most of the time because she was always working. She grew incredibly fond of the sun, but developed an even stronger connection with the moon, especially when it was full and in Aries. It was then she felt the most magical, the most powerful. Even the sun felt a little cold in her presence during that time. She loved magic and used it when she could or when she had to, or even sometimes when she just felt like seeing a little more lightning in a summer storm.

It made for a nice walk through her neighborhood when every single cat and dog flocked to Avery like she had treats in her pockets. It reminded her of the empowering experience she had had in the zoo with the lion, how she had connected to it in such a way that seemed impossible. If she hadn't been so busy, she might have gotten a pet, maybe a cat. She was a witch, after all. But Avery's Apiary was her pet, her baby, and that was enough.

Avery took her first vacation a few years later, closing the store for three weeks while she took a round-the-world trip to Italy, Greece, Norway, Cambodia, Japan and New Zealand, where she collected rocks, stones and other natural objects that she could use in spells. Spellwork was more of a hobby, one that someone enjoys in bursts, like a Netflix binge. In a binge state all she seemed to do was blink, and before she knew it, twelve hours had passed, three spells had been cast, an invocation had been recited, an unextinguishable campfire was burning, two elixirs had been made, along with a spell jar and a charm bag, and she had no idea where the voices were coming from. Some witches might make a joke and call that chaos magick, but Avery called it her day off.

Bisa connected to Spirit and opened her palms, and a swirl of energy rose from her hands and into the air. In the vast cosmos where her spirit was never hungry, she looked for something beyond what she knew, something beyond her known experience. The maintenance of psychic sight required regular check-ins and ensured a well-oiled slip into the ether, and Bisa had been exercising that muscle for longer than any witch she'd known. However, nothing could've prepared her for what she would encounter, and nothing is more exciting, more frightening, than discovering you have found what you've always been looking for. Her psychic eye was wider than it ever had been, and she saw everything that was possible for her to see.

On the days when she fasted or ate very little, her intuition was on fire and she could see the entire universe if she looked the right way. At first, it seemed like more of the same, the way one settles into a new job in the same industry, but soon enough she felt something different about her journey. Her messages were more than messages from spirits, they were spirits *and* people from other timelines, on other planes of existence. Some she couldn't communicate with at all because of language barriers, and she had to rely strictly on her skills of empathy to connect. It was all so fascinating that sometimes she had to set limits for herself. On the days when she discovered something special, she'd fast without meaning to, so wired that she would forget to eat. The whole experience made her want to share it with others.

When she no longer felt so new to the technique, she decided it was time to take on a mentee. No sooner had she considered it than a client asked to be one. This was a client of hers from the past, who had experienced an awakening accompanied by severe headaches and vivid dreams, and knew that her career in marketing wasn't what she was supposed to be doing. Within a few hours of her last reading with Bisa, she'd quit her job and put her trust in her spirit. It was the scariest and most illogical thing she'd ever done. Bisa, being the loving teacher that she was, accepted. There were tears in the woman's eyes when she arrived at Bisa's door, but they were filled with joy.

"What makes you so certain that this journey is for you?" Bisa asked with care in her eyes. "I'm not asking because I don't believe in you. You have a tremendous gift—I've always thought so. I ask only because your life is very full right now, and I would hate for you to let go of all that you've built based on a fleeting thought."

The woman's mouth dropped open as if she'd said something unfathomable. "It's not fleeting, I've ignored it. I've never been so sure about something in my entire life. *This*...whatever *this* is, is what I'm supposed to be doing." The woman gave a smile as she flashed back to one of the first readings she had had with Bisa. "Do you remember what you told me when we first met?"

Bisa shook her head and pursed her lips. "I wish I could. I tend to forget *a lot* when I'm reading for others. It's not really me who's saying things, it comes from somewhere else, so I don't recall very much."

"That makes sense," the woman said, and she seemed lost in thought for a moment before she continued. "When I sat down, right before we began, you looked at me, right into my eyes, and said, 'You're going to be a reader one day.'"

Bisa laughed. "I did? What did you think?"

"I thought you were crazy. *Crazy*. Or like one of those salespeople who tell you that you'd look great in those jeans even though you know they're cut for people three sizes smaller. I was making a hundred twenty thousand a year, so thinking about becoming a spiritual reader and leaving all that behind seemed like something an insane person would say or do. Which, I guess in that way, I'm insane," the woman said with a laugh. "But you were right. You *are* right. This is what I want to do, this is what I'm supposed to do. That doesn't mean that I'm not scared—of course I am. I'm leaving behind a lot that I worked really hard for. It feels right.

"The world isn't going to shut down if I don't develop another brand identity and marketing strategy so I can deliver sales results to the VP. Someone else can fill that spot—we're a dime a dozen. We should...do what we want. I mean, fuck tradition, right? Our lives can't all be KPI and expense tracking, not if we're not happy doing that. We should be able to live how we want to live, and we shouldn't be shamed for wanting to be happier. I just know I have other gifts."

"Everyone is psychic," Bisa said. "We all have that gift. Some have it a little stronger than others. Your gift is blinding."

And the woman wasn't a witch, she was from Idaho.

I never thought I'd be a mentor in that way, but I found more value in watching someone succeed under my tutelage than I ever thought I would. When something speaks to you, you must listen. It's what told me to write, it's what told me to teach, it's what brought me to Louisiana, where my life changed and brought me to where I am now, doing what I am now, with the strength I have now.

Everyone has the ability to connect with their intuition, to travel into the beyond. Even you. We just don't always listen. We're not taught to listen, or to trust it, and so it waits…waiting to be trusted, waiting to be heard, waiting to be developed, waiting to exorcise our logic.

So, I'm going to keep saying this until it sinks in and you start to believe it. Listen.

Listen. Listen. Hear it. Believe it. Trust it. If you can hear it…if you can hear me, and know I'm talking to you…about you…turn the page.

Again...

And again...

And now you're thinking, That was a strange gimmick for the author to do, *because obviously if you went back a page, the same instructions would be there. It's not like the book is talking to you, it's not like the person in the book is actually talking to you...or are they? What if they are?*

What if I am? What if you're only talking yourself out of listening, out of checking...and now you're gonna check...Did you go back and check now? Yes, the words are still there...I'm keeping them there, just to get you thinking. Now finish reading the epilogue.

Bisa opened her eyes. They were as wide as her mind was open. When it came to her psychic abilities, her potential seemed limitless. There were infinite ways for her to explore her power. The things she could do, the knowledge she could learn, the secrets she could discover, the ways she could educate or express an idea. It seemed only natural for her as a writer to challenge herself and try to communicate through something as palpable as a book in another timeline. But now that she knew it could be done, she could eat something, and maybe focus a little more on her own story, which she'd wanted to tell without ever knowing she wanted to tell it.

Bisa looked out the window, where dawn was approaching over the desert. Out of the corner of her eye, a branch fluttered, and she turned to look. A large milky eagle owl flapped its wings and settled onto the branch of the tree. Its eyes fixed on Bisa.

Write...

The corners of Bisa's mouth curled up with wonder and fascination as she watched the owl gaze into her soul. *What do I write?* she wondered.

As with so many other things in her life, Bisa trusted her vibes and knew the answers would come to her. As she rose from her meditation spot, the owl met eyes with her once more.

"So beautiful," Bisa whispered softly as she admired her totem.

It ruffled its feathers and launched from the branch into the air. She watched it fade into the distance, its wings undulating against the clear sky. She watched the sky until it became a celestial blue that reminded her of Monet.

She stretched her arms and headed to the kitchen, where she had a quiet early morning breakfast of tea and toast, slathered with Avery's enchanted honey. *I guess I do know what to write*, Bisa thought as she finished her toast. She took a cleansing bath, and by the time the birds were singing, she found herself at her desk, ready to work. *I see it all now.* The first thing that came to her was the title, *Sage, Smoke & Fire.*

THE
ESOTERIC COMPENDIUM

A collection of key terms, places, spells & recipes

TERMS & PLACES

Astral Fluid: AFD for short. An organic substance present in all beings. A witch's powers and lifeforce are embedded in it. It can be extracted and used.

Bacchanalia: A large, extravagant, and indulgent party with an abundance of food, music, libations and pleasure.

Corporeal: The most recent type of witch to emerge, once thought to be legend. They can sometimes control the elements but cannot summon them. They are the energy alchemists, able to manipulate energy and matter. They possess varying levels of telekinesis, shapeshifting and auric manipulation.

Esoteric Alchemy Fire: A mystical flame that must be conjured through sheer will and not by magical means in order to complete the Union of the Divine Dualities. The flame is said to be purple, blue and green.

The Grand Oriana Hotel: A luxurious, five-star hotel located on Pearl Street in Boulder, Colorado.

HelloMerlot: A conglomerate beast that includes real estate, medical labs, publishing, wine, media and entertainment, a marijuana company that develops, cultivates, manufactures, packages, ships, and distributes regulated recreational and medical-use cannabis.

The Land of Perpetual Midnight: The shadow realm. Existing under an open sky with more stars than one could ever see from even the most remote parts Earth, but no moon. There are occasional celestial activities in the sky that provide some additional light, with open fields of prairie-like grass, forests of evergreen and birch and a single mountain. There are no boundaries, no beginning and no end to its vastness. Access to the land, as well as other astral planes, can be achieved through ritual drug use, sexual trance, deep meditation, and repetition of words believed to contain power.

Nigrum Pullum: Translates to "Black Hen." A magically invoked animal that is the direct result of correctly performing the Union of the Divine Dualities ritual. The hen is the only thing that can locate the rafkolite, as no human, witch or spell is able to do so.

Primordial: The first type of witch to emerge, sometimes referred to as the Elementals. They can light fire, call storms, lightning and can manipulate water. They are especially gifted at using the elements for divinatory purposes. Heightened senses, can detect slight variations in voice pitch, mood and smell. They are physical healers and can communicate, summon and control animals to some degree.

Rafkolite: A vitreous silica projectile rock, silvery green with swirls of smoky purple bubbles that resemble moss. This rock fell to the earth as a meteor around 15 million years ago and is rumored to have many powers but especially known for its ability to create a butterfly effect of positive energy, when used by the right person or group.

Transcendent: The second type of witch to emerge, sometimes referred to as the Spirit Witches. The empathic clairvoyants and the most in touch with the divine. They can communicate with spirits, astral project, and heal emotional wounds and trauma. Their strongest skill is their power to influence others.

The Union of the Divine Dualities: An esoteric ritual designed to invoke the presence of the nigrum pullum.

SPELLS

The Gold Spell – To Become the Highest Version of Yourself:

The journey to becoming the highest and best version of yourself, is to be an alchemist. The past is gone, the future has not happened, and the present is where all active transformation happens. Use this spell when you are aware that you need to realign with or reevaluate your goals, desires, purpose or needs. If you ever feel stuck, or lost, or find yourself at or near rock bottom, this spell can be a useful tool for sharpening your focus so that you may muster the strength to live your life differently, refocus your attention and discover your true potential. There will be obstacles, but think of this spell as the training to move through the obstacles. While gold is often thought of as being the best, we ourselves are never perfect and will never reach perfection. Perfection here is more of a generalized marker for somewhere we aspire to be. Before you begin, imagine yourself in a desert, surrounded by an icy gray fog, and far above you is the bright and shining sun. The goal is to reach the golden sun, your personal goal—your gold.

You will need:
Salt

4	large quartz points
1	gold candle
1	piece of gold (jewelry, flakes, gold leaf)
1	piece of silver (flakes, sterling silver jewelry)
1	piece of mica (lepidolite, aventurine)
1	piece of copper
1	piece of amethyst
1	piece of galena
1	piece of pyrite

1   piece of sunstone

-     Draw a circle of salt, place the four quartz points along the
      salt at each cardinal direction. Fix the gold candle in the
      center of the circle.
-     Place each stone along the salt circle (two between each
      quartz point), and with each placement, recite the follow-
      ing, "what is gray can be gold—bright as the sun, I change
      and grow, it has begun."
-     When all the stones have been placed, light the candle and
      visualize you as the best version of yourself, where you
      want to be, who you want to be and surrounded by what
      you want. Recite, "My spirit is changing, becoming bright,
      with this flame—let my journey ignite."
-     Allow the candle to burn out completely.

To Destroy and Dismantle a Powerful Enemy:

Any spell that involves harm or disruption to another person, be sure
to exercise caution. Know your intention, know and understand
there can and probably will be consequences for you (there is always
a price). It is up to you to decide if a spell is necessary and if you are
willing to accept the risk that comes with it. This spell is incredibly
helpful to defeat and remove someone's power, whether that be
emotional, physical, political, etc. It may not happen immediately,
but it will slowly infect and dissolve the person's power like a
strong weed killer that soaks into the roots of an invasive plant.

You will need:

      dead wasps

      wasp nests

      wax figure of the targeted person

photo of the targeted person

items belonging to or signifying the targeted person (optional)

mortar and pestle

Spanish moss

1 T   sulphur

½ t. black or brown mustard seed

½ t. black pepper

1 t. cayenne

Black Arts Oil

rum

vinegar

storm water

- Douse the Spanish moss with the storm water and vinegar and let it dry.
- Place the photo, moss, personal items (if using), in a pile, douse with rum (can use lighter fluid to help catch fire) and burn until there is nothing left but ashes.
- Where the heart would be, carve out a hollow in the wax figure and fill it with the ashes.
- With a mortar and pestle, make a powder with the dead wasps (reserve some) mustard seeds, black pepper, cayenne, and sulfur.
- Cover the wax figure with Black Arts Oil (be sure to not get any on your skin), blow the powder onto the doll and place on the ground.
- Toss the remaining wasps and pieces of wasp nest onto the figure while chanting, "Find my enemy, seek them out, remove and block their escape routes. Destroy their power—sting, sting, sting—make them weak, dismantle their wings. May the guilty be tortured by the voices of the wronged, bring justice and peace for which we have longed. Remove their power, let it seek a new host, let it go where it is needed most. They are a dangerous, selfish, filthy liar, let them feel the sting of my hell fire."

- Light the figure on fire and let it burn to ashes. When it is cool enough to handle, scoop up the ashes and cast them into the wind from the highest point you can find.

Money Spell:

This spell is best performed during a waning moon, especially when it is in Capricorn or Taurus, which focus on stability, business and money. While not crucial, it does add a helpful edge to the magic. One important thing to remember is that money is a manmade concept, and so what this spell focuses more on is the essence of abundance, prosperity and it is your intention and focus that makes it specific to money. If you focus more on abundance, the results will be greater and more fully realized than if you were to simply wish for money.

You will need:

½ c.	sunflower oil
1 t.	allspice, ground
2 t.	basil, dried
2 t.	peppermint, dried
½ t.	nutmeg, ground
½ t.	lemongrass, dried
1 t.	cinnamon
1 t.	ginger
1 drop	vetiver oil
2 drops	bergamot oil
2 drops	pine oil
2 drops	eucalyptus oil
1	dollar bill (any numerical value of your choice)

Magnetic sand

- Begin to play "Money" by Pink Floyd on repeat.
- In a small pot set over low heat, add the oil to the pan and all of the ingredients (allspice through eucalyptus oil). Bring the oil to a simmer or until the mixture is fragrant. Let cool. Strain the oil, bottle it and hold it to your third eye and charge it with your intention.
- Rub the dollar bill with the money oil, sprinkle with magnetic sand, roll or fold the bill up and place it in your pocket, wallet or purse. Turn off music.

RECIPES

Ollie's Vegan Mac & Cheese:

4 T	olive oil
2 T	all-purpose flour
1 c.	oat milk (unsweetened)
114 g.	plant-based cheese, shredded (such as Violife)
2 T	nutritional yeast
½ t.	garlic powder
½ t.	onion powder
½ t.	smoked paprika
¼ t.	sweet paprika
¼ t.	turmeric
¼ t.	chipotle powder
½ t.	black pepper
2 ½ t.	kosher salt
2 t.	soy sauce
1 t.	apple cider vinegar
1 t.	maple syrup
½ - ¾ c.	water, to thin if necessary
225 g.	cavatappi noodles, cooked

- Cook the pasta according to package directions, strain lightly and set aside.
- Place the olive oil in a medium pan over medium heat. Add the flour and cook for one minute, whisking constantly.
- Drizzle in the oat milk while whisking, and bring to a full simmer. Add the cheese and whisk until melted. Mixture will be a little thick at this point.
- Add the nutritional yeast, garlic powder, onion powder, paprikas, turmeric, chipotle powder, pepper, salt, soy sauce, vinegar, and maple syrup. Taste and adjust for seasoning.

Add some water (up to ¾ c. until the desired consistency is reached.

- Add the cheese sauce to the cooked pasta and stir to combine. Garnish with paprika and black pepper, and serve hot.

Avery's Panzanella:

4-5 thick slices	sourdough, country, or Italian bread, torn into 1-inch pieces (about 390 g.)
7 T	olive oil
Pinch	kosher salt
½ c.	red bell pepper, fine dice
½ c.	red onion, thinly sliced
1 c.	cucumber, seeded and diced
1 ¼ c.	cherry tomatoes, halved (200 g.)

Chimichurri:

50 g.	flat leaf parsley, finely chopped
5	garlic cloves, minced
1 ¼ t.	kosher salt
1 T	fresh oregano, chopped
4 T	red wine vinegar
½ t.	aji triturado (or crushed red pepper flakes)
¼ t.	black pepper
½ c.	olive oil

- Preheat the oven 400°F. Tear the bread into 1-inch pieces and place in a medium sized bowl. Drizzle with olive oil, salt and toss to combine. Place the bread on a sheet tray and roast for 15-20 minutes until a rich golden brown, tossing once halfway through. Remove from the oven and let cool.

- Prepare the chimichurri. Smash and mince the garlic with the salt until you have a rough paste, add to a bowl with the parsley, oregano, red wine vinegar, aji triturado, and black pepper. Mix together until fully saturated and then stir in the olive oil. Let sit for 10 minutes (this can be made a day ahead to let the flavors meld together).
- To a large bowl, add the bread, red bell pepper, red onion, cucumber, and cherry tomatoes. Add the chimichurri and toss to combine. Let stand for 15 minutes, adjust with more olive oil, vinegar and salt if necessary to ensure the bread is saturated but not soggy. Portion and serve. (For the non-vegans, garnish with shaved Reggianito cheese.)

Ollie's Green Fire Juice:

3	kale leaves
1	granny smith apple, cored
2 c.	spinach
½ c.	flat leaf parsley
½	large cucumber
1	lemon
1	orange
1	jalapeño
1	fresh ginger, 1-inch knob
1/3 c.	blueberries

- Bunch the kale and add to the juicer, followed by chunks of apple to make the juicing process of the kale more efficient. Pass remaining ingredients through the juicer and serve over ice.

Honey Cheesecake:

Graham shortbread crust:

10 oz.	brown butter
2 c.	graham cracker crumbs
2 c.	AP flour
1 t.	salt
¾ c.	light brown sugar
2	eggs
1 t.	vanilla

For the crust:

- Brown the butter. Pour into a heatproof bowl and refrigerate until solid. Bring butter to room temperature.
- Whisk graham cracker crumbs, flour, and salt in a bowl. Combine butter and brown sugar in a mixer bowl; beat on medium-high until smooth and fluffy, about 3 minutes.
- Add vanilla and eggs, one at a time, beating well after each addition.
- Add dry ingredients; beat on low speed until just combined. Divide dough in half and wrap in plastic wrap; refrigerate for 2 hours.
- Heat oven to 350°F. Remove one portion of the dough and roll out on a lightly floured board to desired thickness for your 9" springform pan. Form into your pan, pressing into the corners, and blind bake 10-12 minutes. Cool completely before filling.

For the cheesecake:

3 lbs.	cream cheese
4 ½ c.	orange blossom honey
18	eggs
1 ½ T	kosher salt
1 ½ T	vanilla
3 c.	heavy cream
1/3 c.	lemon juice
1 T	lemon zest

- In the bowl of a stand mixer, beat cream cheese until smooth, scrape the bowl. Add the honey and continue beating on low until smooth, scrape down the bowl.
- Add the eggs, 6 at a time, scraping down the bowl between additions.
- Add the salt, vanilla, heavy cream, and lemon juice and beat until thoroughly mixed. Pour custard through a fine mesh strainer to get rid of any lumps. Stir in lemon zest.
- Fill prebaked shortbread crusts with custard, as full as you can without spilling over. Bake in a 300°F oven for 40-60 minutes, rotating after 30 min. When pie is done it will be very jiggly, but not liquid, and will be evenly and slightly browned on top edges. Turn off the oven, crack the oven door with a wooden spoon, and let cool in the oven for an hour to help prevent cracking. Remove from the oven and cool to room temperature, then fully chill before serving.

Ollie's Red Sangria:

750 ml bottle	Spanish red wine (any fruity, full-bodied merlot, cabernet sauvignon, rioja, or shiraz will work)
750 ml bottle	white wine (any fruity vidal blanc, chardonnay, or pinot gris)
1	lime, juiced
1	lemon, juiced
½ qt.	orange juice
½ qt.	pineapple juice
½ qt.	apple juice
4 ½ oz.	Cointreau
5 oz.	pomegranate liqueur
2 ¼ t.	kosher salt
3 oz.	honey, slightly warmed
1	granny smith apple, sliced thinly
1 c.	green or red grapes, halved
1 c.	strawberries, halved
2	cinnamon sticks, roasted

- Pour the wine into a pitcher and squeeze the lime and lemon juice into the pitcher. Mix all remaining ingredients together in the pitcher (orange juice through honey) with a whisk. Add in apples, grapes, strawberries and cinnamon sticks; stir, cover and refrigerate for at least 4 hours or overnight. Serve over ice.

Ollie's Roasted Carrot Soup:

6	carrots, peeled, cut into 3-inch batons
½	yellow onion, diced
4	garlic cloves, dry roasted
1 ½ t.	cumin
1 t.	basil
1 ½ t.	dill
½ t.	coriander
½ t.	thyme
1 T	fresh ginger
Zest	1 orange
Zest	1 lemon
Zest	1 lime
1 T	maple syrup
Juice	orange, lemon
28 oz.	canned tomatoes
1 c.	vegetable stock
½ c.	coconut yogurt, unsweetened (or vegan sour cream)
Salt	
Black pepper	
2 T	pepitas, toasted (optional)
1 T	red pepper flakes (optional)
1 T	dill (optional)

- Toss the carrots with olive oil, salt and cumin. Roast at 400°F for 25-30 min. Set aside.
- Dry roast the garlic over medium heat, unpeeled, in a dry pan for 5-10 min. Cool, peel and rough chop.
- In a pot, sauté the onion with olive oil and salt until slightly caramelized. Add the garlic, cook one minute. Add the cumin, basil, dill, coriander, thyme, ginger and zests. Cook an additional minute. Add the tomatoes (with juices), the

reserved carrots, salt and pepper. Bring to a gentle simmer and cook for 10 minutes, until fully heated through.

- Blend with an immersion blender. Thin with vegetable stock. Add the maple syrup, lemon and orange juices and yogurt. Blend again. Adjust seasoning as necessary as well as stock to thin it to desired consistency.

Kale & Brussels Sprouts Salad with Vegan Green Goddess Dressing:

175 g.	avocado, diced
175 g.	vegan mayo
3 T	lemon juice
¼ c.	oat milk, more as needed
¼ c.	chives, chopped
¼ c.	flat leaf parsley, minced
1 t.	tarragon, minced
½ c.	dill, minced
30	basil leaves, minced
2 t.	red wine vinegar
1 ½ t.	garlic powder
2 t.	salt
1 t.	pepper

2 bunches	kale, sliced, blanched and shocked in ice water
12 oz.	brussels sprouts, grated or thinly sliced
2 T	olive oil
1/3 c.	walnuts, coarsely chopped
¼ t.	Aleppo pepper

- In a large bowl, add the ingredients from the avocado to the pepper, and whisk vigorously to combine. If wanting to save time and effort, use a food processor. Taste for seasoning and adjust with oat milk to reach your desired consistency. Set aside in the fridge.
- Mix thinly sliced blanched and shocked kale and shredded brussels sprouts in a large bowl.
- Add 2 T of olive oil into a small skillet and heat over med-high heat. Add walnuts and stir until toasted, 2-3 minutes. Transfer to paper towel and sprinkle with salt.
- Add dressing to kale mixture, toss to coat (you may not need or want all of the dressing). Garnish with Aleppo pepper and chopped walnuts.

Ollie's Vegan Brownies:

180 g.	vegan 70% chocolate, melted
115 g.	vegetable oil
2 T	ground flax seed
6 T	hot water
250 g.	sugar
50 g.	dark muscovado sugar
1 ¼ t.	salt
½ c.	brewed coffee
2 t.	vanilla extract
180 g.	all-purpose flour
40 g.	Dutch processed cocoa powder, sifted
¼ t.	baking powder
80 g.	70 % chocolate, chopped for chips

- Preheat oven to 350°F. Line an 8×8 pan with parchment paper with overhang and grease the pan with cooking spray.
- In a bowl set over a double boiler, add the 180 g. of chocolate and the vegetable oil, and melt together, whisking occasionally until fully smooth and the chocolate is melted.
- In a small bowl, whisk ground flax seed and 6 T of hot water. Set aside.
- In a medium pot set over medium high heat, add the sugar, muscovado sugar, salt, and coffee. Bring just to a boil, then add in the vanilla. Pour into the bowl with the chocolate and vegetable oil mixture, whisk to combine and then whisk in the flax egg. Transfer to a large bowl.
- In a medium bowl, whisk together the flour, cocoa, and baking powder. Add to the bowl with the rest of the ingredients. Mix with a spatula until about 75% incorporated, then add in the 80 g. chopped chocolate and fold in until no more flour is visible. Do not overmix.
- Pour batter into greased pan. Bake for 40-45 minutes. A toothpick may not come out clean since they are fudgy, it doesn't mean they are not fully baked.
- Remove from the oven and let cool for an hour, then place in the freezer overnight. Remove from freezer, unmold, and slice into desired portions using a hot knife. completely before slicing. Store brownies in an air tight container in the fridge.

ACKNOWLEDGEMENTS:

Writing is a solitary practice, and writing a book, in addition to being incredibly challenging and exhausting, yet deliciously rewarding, wouldn't be entirely possible without the help, interest, support, and generosity of the collective. No matter how much you prepare, outline, or plan, books and the characters within them tend to write themselves—regardless of what you had planned for them. So much of this story has taken shape because of the people in my life and the experiences I've had. When I stand back and look at the book, I feel less like an author and more like the curator for an extraordinary collection of influences from every person, experience, place, thing, hope and dream I've ever come in contact with. Every observation sparks an idea, every flutter of the heart inspires a character, every conversation conjures truth and authenticity. Esoteric Alchemy is our exhibit that we made and collaborated together to create. Thank you.

To my mother and stepfather, Carol & Eric Dahlen: there are a lot of words in the number of pages you've read over the years. Your continued support and hope for my success have never gone unnoticed—thank you very much.

To my editor, Laurel Robinson: I don't know what I would've done without your keen eye and hard work. You always set me up for success while allowing my style and voice to come through. Thank you.

To my designing Scorpio, Allison Layman: "I love the cover" is one of the very first things I hear from so many people who've reached out to me about the book. Thank you for interpreting what I want, while also knowing I have no interest in playing by the rules of what fantasy readers have come to expect as far as a cover. Thank you for helping me create something that no one has seen before.

To my editor at Witches Magazine, Laura O'Rourke: the magazine has been a place for me to flex my writing muscles and express ideas without judgement or censorship, and you've made an effort to help me whenever I ask for it. Thank you.

To my Libra, Erik McLinn: for someone who doesn't write, you certainly are creative. You've helped me solve many writing blocks and break through walls I've encountered with my story, and if whether it be food or plot, you always tell me the truth about what you think, and for that, I will always be grateful. Thank you.

To my Taurus, David Petrusich: you and I both know this story would never have come to be had we not planted the seed so many years ago. Thank you for that, and for your continued support in all endeavors.

To all the rest of you who have played a part in this story of getting me to where I am now: Sarah Day, Patrick English, Micaéla Royal, Sandra Szatkowski, Cody Torbert, the staff at Blue Cypress Books, and the many others that I haven't mentioned here or accidentally overlooked because I forget everything, and if I have—I apologize—it shouldn't suggest I am not appreciative.

To my angels, my ancestors, my guides, the natural world and beyond: thank you for allowing me to be here today. Thank you for guiding me through the peaks and valleys of my life. Thank you for your lessons, even when I don't understand them. Thank you for all the things I have yet to experience, see, feel, taste, and touch. With much love—thank you.

ABOUT THE AUTHOR

Ryan Kurr is an author, pastry chef, massage therapist, and mystic practitioner. *The Black Hen* is the third and final novel in the *Esoteric Alchemy* series. The first two in the series, *Sage, Smoke & Fire*, and *Powdered Oak & Seven Metals*, were both bestsellers in the LGBT Fantasy genre on Amazon. His debut memoir, *Sugar Burn: The Not So Hot Side of the Sweet Kitchen*, was released in 2015. His freelance work on spiritual and metaphysical witchcraft has been published by Witches Magazine. He currently lives in New Orleans.

www.ingramcontent.com/pod-product-compliance
Lightning Source LLC
Chambersburg PA
CBHW060518220726
48290CB00015B/1750